"Gith's blood!" one of the bandits cried out from beyond the wall. "I smell halfling!"

The wind had shifted, but Sorak had not thought the humans would have been able to catch his scent.

"I knew something was bothering the crodlu!" one of the others cried.

There were sounds of commotion beyond the wall as the bandits jumped to their feet and snatched up their weapons. Sorak realized it would be pointless to run. The trail was open in both directions and he would present an easy target for their bows, or they could mount up and ride him down with their crodlu before he had gone a hundred yards. There was nothing to do but stand and face them.

TRIBE OF ONE

Simon Hawke

The Outcast

SIMON HAWKE

TRIBE OF ONE TRILOGY
Book One

THE OUTCAST

All characters in this book are fictitious. Any resemblance to actual persons, living or dead, is purely coincidental.

All TSR characters, character names, and the distinct likenesses thereof are trademarks owned by TSR, Inc.

This book is protected under the copyright laws of the United States of America. Any reproduction or other unauthorized use of the material or artwork herein is prohibited without the express written permission of TSR, Inc.

Random House and its affiliate companies have worldwide distribution rights in the book trade for English language products of TSR, Inc.

Distributed to the book and hobby trade in the United Kingdom by TSR Ltd.

Distributed to the toy and hobby trade by regional distributors.

DARK SUN is a registered trademark owned by TSR, Inc.

The TSR logo is a trademark owned by TSR, Inc.

Cover art by Brom.

First Printing: December 1993

Printed in the United States of America

Library of Congress Catalog Card Number: 92-61104

9 8 7 6 5 4 3 2 1

ISBN: 1-56076-676-X

TSR, Inc.	TSR Ltd.
P.O. Box 756	120 Church End, Cherry Hinton
Lake Geneva, WI 53147	Cambridge CB1 3LB
United States of America	United Kingdom

For Troy Denning
with thanks for allowing me to come
and play in his world.

Acknowledgments

With grateful acknowledgments to Rob King and Jim Lowder for their editorial support, and Heather Richards, Megan McDowell, Bruce and Peggy Wiley, Rebecca Ford, and Daniel Arthur for providing helpful feedback, and Pat Connors for helping to gametest "Hawke's Gambit" on a group of unsuspecting victims at Tuscon XIX.

Special thanks to Adele Leone and Richard Monaco, who performed services well above and beyond the call of duty, and to Robert M. Powers, who kept telling me to cheer up, things would only get worse.

And a very special thanks to Bruce Miller, who extends extraordinary generosity to friends and doesn't want anyone to know. They know, Bruce, that's why they love you.

Hey, Cheryl? Hugs . . .

PROLOGUE

As the twin moons cast their ghostly light upon the endless wasteland, Lyra stood alone atop the Dragon's Tooth, waiting for the sunrise. Once each year, for the past thousand years, she had made her pilgrimage to the summit of the highest peak on Athas to reaffirm her vows and dream the dream she would never live to see. A thousand years, she thought as she shivered in her cloak. I am growing old.

It was nearly dawn. Soon the dark sun would rise to glow like a dying ember in the dust-laden orange sky, and its rays would beat down on the desert like a hammer on an anvil. Only at night was there any respite from the searing heat. The desert sands would cool, the temperatures would plummet, and the deadly creatures of the night would leave their nests and burrows to prowl for food. The day brought other dangers, no less lethal. Athas was not a hospitable world.

Lyra Al'Kali dreamed of the world as it once was, long before her birth. In the moments before dawn, she would imagine that the sun would rise over the horizon to reveal verdant plains stretching out below her instead of barren desert tablelands. The foothills of the Ringing Mountains would be forested rather than strewn with broken rock, and the song of birds would replace the mournful wailing of the wind over the ruined landscape. Once, the world was green. The sun was bright, and the plains of Athas bloomed. But that had been before the balance of nature was destroyed by those who thought to "engineer" it, before the color of the sun had changed, before the world had been despoiled by defiler magic.

The pyreens were the oldest race on Athas, though with the passing centuries, their numbers had grown ever fewer. They recalled the Green Age in their legends, the stories that were passed on from generation to generation as pyreens matured and took their vows. There are not many of us left, thought Lyra. Each year, she encountered fewer of her kind during her wanderings. She was an elder herself now, one of the oldest pyreens remaining. Our time is passing, she thought. Even though our lives span centuries, there will not be enough time to restore the dying planet. We are too few, and we cannot do it all alone.

Each year on the anniversary of her vow-taking, Lyra made the journey to the Dragon's Tooth and climbed the towering mountain. For any of the humanoid races of Athas—even the tireless, fleet-footed elves and the nimble, feral halflings—the tortuous climb to the summit would have been nearly impossible, but Lyra did not make it in her humanoid form. Only once, when she first took her vows, had she made the climb unaided by her shapeshifting abilities, and it had nearly killed her. Now, she was no longer young, and even in the form of a tagster or a rasclinn, the climb was difficult for her. Still, she continued to make it every year, and she would do so as long as she still drew breath. And when she could no longer make the climb, she would at least die in the attempt.

The first smoky orange rays of sunlight began to tint the sky at the edge of the horizon. Lyra stood upon the windswept summit, her long white hair billowing out behind her, and she watched as the dark sun rose slowly and malevolently to burn the desert tablelands below. As she had done a thousand times before, from the time she had reached her quickening and began the counting of her years, Lyra started to recite her vows aloud into the morning wind.

"I, Lyra Al'Kali, daughter of Tyra Al'Kali of the Ringing Mountains, do hereby take my solemn vows and acknowledge the purpose of my life, as every son and daughter of the pyreen has done before me, and shall do after me, until Athas once again grows green. I vow to follow the Path of the Preserver, using my powers to protect and restore the land, and to foil and slay defilers who would steal its life for their own perverted gain. I vow allegiance to the elders, and to the Eldest Elder, Alar Ch'Aranol, Peace-Bringer, Teacher, Preserver, Dragonslayer. I herewith dedicate my life to follow in his noble path, and pledge my soul to the service of the Druid Way and the rebirth of the land. So do I vow, so shall it be."

Her words were lost upon the wind as the light from the dark sun flooded the desert landscape far below her. Just as all our dreams may be lost upon the wind, she thought. Perhaps there would never come a time when Athas would be green again, not so long as the sorcerer-kings still lived and drained the planet of its life to fuel their spells, and not so long as dragons walked the world, leaving waste and desolation in their wake. The Eldest Elder had vowed death to the dragons of Athas, but alone he was no match for their magic. Even all the pyreen together could not stand against them. For as long as Lyra had been alive,

Ch'Aranol had been seeking to overcome the dragons who had once walked as men, but preserver magic had never been as strong as that of defilers, and no defiler was as powerful as a fully metamorphosed dragon.

Many adventurers had met their deaths in trying to do combat with the dragon, and many more would die if the sorcerer-kings continued to grow in power. Each of them had already embarked upon the path of metamorphosis that would transform them into dragons. The process was a slow and painful one, requiring powerful enchantments, spells that drained the earth of life and sapped the souls of unfortunates who fell under the sorcerer-kings' dominion.

The Path of the Preserver called for restraint and purity in use of magic, with the spellcaster either drawing on his or her own life energy, or merely "borrowing" life energy from plants and the earth, taking only small amounts so that the plants would be able to recover and the earth would not be left forever barren where the spellcaster had passed. Defilers, on the other hand, eschewed respect for living things and were motivated solely by greed and lust for power. Defilers cast spells that killed off all the vegetation in the area, left animals dropping and writhing in their tracks, and leeched all nutrients from the earth, so that nothing more would ever grow there. Nor did defilers stop at that. Those with enough magical might would not hesitate to drain power from sentient life-forms, be they elves or halflings, dwarves or thri-kreen, or any of the humanoid races of Athas—or even the pyreen.

There was madness in defiler magic, Lyra thought, especially in the devastating spells cast by the sorcerer-kings in their lust to metamorphose into dragons. If she lived another thousand years, she would never understand it. What did it profit them to gain such incalculable power if all that was left for them to rule would be a barren world, devoid of life? Where, then, would they turn to seek the enormous amounts of energy that full-fledged dragons needed to survive? They would kill off everyone and everything, and then, like the maddened beasts they were, they would turn upon each other until there would be only one left, and that one would hold dominion over a drained husk of planet. As it gazed out on the ruined world of Athas, that last dragon would have the brief satisfaction of knowing that its power was unchallenged and supreme—before it slowly starved.

How, thought Lyra, as she sadly gazed out over the parched landscape, could they not see it? How could the defilers fail to comprehend where it all would lead? The only possible explanation was that the sorcerer-kings were insane, driven mad by their lust for power, living only to feed that lust. As their powers increased, their appetites grew. There had to be a way to stop them, but the only way to do that would be to destroy them, and defilers could accumulate power much faster than any preserver. No ordinary magic-user could ever stand against them. There was only one chance, one being that could hope to match their power—the avangion.

There had never been an avangion on Athas. The sorcerer-kings and their minions had seen to that. They ruthlessly hunted and exterminated any rivals, either defilers or preservers, and the birth of an avangion took far longer than the creation of a dragon, for it entailed only preserver magic. The path of metamorphosis was long and painful, involving selfless dedication and excruciating patience. Yet, after over a thousand years, there was at least a glimmer of hope. An avangion was now in the process of being born. It would take many, many years, and the sorcerer-kings would do their utmost to seek it out and destroy it before the cycle was complete. But if their efforts failed and the avangion took flight, then the dragons would start to tremble in their lairs.

Still, what were the odds? Before the avangion cycle of creation could become complete, it was more than likely that all the remaining sorcerer-kings would fully metamorphose into dragons, and then it would be many against one. The surviving pyreens would gladly dedicate the remainder of their lives to guarding the avangion until its cycle was complete, but no one knew where the solitary wizard who pursued the arduous metamorphosis could be found. Perhaps, thought Lyra, it is better that way. If we cannot find him, then neither can the sorcerer-kings. But that will not stop them from looking.

Lyra was abruptly startled out of her reverie by the sound of an anguished, desperate cry. A child's cry, she thought, blinking with surprise and glancing around quickly. But that was clearly impossible. A child could not have climbed the Dragon's Tooth. Perhaps some freak trick of the wind had deceived her. . . . And then she suddenly realized she hadn't actually *heard* the cry. It had echoed *in her mind*. It was psionic cry for help, a tormented, unarticulated scream, almost like the dying wailings of some animal. Yet it had been a child, Lyra was certain of it. A lifetime of devotion to the discipline of psionics meant she could not have been mistaken. Somewhere, a child was in desperate trouble, but for the psionic cry to have been projected as far as the summit of the Dragon's Tooth meant that it was a child gifted with incredible, inborn psionic powers. She had never encountered anything even remotely like it before, and she could not possibly ignore it.

Spreading her arms out wide, Lyra started to twirl in place, picking up speed as her form blurred and grew less and less distinct until, within seconds, she had taken on the form of an air elemental, a whirling funnel of wind that left the ground and swept down the mountainside, heading for the foothills. Lyra focused on that cry, trying to judge the direction from which it came, and then she heard it once again, much weaker this time, as if it were a sob of resignation. She locked onto it and veered slightly to the west, heading directly for the origin of the psionic cry. As she rapidly closed the distance, she marveled at its strength, even in the weakness of it. She swept over the rock-strewn foothills and headed out into the desert. Could it be possible? What would a child be doing out in the desert at night? Perhaps it was with some caravan that had run into trouble. In the desert, disaster always awaited the next step. . . .

And then she saw it. As she skimmed over the desert, she almost overshot it in her anxiety. There was no caravan. There wasn't even a solitary wagon, or a party on foot. There was but one child, stretched out motionless in the sand, with what appeared to be a feral tigone cub moving in for the kill. She had found it just in time.

Still whirling, Lyra settled to the ground and moved toward the cub, trying to get between it and the child. Even as it flinched and squinted in the powerful blast of sand she raised, the cub would not move away from the prostrate child. Tigones were psionic cats, using their power to stalk prey such as this, but their natural habitat was in the foothills and on the high slopes of the Ringing Mountains. This was the first time Lyra had ever seen one venture down into the desert. She guessed the hungry young cub had picked up the child's psionic cry as she had, and responded to it instinctively. She changed shape once again, this time assuming the form of a full-grown tigone, and she directed a basic, animal-level psionic thought at the young cub.

"*Mine. Move away.*"

She sensed sudden apprehension in the tigone cub, and the thought that came back at her was both challenging and surprising. "*No. Not prey. Friend. Protect.*" The young cub bared its fangs in warning.

Lyra was completely unprepared for such a response. Not only was the cub not interested in the child as food, but it was fully prepared to take on a full-grown tigone to protect it. Lyra reverted to her humanoid form.

"Easy, now," she said to the cub aloud, reinforcing her tone with soothing thoughts. "I have come to help your friend."

Warily, the cub allowed her to approach, but remained poised to attack if she made the slightest hostile move toward the motionless child. This, too, surprised Lyra. Ordinarily, she had no difficulty in using her psionic skills to control beasts, but even as she exercised her domination over the young cub, it refused to submit completely to her will, intent above everything else on protecting the child.

Slowly, keeping a wary eye on the cub, Lyra crouched beside the small body of the child and gently turned it onto its back. And she was confronted with yet another surprise. "What have we here?" she said.

The child, at first glance, looked human. It was

male, only five or six years old, and yet, as she turned him over, she saw the pointed ears and the sharply defined features—high cheekbones, angular jawline tapering down to a slightly pointed chin, a narrow and well-shaped nose over a wide, thin-lipped mouth. . . . All these things indicated that the child was an elf, and yet he did not possess the long and extremely thin, exaggerated frame of an elf. His limbs were proportioned as a human's, not an elf's. The legs and arms were too short, and the ears, though delicately pointed, were too small. They were the same size as human ears, except that they had points.

The boy also had some of the features of a halfling—the deeply sunken eyes, the thick and almost manelike hair that cascaded to his shoulders, the delicately arched eyebrows. Halflings, too, had pointed ears, but the child was too large to be a halfling. And yet, he possessed the physical traits of both halflings and elves.

A half-breed, Lyra thought with astonishment. But elves and halflings were natural enemies. And it was unheard of for an elf to mate with halfling, although she supposed there was no reason why it should not be possible. Clearly, it was, for she was looking down at the result of just such a mating. And that explained what the child was doing alone in the desert. Lyra felt a tightness in her stomach. He had been cast out. The result of a forbidden union, he had doubtless, up to this point, been hidden and protected by his mother, but as he grew, it became obvious what he was, and the poor thing had been taken out into the desert and left to die.

However, the child clearly possessed a strong will, for, unaided and without food or water, he had almost succeeded in reaching the foothills of the

Ringing Mountains. Not only that, but he was gifted with incredible psionic talent. Young and untutored as he was, he had nevertheless been able to project his anguished mental cry of rage and despair to reach her at the very summit of the Dragon's Tooth. Few adult psionicists she knew, even those who had studied the discipline for years, could hope to match such a feat.

She had to save him. He was not yet dead, but he was unconscious and very, very weak. That last mental shout had been his mind, pushed to its final extremity, howling out fury and frustration at having come within sight of his goal and yet failing to attain it.

"Never fear, little one," she said. "You shall not die."

She scooped out a bowl in the desert sand and shut her eyes, reaching deep within herself to summon up the necessary stored energy for a spell to create water. As she concentrated, water slowly bubbled forth in the depression she had scooped out. She dipped her fingers into it and sprinkled a few drops on the boy's lips. His mouth twitched, and a parched tongue slowly emerged to taste the precious drops. Gently, she probed his mind . . . and then recoiled sharply at what she found. As the boy's eyes flickered open and he stared up at her, she shook her head sadly and said, "Oh, poor little elfling! What have they done to you?"

* * * * *

The young priestess hesitantly approached the high mistress at her loom and waited to be recognized. Sensing her presence, the older woman spoke to her without turning around and taking her eyes off her weaving.

"Yes, Neela, what is it?"

"Mistress, we have a visitor who wishes an audience with you. She awaits outside your chamber."

The high mistress frowned and turned to face her. "Outside my chamber? You mean she was admitted through the gates? You know we do not allow outsiders on the temple grounds, Neela. Who is responsible for this?"

"But, Mistress . . . she is pyreen."

"Ah," the high mistress replied. "That is a different matter. The druid peace-bringers are always welcome here. Did she give her name?"

"She is called Lyra Al'Kali, Mistress."

"And you have kept her waiting?" the high mistress said, her eyes growing wide. "Foolish girl! She is one of the pyreen elders! Show her in at once!"

The young priestess hesitated. "Mistress . . . there is but one more thing. . . ."

"Well? What is it? Be quick about it!"

"She has a child with her. A male child."

"A male? In a villichi temple?" The high mistress considered. "The child is pyreen?"

The young priestess moistened her lips nervously. "No, Mistress. I . . . I do not know *what* it is. I have never before seen such a child. And there is a tigone—"

"A tigone!"

"A mere cub, Mistress, but she says it will not leave the child, and is bonded to it."

"How very curious," the high mistress replied. "Show Elder Al'Kali in, Neela. We have already kept her waiting too long."

The young priestess went out and returned a moment later with Lyra and a small boy, whom the pyreen held by the hand. A young tigone cub trotted in after them, staying close to the boy. When they stopped, the cub lay down at the boy's feet. The high mistress first noticed the boy's emaciated appearance and vaguely unfocused stare, but then she quickly saw what Neela meant when she said that she had never seen such a child before. In her sheltered life at the temple, Neela knew little of the outside world, but the high mistress immediately saw that the boy was a half-breed, which in itself was not uncommon on Athas. However, he appeared to have been born of a union between a halfling and an elf, and *that* was an unheard of rarity.

"Peace to you, Mistress Varanna," Lyra said.

"And peace to you, Elder Al'Kali," the high mistress replied. "You honor this temple with your presence."

Lyra inclined her head slightly in acknowledgment of the compliment. "You are wondering about this child I have brought with me," Lyra said. "I know that males are not admitted to the villichi temple, unless they are pyreen, but then this is no ordinary male child, as you can plainly see. However, rather than explain further at this point, I invite you to ascertain that for yourself, using your abilities."

With a slightly puzzled expression, the high mistress nodded and said, "Very well." Then she directed a subtle psionic probe at the child. Almost immediately, she gasped and her eyes grew wide. The child had displayed no visible reaction to the probe. In fact, he seemed to be displaying no reactions whatsoever. It was as if he were in a fugue state. Yet, when she touched his mind with hers, she had been hurled back with such startling force that it took her breath away. However, in that brief instant of contact, she had discovered why the pyreen had brought the child to her.

"*A tribe of one?*" she said softly, with astonishment.

Lyra nodded. "You have, no doubt, experienced his latent power, as did I."

"But . . . so strong!" said the high mistress. "I have never before encountered its like in one so young!"

"Nor have I, in all my years," Lyra replied. "You see why I have brought him to you."

"Where did you find him?"

"In the desert, struggling to reach the foothills," Lyra replied. "He was cast out by his tribe and near death when I came upon him. His call reached me at the summit of the Dragon's Tooth."

"*So far?*" asked the high mistress, amazed. She shook her head. "And he has had no training?"

"How could he have?" Lyra replied. "He is no more than five or six years old, at most. Until recently, he must have been hidden by his mother, who would have known his fate if his origin was discovered. And in an elf or halfling tribe, whichever cast him out, he would not have received any schooling in psionics."

"No, obviously not," the high mistress said. "To think of such incredible potential nearly being destroyed . . . to say nothing of the savage cruelty of leaving a mere child to such an awful fate. His ordeal must have been responsible for the fragmentation of his mind, and it may also have brought forth his latent talents. It is very rare to encounter a tribe of one. I have seen it only twice before, both times in girls who had been born villichi and were violently abused before they were cast out. This is the first time I have ever seen it in a male. Poor child. To think of the terrible torment he must have suffered. . . ."

"I could think of no one else who would be capable of understanding it," said Lyra. "It was my hope that, despite his being male, you would agree to grant him shelter at the temple."

"Of course," said the high mistress, with an emphatic nod. "There has never been a male in residence at the villichi temple, but this time an exception must be made. Who but the villichi could ever accept and understand a tribe of one? And who but the villichi could properly develop his potential? You may leave him with us, and I shall personally see to his care. But . . . what of the tigone?"

"The beast is psionically bonded to him," Lyra said. "It is his protector. Some part of him communicates with it. Such a bond is rare and must not be broken."

"But as the boy grows, so shall the cub," said the high mistress. "Even when young, a tigone is dangerous. When full-grown, even I shall not be able to control it."

"So long as no one threatens or mistreats the boy, you need have no fear of the tigone," Lyra said. "However, I would suggest that you do not attempt to feed it. Allow it to roam free outside the temple grounds at night and hunt for its food, as it was meant to do. It shall always return to the boy, and it will accept those at the temple as members of his 'pack,' and guard them as it does the boy."

"I shall defer to your wisdom in such matters, Elder Al'Kali," the high mistress said. "What is the boy's name?"

Lyra shook her head. "I do not know. I do not even know if he knows. He has not spoken a word since I found him."

"We shall have to call him something," the high mistress said. She thought a moment. "We shall call him Sorak."

"An elvish word for a nomad who always travels alone," said Lyra with a smile. "It seems appropriate. But then, he is no longer alone."

The high mistress shook her head. "He is a tribe of one, Elder Al'Kali. One who is also many. And for that, I fear he shall always be alone."

ONE

Varanna stood out on the balcony of her private chambers in the temple, watching as Sorak practiced with blades in the courtyard below. Though the villichi were all schooled in the discipline of psionics, they were trained in the use of weapons as well. At the convent, weapons training was stressed not only as a martial art and a means of keeping fit, but also as a discipline to help hone the mind and train the instincts. Years of intense training in the arts of combat, coupled with psionic abilities developed to perfection, made the villichi extremely formidable fighters. Even a mul gladiator would think twice before attempting to take on a villichi.

As the high mistress watched Sorak's quick, confident and graceful movements, she recalled the small, emaciated child Elder Al'Kali had first brought to the temple. Ten years had passed since then, which made him perhaps fifteen, sixteen, or seventeen. Sorak himself did not know how old he was, and psionics could not pinpoint his age. He had such formidable psionic defenses that not even Varanna could probe past them, and that was only one of the difficulties she had faced with the young elfling.

To begin with, no male had ever been admitted to

the convent before. There were approximately five
hundred villichi in residence at the secluded sanctuary
in the Ringing Mountains. The senior priestesses and
the high mistress resided in the temple itself, while the
others shared common living quarters in the outbuild-
ings on the convent grounds. At any given time, there
were between seventy-five and a hundred priestesses
absent on pilgrimages. That left at least four hundred
women in residence at the convent, ranging in age
from six to sixty, not including the senior priestesses.
The youngest of these was eighty-five and the oldest,
Varanna herself, over two hundred. All these resi-
dents—and one young elfling male.

It was an unprecedented situation. Within living
memory, no male on Athas had ever been born villichi. Villichi were always human females, and they
were born with the gift—some said the curse—of
strong psionic talent. Because of the dangerous raw
power of their psionics, villichi were almost always
shunned. Sometimes, they were even cast out of their
homes, though to do so was considered a bad omen.

Not cruel, thought Varanna wryly, merely unlucky.

Psionic powers could be developed by anyone to
some extent, provided the person possessed the intelligence, patience, and dedication to persevere in
studying the art. Most people were born with the
latent capacity for at least one psionic talent, but that
talent was usually "wild," which meant it could not
necessarily be tapped at will. Many people didn't
even know they had the ability. It required years of
intense training under a master for even minor talents
to be fully brought forth. Even then, few could
develop their psionic skills to the same extent as the
villichi, who were born with the ability in full flower.

They were different in other ways, as well. Females

born villichi had longer life spans than was normal for humans. They were taller than average, more slender, and with longer limbs, rather like elves, although in elves, those physical traits were even more pronounced. They were extremely fair-skinned—not quite albino, but very pale, so that the sun burned rather than tanned them. To protect themselves, they wore their hair very long, and donned light cloaks whenever they went out into the daylight.

No one seemed to know what caused a girl to be born villichi. A villichi child was usually born to perfectly normal human parents, and such parents often considered the daughter a curse. Not only did she look different, freakish by most people's standards, but she possessed fully developed psionic abilities. She was capable of reading her parents' thoughts, and the thoughts of all their friends and neighbors who came to visit. As a result, she developed intellectually much faster and much earlier than ordinary human children. But just as normal human infants master elementary physical movements, such as crawling, before they begin to walk, so did villichi infants need to master their inborn abilities before they could fully control them. Frequently, villichi infants unintentionally caused objects to fly around the house, creating much damage and consternation. They could direct blasts of psionic force at their parents and anyone unlucky enough to be in their vicinity. A villichi baby who was hungry often did much more than merely cry for milk.

For such reasons, the parents of villichi children were often completely unequipped to deal with them, and both the parents and the child led a miserable existence. The phenomenon of villichi birth was uncommon, and there was no one to whom the parents of such a child could turn for help. If there was a master psionicist residing nearby, they might go to him for counsel, but he often had students of his own, who either traded for his teaching with indentured servitude or else paid for their studies. A villichi child would be an unnecessary burden to him, and would usually possess psionic abilities rivaling his own. Sometimes kindhearted masters took in villichi children, at least until a villichi priestess could be found to relieve them of the responsibility. But most masters simply refused.

One way or another, girls born villichi often became outcasts. If they were not located by a priestess on a pilgrimage, they eventually made the journey to the Ringing Mountains on their own. There, in a high, secluded valley, they would find a place where their talent could be nurtured, guided, and developed. They would find their own society, one that was devoted to study, discipline, and contemplation. They would never marry or have children, for villichi were born sterile, and most would remain celibate.

When her turn came, each of the priestesses would make a pilgrimage to learn about the state of the outside world and to seek out other villichi. At such times, there were occasionally opportunities to indulge in the pleasures of the flesh. Varanna neither forbade nor encouraged such activities, for she felt that each priestess needed the freedom to make such choices on her own. Though some priestesses succumbed to curiosity, most of the women tended to avoid the company of men. They did not find their thoughts attractive.

Sorak was different. His thoughts were completely inaccessible, even to Varanna, who had devoted over two centuries to mastery of the psionic arts. When the others first learned that a male had been accepted at the convent, their reactions were almost all negative. The strongest reactions came from the younger priestesses, who were aghast at the idea of a male in their midst, especially a male who was part elf and part halfling.

Human males were bad enough, they claimed, but elves were never to be trusted and halflings were savage, feral creatures who ate not only the flesh of animals, but human flesh, as well. The reactions of the priestesses ranged from astonishment and dismay to anger and even fear. None of them truly understood what it meant to be a 'tribe of one,' and lacking that understanding, they were frightened. Some of them even formed a delegation to make a formal protest to Varanna, an action without precedent, for the word of the high mistress had always been accepted without question. However, Varanna had held firm. Sorak was a male, and he was not human, but in every other respect, he may as well have been born villichi.

"He is gifted with powerful psionic talents," Varanna had explained to them. "The strongest I have ever seen. Such talents must be nurtured and properly developed. He is also an outcast. You all know what that means. Every one of you has known how it feels to be shunned and rejected, to be looked upon with distrust and even fear. Every one of you has known the pain of being unwanted and misunderstood. When you first came here, you were all granted shelter and acceptance. Are we to deny the same to Sorak merely because he is a male, and an elfling?"

"But males seek only to dominate women," one of the young priestesses replied.

"And elves are notoriously duplicitous," one of the others said.

"And halflings eat flesh," added another with disgust.

"As do humans," Varanna replied calmly. "We villichi do not eat flesh by choice, out of respect and veneration for other living creatures. Sorak is but a child, and he can be taught that same respect. Elves lie, cheat, and steal because that is the way of their society, where skill in such things is a measure of accomplishment. That is not our way, and that is not how Sorak shall be taught. As for the attitudes of males toward women, such attitudes result from the society in which they are brought up. If you treat Sorak with respect and accept him as an equal, he shall respond in kind."

"But even so, Mistress," said Kyana, the priestess who had been chosen to present their arguments, "the mere presence of a male in the convent will be disruptive. He is not truly one of us, and never can be, for he was not born villichi."

"No, he was not," agreed Varanna. "In some respects, he is as different from us as we are different from other humans. And because we were born different, we were shunned. Should we now treat Sorak the way others treated us?"

"It is not a matter of how we shall treat him, Mistress, but how he shall treat us," Kyana had replied. "He is a tribe of one. How much is known about this rare malady? You, yourself, Mistress, have said that you have only seen it twice before, and that only when you were very young. None of us has any way of knowing what this elfling may be capable of. He does not possess a normal mind. How do we know that we have not taken a serpent to our bosoms?"

"He does not possess a normal mind?" Varanna said, echoing Kyana's words. "Is that what you truly said? Are any of *us* normal? Each of us is here because others have said the very same things about us. We do not judge people by their appearance, by their gender, or by their capabilities, but by what is in their hearts. We do not condemn anyone simply because they are different. Or do the things that we believe and teach here at the convent matter to us only when it is convenient? If we shrink from those beliefs when they are put to the test, then we make a mockery of them. I shall not discuss this matter any further. Let the choice be yours. But if you choose to expel Sorak from the convent, then you shall have to choose a new high mistress, as well. I promised the pyreen elder to give the elfling shelter and to care for him. I shall not break my word. If Sorak leaves, then so shall I."

That had settled the matter of Sorak's staying at the convent, but other problems remained to be solved. For a long time, Sorak did not speak, and Varanna was not certain if the silence resulted from his not knowing the human tongue, or from the trauma he had suffered. Varanna did not know whether he had been cast out of an elvish tribe or a halfling tribe, and thus wasn't sure which language he had been exposed to. Then Sorak started having nightmares during which he cried out while he slept. He cried out in the halfling tongue for the most part, which suggested he had spent his first few years among a halfling tribe, but occasionally his words were elvish.

When he was awake, he never spoke at all.

Elder Al'Kali had done much to bring him back from the pitiful condition in which she had found him, but he was still weak, and his strength returned slowly. During his first few weeks at the convent, Sorak stayed with Varanna in her private chambers in the temple. Her repeated attempts to probe his mind continually met with failure. Either she was unceremoniously "tossed out," or else it was as if she had encountered a stone wall. Nevertheless, she kept on trying.

When Sorak had started to recover his strength, she decided it would be best for him to take up quarters with the priestesses. It would help him assimilate into life at the convent, and would discount claims of favoritism. However, once again, when Varanna brought Sorak to one of the residence halls, there had been alarmed reactions. The priestesses did not have their own individual rooms or cubicles. They slept on the upper floors of the residence halls, with their beds all lined up against the walls. The lower floors were set aside as large common rooms, where they could work at their looms or other crafts, or merely socialize. When Varanna had a bed installed upstairs for Sorak, the other women, especially the younger ones, became rather disturbed.

"But . . . he cannot sleep here!" one of them had said, a fifteen-year-old whose bed would have been next to his.

"And why not?" Varanna asked.

"But, Mistress . . . how shall we disrobe?"

"By pulling your robes over your heads, the way you usually do," Varanna said. "Unless there is a new method of disrobing I am not familiar with."

"But, Mistress . . . the boy shall *see*!" the young priestess protested.

"What of it?" asked Varanna, testily. "Are you ashamed of your body? Or does your nakedness make you feel vulnerable before a male, even one who is merely a boy? If that is the case, then you shall always feel vulnerable, for clothing makes the poorest sort of armor."

"It . . . it is not seemly," another young priestess

stammered hesitantly.

Varanna raised her eyebrows. "Are you suggesting that my actions are improper?"

"N-No, Mistress, but . . . but . . . he is a male, after all, and if he should see us naked, it will give him lewd ideas."

"Will it, indeed?" Varanna asked. "What sort of lewd ideas?"

The priestess blushed. "You . . . you know."

"No. Tell me."

The priestess took a deep breath while the others gathered around, watching to see how she would reply. "Males think of only one thing when it comes to women," she said.

"Ah, I see," Varanna replied. "And you are all so frightened and defenseless that you are afraid of a mere boy?"

"No, Mistress, of course not, but . . . " she took a deep breath and plunged on. "It will create tension and disharmony."

"Only if you allow it to," Varanna replied. "Sorak is but a child. His thoughts and attitudes about such things are not yet formed. If you accept him and treat him as a brother, then he will grow to love and accept you as his sisters. If you teach him respect for women, that is what he shall learn. But if you hide your bodies from him, as if they were unnatural, then he will grow curious and come to look upon a naked female body as forbidden fruit. And if you treat him differently simply because he is a male, then he will grow to treat women differently, simply because they are female. If there are things about the way that males act and think you find objectionable, then here is your opportunity to form the character of a male who does not act and think that way. And if your best efforts fail in

this task, then perhaps there is some fault in the way
you act and think."

"He may place his bed beside mine, Mistress," said
a firm, young voice. "I am not afraid."

Varanna turned toward Ryana with a smile. At six,
she was the youngest priestess at the convent, and in
many ways she was different from the others. Unlike
most villichi, who were born with blond hair and blue
or light gray eyes, Ryana's hair was absolutely white
and her eyes were a striking bright green. She was
also more normally proportioned, tall for a girl and
slender, but lacking the elongated limbs and neck of
most villichi. Judging by outward appearance alone,
it would have been difficult to tell she was villichi.
However, she had been born with powerful psionic
abilities and a strongly independent spirit, which
resulted in her being intelligent beyond her age. She
had been at the convent only a little less than a year.
Her frustrated and beleaguered parents were poor
people from Tyr with four other children, all of whom
had been born normal. They had been more than
happy to surrender the responsibility of caring for
Ryana, who had proved more than they could handle.

"You see?" Varanna said. "The youngest and the
smallest among you has a heart that is stouter and
braver. The rest of you should look to Ryana for an
example of what it truly means to be villichi."

Ryana's words had shamed the others, and they
had grudgingly accepted Sorak in their hall. His bed
was placed next to Ryana's, and from that day forth,
she had assumed responsibility for him like a protective older sister, even though they were roughly the
same age. It was Ryana who daily reported to Varanna
on Sorak's progress, and the first time Sorak ever
spoke, it was to utter Ryana's name. The two became

practically inseparable.

The fears of the other young priestesses about a male elfling in their midst proved groundless, and soon they were all calling him "little brother." They adopted the tigone cub as if it were their pet, but while it tolerated their caresses, it was clearly Sorak's beast. He called it Tigra. At night, they would let Tigra out to hunt for food, and shortly before daybreak, the gatekeeper would always hear it scratching at the heavy wooden doors. When it wasn't out hunting, it slept at the foot of Sorak's bed or followed him as if it were his shadow. And as time passed, it grew to be a very *large* shadow.

Sorak grew as well. As Varanna watched him practicing down in the courtyard, his leanly muscled chest and arms gleaming with sweat, she recalled how scrawny and emaciated he had been when Elder Al'Kali had first brought him to the temple. He had grown into a fine, strong, and very handsome young man. No, she thought, mentally correcting herself, not a man, for he wasn't human, after all. However, the blend of elf and halfling parentage had resulted in his looking almost completely human, except for his pointed ears, which his thick, shoulder-length, black hair often hid. He was tall, just under six feet, and his features, so delicate and elfin when he was a child, had grown sharp and rather striking. However, he did not possess any of the exaggerated features of an elf. Exaggerated, at least, from a human perspective. His ears were the same size and appearance as human ears, except for their sharp points. His eyes were deeply set and very dark. The eyebrows were no longer as delicately arched as they had been when he was a child, but high and narrow. The nose was sharp and almost beaklike, yet not unattractive. The cheekbones were prominent, and the face was narrow.

Overall, Sorak had a rather feral, haunted look about him. He had the kind of face people would immediately notice and remember, just as they would remember his direct, unsettling gaze. It was the sort of gaze that would make people look away. There was something in that gaze that would always mark Sorak as different. Varanna could not say exactly what it was, but she knew no one could fail to notice it. There was a turbulence in his gaze that hinted at the storm behind it.

In all her years, Varanna had only twice before encountered the phenomenon the villichi called *a tribe of one.* Both of the affected people were female, both were born villichi, and both had suffered terrible abuses as small children. The two women Varanna had known were senior priestesses at the temple when she was a mere girl, and had died long since. Varanna had never even heard of any others. The condition was so rare that, to Varanna's knowledge, no one on Athas knew about it save for the villichi. Yet, she had long suspected that being a tribe of one did not result from being born villichi, but from some painful and unbearable experience in an early stage of life that the young mind simply could not cope with. And so the mind fragmented into discarnate entities.

She was not certain if it had anything to do with psionic talent, but there did seem to be a relationship between the two. It was as if the fragmentation of the mind somehow resulted in a compensation of abilities.

For all Varanna knew, this fragmentation could happen to anyone, and there may well have been other, similar cases among normal humans, perhaps even among the other humanoid species of Athas, though she had never heard of any. Of course, if no one understood the condition, or were even aware it could exist, it might simply pass for madness.

Most people, she thought, would undoubtedly consider it madness, yet it did not seem to result in delusions or irrational behavior. Sorak, however, showed an inconsistency of behavior that could seem irrational because it was not the behavior of the same individual, but of different individuals sharing the same body, each with his or her own distinct voice and personality. And, Varanna soon discovered, each with distinct abilities.

Varanna was not certain how many of them there were. In the beginning, Sorak had not conspicuously displayed any of his other personalities, but he did experience occasional lapses—periods of time he later could not account for, could not remember. It was as if he had been asleep, but his behavior did not seem to change dramatically during those times. However, Varanna knew that during those lapses, one of his other personalities was in control, and she learned to watch for changes in behavior that would signal such lapses.

The changes were often subtle, but they were nevertheless discernable to anyone who knew Sorak well. It was as if the other entities residing in his mind were cautiously attempting to conceal their emergence. As Varanna observed Sorak's different aspects, she soon learned to differentiate them.

The first one she had met was called the Guardian. The first time she had knowingly spoken with the Guardian, Sorak was ten or eleven years old.

A curious pattern had developed in his education, a pattern that exasperated his instructors. They knew Sorak had unusually powerful abilities, but he did not seem to respond well to psionic training. He grew frustrated with his repeated failures, yet stubbornly kept trying. Regardless of the effort, however, he could not perform even the most elementary psionic exercises. He would concentrate until his face turned red and sweat started to break out on his forehead, all to no avail. Then, when he was utterly exhausted and apparently had no energy left to continue, he would suddenly accomplish the exercise successfully, without even being aware of having done so. His instructors were at a loss to account for this peculiarity, and Varanna decided to look into it herself. She summoned Sorak and gave him a simple exercise in telekinesis.

She placed three small balls on a table before him and told him to lift as many as he could with the power of his mind. He concentrated fiercely, but to no avail. He could not even move one. Finally, he gave up and covered his face with his hands.

"It is no use," he moaned miserably. "I cannot do it."

The three balls suddenly rose into the air and began to describe graceful and complicated arabesques, as if manipulated by an invisible juggler.

"Yes, Sorak, you can," Varanna said. "Look."

And when Sorak looked up, the three balls all dropped to the floor.

"You see? You did it," said Varanna.

Sorak sighed with frustration. "It happened again," he said. "When I try, I cannot do it. When I stop trying, I succeed, but I do not know how!"

"Perhaps you simply try too hard," Varanna suggested.

"But even when I try only a little, I still cannot do it," he said with exasperation. "It simply seems to happen by itself."

"Nevertheless, it is *you* who are doing it," Varanna replied. "Perhaps, in your anxiety, you are creating a block for your abilities, and when you give up in frustration, the block is dissipated, allowing the task to be accomplished, if only for a moment. If you would allow me to probe your thoughts, perhaps I could discover where the problem lies."

"I have no objection, Mistress," Sorak said, "and yet a part of me seems reluctant to allow it. I do not know why."

Varanna knew why, but up to that point, Sorak seemed unaware of his true nature, and she did not wish to prod him in directions he was not yet ready to explore. "You know you have nothing to fear from me, Sorak," she said.

"I *know* that," he said, frustrated. "I cannot understand what it is. Each time we try, I am perfectly willing, and yet some part of me seems anxious to prevent it. I try my best to be receptive, but . . . " His voice trailed off, and he simply shrugged helplessly.

Varanna had a sudden intuition. "Let us try it the same way it happened with the balls. Do not attempt to be receptive. Simply give up and relax. Empty your mind."

"Very well." He slumped slightly on the bench and lowered his head, emptying his lungs with a heavy sigh. Before Varanna could attempt to make her probe, however, he abruptly raised his head and stared at her with a challenging gaze.

"Why do you persist in attempting to invade our thoughts? What do you want of us?"

Varanna suddenly realized that it wasn't Sorak speaking. At least, not the Sorak she had known up to that point. The voice was the same, and yet the tone was completely different, more demanding, more mature, more self-assured. Even Sorak's physical demeanor had undergone a subtle change. The language of his body, a language that often spoke more eloquently than words, had become suddenly defensive.

"Who are you?" she asked in a soft voice, leaning forward slightly.

"You may call me the Guardian. I know who you are. You are the mistress."

"If you know who I am, then you should also know that my only intentions are to help you," replied Varanna. "All of you," she added.

"With this?" the Guardian said as Sorak indicated the fallen balls with his outstretched hand. Suddenly, they rose into the air and hovered there.

"With that, and other things, as well," Varanna replied.

"The boy is confused," the Guardian said. "You are causing him distress. You make him think he can do this, but he cannot. He does not have the ability."

Varanna suddenly understood. "But you do," she said, with a nod. "I see that now."

The balls leaped over one another briefly in midair, then fell bouncing to the floor. "I fail to see the point in this. It is meaningless and serves no purpose."

"It is *not* meaningless, and it *does* serve a purpose," Varanna countered firmly. "It is an exercise designed to sharpen telekinetic skills."

"I have no need of such exercises," the Guardian said curtly. "I have only cooperated to ease the boy's frustration, which you and others cause."

None of the other priestesses would have dared to speak so to the high mistress, and Sorak would certainly never have addressed her in so challenging a tone. Then again, Varanna thought, this wasn't Sorak.

Even though she had some understanding of what it meant to be a tribe of one, she had to keep reminding herself of that. This entity seemed much more mature than Sorak, she thought, more confident, and certainly more combative. Then with a flash of insight she suddenly realized that this was precisely its role. The name alone should have alerted her, and she mentally castigated herself for not seeing it at once, but the shock of the Guardian's emergence had thrown her.

"You seek to protect the boy," she said. "I only seek to teach him."

"He cannot learn that which you would teach," the Guardian replied. "And the rest of us have no need for such instruction."

"Then there are others among the tribe, beside yourself, who possess psionic talent?" asked Varanna, leaning forward intently. Here, at last, was the explanation for Sorak's failure to display his psionic powers. He did not really have them, in a sense. The other members of his inner tribe did.

"Tribe?" said the Guardian. "Why do you call us that?"

"You are many who form a tribe within one body," said Varanna, "a 'tribe of one.' It is rare, yet not unheard of. I, myself, have known two others, though it was many years ago. And you are doing Sorak no service by sheltering him from his true nature. He knows that he is unlike others, and not merely because he is an elfling. He knows that he possesses powers he cannot summon forth, yet he does not understand why. This is what confuses him and causes him distress. You cannot protect Sorak from the truth about himself. If you persist in your efforts to shelter him, then you shall only cause him pain and suffering."

"The boy suffered when he was abandoned in the desert," said the Guardian. "We sheltered him from his suffering. He was prepared to surrender to death. We gave him the strength to go on."

"But there is a limit to how much strength you can give him," said Varanna. "Despite your efforts, the boy would have died had not the pyreen found him. She brought him here so that we could give him shelter and the knowledge necessary to comprehend his nature. He will be stronger for this knowledge of himself, and with the proper training, he can learn to live more easily with what he has become and call upon his abilities much more effectively. There is strength in a tribe that is united. But so long as you shelter Sorak from the truth about himself, he shall always remain weak."

The Guardian was silent for a while, considering what she had said. When the Guardian spoke again, it was in a more relaxed tone, though still a cautious one. "There is wisdom in your words. Yet, if you have known the truth about us all along, you could have told Sorak all these things yourself. Why have you refrained?"

"Because I, too, care for Sorak's welfare," said Varanna. "And it is not enough merely to tell someone the truth. He must be prepared to hear it."

"Perhaps the time has come, then," the Guardian replied. "The boy bears great affection and respect for you. Prepare him to experience this truth. Then, in our own way, we shall reveal it to him."

The next thing she knew, Sorak was gazing at her once again, a puzzled expression on his face. "Forgive me, Mistress," he said. "I must have fallen asleep. I had the most peculiar dream. . . ."

That had been the beginning of Sorak's true awakening. Gently, and with great care, Varanna had told him the truth about himself, a truth he had, up to that point, not even suspected. And as she spoke, the Guardian gently eased Sorak's anxiety and apprehension. In the coming weeks, the Guardian gradually allowed Sorak to discover more about his multiplicity. Initially, this strange learning process took place, for the most part, while Sorak slept and dreamed. Then, when the context of his situation started to become familiar to him, Sorak experienced the gradual emergence of his other personalities, without suffering lapses, but remaining conscious on some level while they were dominant in his body. It was a slow process, however, and one that was still unfolding.

From the beginning of Sorak's inner journey of self-discovery, the Guardian had been his guide and Varanna his mentor. She studied the journals of the two priestesses who had had the same condition, spending hours each day in the temple library, trying to relate their experiences to Sorak's. In some ways, it was easier for Sorak because the alternate personas of his inner tribe were inclined to be cooperative, and there did not seem to be any competition between them. Varanna believed this was the result of Sorak's ordeal in the desert. His young mind had fragmented because it could not endure the pain and suffering inflicted on him. To survive in the desolate Athasian desert, his different aspects all had to work together.

Every evening, Sorak would come to Varanna's chambers, and they would discuss the Guardian's gradual revelations. In time, Sorak came to accept and understand his condition. As the years passed, he learned how to communicate with his inner tribe and how to function with them, as well as how to give way and allow them to work through him. It was, however, a journey that was far from finished. Both Varanna's intuition and the knowledge she gleaned from the others' journals told her that new discoveries still awaited him. And, recently, she had come to the conclusion that there would be yet another journey for Sorak to undertake, a physical journey, and that he would be embarking on it very soon.

She returned her attention to the weapons practice session down in the courtyard, where Sorak and his instructor engaged in mock combat with wooden practice swords. Tamura was the head weapons instructor at the convent, and at the age of forty-three, she was still young for a villichi. Her physical condition was superb, and none of the other priestesses could even come close to matching her skills with weapons. Yet, though still in his teens, Sorak was already a match for her. That, Varanna thought, was his particular gift. Each of his personalities possessed a talent of his or her own, and Sorak's was mastery of the blades. He handled the sword and dagger as well as any champion gladiator, and Tamura took great pride in her prize pupil. She yelled encouragement to him with each well-placed blow he struck, and as her other pupils watched their match, no one looked on with more admiration than Ryana, whose own skill with the blades was almost the equal of Sorak's.

The two had always been extremely close, Varanna thought, but as they had matured, Ryana's feelings toward Sorak had grown unmistakably stronger. And they were not the feelings of sister toward brother. There was, on the surface, nothing wrong with that, Varanna thought. They were not related by blood. However, with Sorak, there was a great deal beneath the surface, and Varanna felt concern about this new development.

Ryana was villichi, but she was still human, and Sorak was an elfling—perhaps the only one of his kind. If they were to spend the remainder of their days at the convent, a relationship between them might not pose a problem, but in the outside world, it would not be easily accepted. Further, Varanna did not know if Sorak was capable of fathering any children. Half-breeds were often sterile, but not always. As a villichi, Ryana would never bear any children of her own, whether Sorak would want them or not. These potential problems were, perhaps, insignificant, but there were others that were not.

"He fights like a fiend," Neela said, coming up behind the high mistress. She stood beside her, watching the contest in the courtyard below. "He is still young, yet already he has surpassed Tamura. Perhaps it is time he took over as instructor."

Varanna nodded. "Indeed, he is masterful, but he still has much to learn. Perhaps not about the blades, but about himself, the world, and his place in it. I do not think he will be remaining with us much longer."

Neela frowned. "He has spoken of leaving the convent?"

Varanna shook her head. "No. Not yet. But soon, Neela. I can sense it." She sighed. "This has been a good place for him to grow, to get his two feet firmly on the ground, but now he must set those feet upon the path that he will walk in life, and that path shall take him away from us."

"He may have a compelling reason to remain," said Neela.

"Ryana?" Varanna shook her head. "No, she will not be reason enough."

"They love each other," Neela said. "That is clear

for anyone to see."

Varanna shook her head again. "That Ryana loves him, I shall not dispute. But as for Sorak . . . " She sighed. "Love can be difficult enough for ordinary people. For Sorak, it poses problems that may well be insurmountable."

Neela nodded. "Then he shall leave us, and that will solve the problem. Ryana will be broken-hearted, but broken hearts can mend."

Varanna smiled, sadly. "Tell me, Neela, have you ever been in love yourself?"

Neela glanced at her with surprise. "No, Mistress, of course not."

Varanna nodded. "I did not think so."

TWO

The courtyard echoed with the cracking of wooden practice swords as Sorak and Tamura moved back and forth in the intricate choreography of combat. Sorak was less than half Tamura's age, and despite having just gone through an intense workout, he was still possessed by the energy of youth. However, Tamura was by no means at a disadvantage. She was the head weapons instructor at the convent for one reason only—she was the best.

At the age of forty-three, Tamura's physical condition was superior to that of most women half her age, and her reactions were as quick as ever. She fought in a light robe to protect her pale skin from the sun, her blond hair tied back loosely behind her neck. Sorak, having already worked up a sweat during the training session, fought bare-chested, his darker skin far less vulnerable to the sun's rays. His black hair hung loose past his shoulders and his lean muscles stood out sharply, defined by the glistening sweat. Ryana felt excited as she watched him.

For years, she had looked upon him as a brother, though they were not related by blood and were not even of the same race. Recently, however, Ryana had become aware of a dramatic change in her feelings toward Sorak. These feelings had come upon her gradually, so there had never been a moment when she found herself shocked to suddenly discover that she wanted him. There had been time for her to analyze these feelings and to become accustomed to them, though it was something she and Sorak had never actually discussed. Still, she knew he must be aware of how she felt. They were too close for him not to know. Yet, he had never said or done anything to indicate to her that he felt the same way.

The others all knew, Ryana was certain of that. Everybody knew. It was something she simply could not hide, nor did she wish to hide it. She told herself that there was nothing wrong in what she felt. With only rare exceptions, villichi priestesses were celibate, but that was not as a result of any rule; it was simply their choice. She felt sure her love for Sorak did not violate any taboos at the convent. Nevertheless, there were those among her sisters who sought to discourage it.

"You are treading on dangerous ground, Ryana," Saleen had told her while they were working at their looms. Saleen was older, almost twenty-two, and saw Ryana watch as Sorak walked past their window. He was on his way to see the high mistress and had Tigra trotting along at his heels.

"What do you mean?" Ryana replied.

"Sorak," said Saleen. She smiled. "I have seen the way you look at him. Everyone has seen."

"What of it?" asked Ryana, in a challenging tone. "Are you saying it is wrong?"

"Perhaps not," Saleen had replied gently, "that is not for me to say, but I think it is unwise."

"Why? Because he is an elfling and a tribe of one?" Ryana had said. "That makes no difference to me."

"Yes, but it may make a difference to him," replied Saleen. "You are closer to Sorak than any of the rest of us, but your very closeness may be preventing you from seeing what the rest of us have seen only too clearly."

"And what would that be?" she asked defensively.

"You look upon Sorak as a woman looks upon a man she loves," Saleen said. "Sorak looks upon you as a brother looks upon a sister."

"But he is not my brother," Ryana protested.

"That makes little difference if he merely looks upon you as a sister," said Saleen. "Besides, you know that loving Sorak could never be the same as loving any other male. I do not pretend to be wise in the ways of the world, Ryana, but from all that I have heard, it is often difficult enough for just two people to find love together. With Sorak, there are more than two people involved."

"I am well aware of that," Ryana said sharply. "I am not a fool."

"No," Saleen said. "No one is saying that. Nor am I suggesting that you do not know what is involved. His other aspects speak through him only to you and the high mistress. The rest of us have never been so favored. But that is still no indication that *all* of Sorak's inner aspects can feel love for you. It is not enough for you to love all of Sorak. All of Sorak must also love you. And even if they could, where would it lead? Where *could* it lead? Villichi do not marry. We do not take mates."

"I am aware of no rule that forbids it," said Ryana.

"Have you forgotten your vows? ' . . . to devote my heart and soul completely to the sisterhood; to devote my energies to the teaching of the disciplines we all hold true; to seek out others like myself and grant them aid and shelter; to cleave to one another above all personal desires and material comfort.' Those are the vows you took, Ryana."

"But there is nothing there forbidding marriage or the taking of a mate," Ryana said.

"Perhaps that is your interpretation," said Saleen, "but I doubt the high mistress would agree with it. Remember, also, that Sorak was never asked to take those vows, because he is not villichi. And he is no longer a child. He is almost a grown man. Our life is here, at the convent, with our sisters. Sorak is a male—part elf, part halfling. Elves are true nomads and halflings somewhat so. It is in their blood, in *his* blood. Do you truly believe that Sorak could be happy to remain here the rest of his days? If he should choose to leave, Ryana, there is nothing to prevent him. But you have taken vows."

Ryana felt a hollow feeling in the pit of her stomach. "He has never said anything about leaving the convent. He has never even indicated the slightest wish to leave."

"Perhaps because the time was not yet right," Saleen said. "Or perhaps because, knowing how you feel, it is a subject he has purposely avoided. He came to us half dead, weak in body and in spirit. Now he is strong in both, and vibrantly alive. He does not need the convent anymore, Ryana. He has outgrown us, and you are the only one who cannot or will not see it. Sooner or later, he must leave to find his own way in the world. What will you do then?"

Ryana did not know what she would do. The possibility of Sorak's leaving the convent was something she had never even considered, perhaps because, as Saleen suggested, she had been afraid to consider it. She had assumed that she and Sorak would always be together. But what if Saleen was right? The thought of losing him was more than she could bear. Ever since that conversation with Saleen, the uncertainty had been gnawing away at her. Nor was Saleen the only one who had sought to caution her in that regard.

At first, she had tried to tell herself that the others were merely jealous, or that they were somehow threatened by the prospect that she and Sorak might become lovers, but she could not deceive herself that way. She knew her sisters cared for her, just as they cared for Sorak, and had only her best interests at heart. But what did Sorak feel?

Outwardly, nothing in their relationship had changed. She had given him every opportunity to reveal if he felt the same way she did, yet he seemed not to notice her attempts to steer their relationship in a new, more intimate direction. Perhaps, thought Ryana, I have been too subtle. Males, she had been told, were not very perceptive. However, that did not seem to apply to Sorak. He was unusually perceptive, and possessed of a strong intuitive sense. Perhaps, she thought, he has merely been waiting for me to make the first move, to openly declare myself. On the other hand, what if he did not share her feelings? Either way, she could stand the uncertainty no longer. One way or the other, she simply had to know.

"*Enough!*" cried Tamura, raising her hand and lowering her wooden sword. Both she and Sorak were breathing heavily from their exertions. Neither had managed to score a telling blow. Tamura grinned. "I knew this day would come," she said. "We are evenly matched. There is no more I can teach you."

"I find that difficult to believe, Sister," replied Sorak. "You have always beaten me before. I was merely lucky today."

Tamura shook her head. "No, Sorak, the past few times we have tried each other's measure, it was *I* who have been lucky. I have held nothing back, and you have taken the best that I could give. The pupil has now become the master. You have made me very proud."

Sorak bowed his head. "That is high praise, indeed, coming from you, Sister Tamura. I am not worthy."

"Yes, you are," Tamura said, clapping him on the shoulder. "For a teacher, there can be no greater satisfaction than to see a pupil surpass her."

"But I have not surpassed you, Sister," Sorak protested. "The match was, at best, a draw."

"Only because I stopped it when I did," she said with a smile. "I remember all the nasty whacks I gave you while you were still learning, and I did not wish to be repaid in kind!"

The others laughed. They had all felt the sharp crack of Tamura's wooden sword on more than one occasion, and the thought of her receiving some of her own medicine was tantalizing.

"The lesson is finished for the day," Tamura said. "You are all free to go bathe."

The other pupils whooped and ran to put away their practice swords before they raced down to the shaded pool. Only Ryana lingered, to wait for Sorak.

"You two are the best pupils I have ever had," Tamura said to them. "Either one of you could take over the training of the others now."

"You are too kind, Sister," said Ryana. "And Sorak is still the better fighter."

"Yes, but not by much," agreed Tamura. "He has a special gift. The sword becomes a part of him. He was born to the blade."

"You did not seem to think so when I began to

study with you," Sorak said with a grin.

"No, I saw it even then," Tamura said. "That is why I was so much harder on you than on any of the others. You thought it was because you were a male, but it was because I wanted to bring out your full potential. As for you, little sister," she added, turning to Ryana and smiling, "I have always known that you resented me because you thought I was being unfair to Sorak. That is why, for all these years, you have worked twice as hard as any of the others. I know you wanted to repay me for all of Sorak's bruises, and for your own, as well."

Ryana blushed. "It is true, I must confess. There were times I almost hated you. But I feel that way no longer," she quickly added.

"And a good thing, too," Tamura said, reaching out to ruffle her hair playfully, "because you have reached the stage where you could do some damage. I think it is time you two took over the training of the novices. I think you will find, as I have, that teaching has its own rewards. Go on now and join the others, or we shall all have to sit upwind of you at supper time."

Ryana and Sorak went to put away their practice swords, then they walked down to the gate together, heading toward the pool. A short distance from the entrance to the convent, a thin stream bubbled up from beneath the mountains, cascading down in a waterfall that formed a pool around its base. As Ryana and Sorak approached, they could hear the others shouting as they enjoyed the bracing, ice-cold waters of the pool.

"Let us go this way, Sorak," said Ryana, beckoning him down a path that led away from the pool, toward a point farther down, where the water flowed over some large rocks in the stream. "I am in no mood to splash and wrestle with the others. I feel like simply lying back and letting the waters engulf me."

"Good idea," Sorak said. "I have no energy to frolic either. I am sore all over. Tamura has exhausted me."

"No more than you have exhausted her," Ryana replied with a grin. "I felt so proud of you when she said you were the best pupil she ever had."

"She said we were *both* the best pupils she ever had," Sorak corrected her. "Did you really want to pay her back for all my bruises?"

Ryana smiled. "And for my own, as well. But I used to think she singled you out for mistreatment because you are male. I always thought that she resented your presence among us. Now I know better, of course."

"Yet, there *were* those who resented my being here, at least in the beginning," Sorak said.

"I know, I remember. But you proved them wrong and won them over."

"I could never have done it without you," said Sorak.

"We make a good team," she said.

Sorak did not reply, and Ryana suddenly felt flooded with uncertainty again. They walked a while in silence, until they reached the bank. Sorak waded right in, without bothering to strip off his high moccasins or leather breeches. He lay back on a large flat rock and put his head in the water, soaking his hair. "Ahhh, that feels good!" he said.

Ryana watched him for a moment, then removed her robe, unlaced her moccasins and untied the leather thong holding back her long, white hair. She and Sorak had seen each other naked more times than she could count, but suddenly, she felt self-conscious. She waded out and took her place beside him on the rock. He moved over to make room for her. Now was the time, she thought. If she didn't ask him now, she did not know if she would ever get up the courage.

"Sorak . . . there is something I have been meaning to ask you," she began hesitantly. She did not quite know how to put it into words. It was the first time in her life she had ever felt awkward about expressing any of her feelings.

"I know what you are going to ask," said Sorak before she could continue. He sat up and faced her. "I have known for quite some time now."

"And yet, you have said nothing," she said. Her mouth suddenly felt dry, and there was a tightness in her chest. "Why?"

Sorak looked away. "Because I have been wrestling with it myself," he said. "I knew this moment would come, and I have dreaded it."

Ryana felt as if she were teetering on the brink of an abyss. Those last words had said it all. "You need not go on," she said flatly. She looked away and bit her lower lip, trying to keep it from trembling. "It was just that . . . I had hoped . . . "

"Ryana, I *do* care for you," Sorak said, "but we can never be anything more to each other than what we are now." He sighed. "I could accept you as my lover and my mate, but the Guardian could not."

"But . . . *why*? In all the times that I have spoken with the Guardian, he has never indicated any disapproval of me. What is his objection?"

"Ryana . . . " Sorak said gently, "the Guardian is female."

She stared at him, thunderstruck by this sudden revelation. "*What?* But, he never . . . I mean, you never said . . . " Her voice trailed off and she shook her head in confusion. "The Guardian is *female?*"

"Yes."

"But . . . how can that be possible?"

"Ryana, I do not know," said Sorak helplessly. "Even after all these years, there is much about the way I am I do not fully understand. I do not recall my childhood, my infancy that is, before I was cast out into the desert. The high mistress thinks that the Guardian is female because my mother was my first protector. Perhaps after I had been cast out of the tribe, my young mind somehow created a maternal entity to take over that function. But there is no way of knowing for certain how or why it came to pass. It simply happened. The Guardian is female. Nor is she the only one. At least two of my other aspects are also female. For all I know, there may be others I am not even aware of yet. Perhaps the way I have grown up here at the convent had something to do with it. Who knows? After all, I have been surrounded by females all my life. I have never known another male, nor even seen one."

Ryana felt utterly confused. "But . . . *you are male!* How can a part of you be female? It makes no sense!"

"The mistress says we all have male and female aspects," Sorak replied. "In my case, those aspects have become separate identities. Different people. The *body* that we share is male, and I, Sorak, am male, but the Guardian was born female. As were Kivara and the Watcher."

Ryana stared at him in complete bewilderment. "*Kivara? The Watcher?* Who are they? I know nothing of them! In all these years, you have never even mentioned them before!"

"And I would not have mentioned them now, save that they felt it was important in this current circumstance," Sorak replied.

Ryana suddenly felt angry. "After all the years we have known each other, after all we have meant to one another . . . *how could you have kept this from me?*"

"*I* could not have kept it from you," Sorak said, "but *they* could, and they *did*." He brought his hands up to his head and pressed his fingertips against his temples. It was a sign, Ryana knew, that one of his other aspects was trying to emerge, but that Sorak was struggling to retain control. It caused him terrible headaches, and she had not seen such an inner struggle for a long time.

"How can I possibly explain it you?" he said in a tormented voice. "We have known each other for ten years, Ryana, and yet still you do not truly comprehend what it is to be a tribe of one. You simply do not understand. Perhaps you never shall."

"How can you say that?" she countered, feeling hurt and angry. "I was the first to speak up for you! I was the first to hold out my hand to you in friendship, and for ten years we have been as close to one another as two people can be. I had hoped we could grow closer, but now . . . great dragon! Now I do not know *what* to think!"

He took her hands. "Ryana . . . " She tried to pull away, but he held on firmly. "No, Ryana, *listen* to me. Please. I cannot help being the way I am. I, Sorak, can control but my own thoughts and actions. The others with whom I share this body all think the way they choose to think and act the way they choose to act. I can look upon you and see a warm, compassionate, intelligent, and beautiful young woman for whom I can feel desire. But the Guardian, Kivara, and the Watcher are not capable of feeling desire for a woman. Well, Kivara, I must admit, has a certain curiosity, but the Watcher and the Guardian are repelled by the idea of us becoming lovers. They could not allow it." He brought his hands up to clutch his head and winced with pain. "No! Let me finish!"

Then, abruptly, his hands came down, and a calm, stoic expression came over his features. It was not Sorak anymore. "We should not continue this discussion," said the Guardian flatly. "It is causing Sorak great distress."

"Damn you," said Ryana. "How can you do this to us? You never told me that you were female!"

"You never asked," the Guardian replied.

"How could I have thought to ask? Whenever you spoke to me, it was always with a man's voice, as you speak to me now!"

"It is not my fault that I exist within a male body," the Guardian replied. "Had I a choice, it is not the choice I would have made. However, it is something I have learned to accept, as you must learn to accept it."

"This is ridiculous!" Ryana shouted. "Sorak is a *man!*"

"No, he merely looks like one," the Guardian replied in a calm voice. "In fact, he is an elfling. He cannot be a man, because he is not human. Or have you forgotten that, as you seem to have forgotten his needs and his feelings in the face of your own selfish desire?"

Reacting instinctively, Ryana slapped the Guardian's face, but in doing so, she also slapped Sorak, and suddenly realized what she had done. Her hand went to her mouth and she bit down on her knuckle as her eyes went wide with shock. "What have I done? Sorak. . . ."

"Sorak understands, and he forgives you," said the Guardian. "And for his sake, I shall try to do the same. But you are behaving like a foolish, thoughtless girl who is merely angry because she cannot have her way. And you are only causing Sorak pain. Is that truly what you wish?"

Ryana's eyes flooded with tears. "No," she said in a small voice. She shook her head. "No, that is the very last thing I would wish to do." She stifled a sob, then rose quickly and splashed back to the bank, where she had dropped her robe and moccasins. Without even bothering to put them on, she simply snatched them up and ran back toward the convent.

As she stumbled up the path, tears blurring her vision, Ryana cursed herself for a fool. She felt angry, hurt, humiliated, and more miserable than she had ever felt in her entire life. A storm of conflicting emotions surged through her. She ran, as if trying to escape them, and when she was about halfway back to the convent, she simply sank to her knees on the path and pounded her fists on the ground in helpless frustration, sobbing in both pain and anger.

Fool, fool, she thought. Why, oh, why did I not listen to the others? They only sought to warn me, to protect me. . . . And the sudden thought came, just as the Guardian is protecting Sorak. But from what? From her love? From his own feelings? Was it not the Guardian who was being cruel and selfish? Ten years, she thought, bitterly. *Ten years* we knew each other, and he never told me. *They* never told me. The others wouldn't let him. And then, abruptly, her feelings of pity and despair shifted from herself to Sorak.

He had told her that he cared for her, that he had wrestled with this problem, but he could not go against his own nature. She thought, with anguish, what must it be like for him? He had said she did not understand. Well, he was right. How could she? How could she possibly know what it was like to share her body with other entities who had thoughts and feelings of their own? It was not his fault. It was not something he had chosen, but a curse that he was doomed to live with, most likely for the remainder of his life. And in declaring her feelings for him, she had just made things that much worse for him.

Oh, Sorak, she thought, what have I done to you? As she knelt on the ground and wept, the shouts of the other priestesses frolicking in the nearby pool drifted toward her. She could hear them laughing as if they didn't have a care in the world. Why couldn't she be like them? They did not suffer for the lack of males in their lives. They were content to accept Sorak as a brother. Why wasn't that enough for her? Perhaps they knew nothing of love, but if this was love, then with all her heart, she wished them continued ignorance.

With an effort, she struggled to pull herself together. She didn't want the others to see her like this. What had just passed between herself and Sorak did not concern them. She stood and put on her robe and moccasins, then brushed the tears from her eyes. The Guardian was right, she thought. She would simply have to learn how to accept this. Right now, she did not know how she could, but she simply had to somehow, or else her presence around Sorak would only cause them both continued pain. She took a deep breath, trying to collect herself, and started walking purposefully back toward the convent gates. There was only one thing she could think to do right now. It would be best for Sorak if he did not see her for a while. She, too, needed time to sort things out, to be apart from him.

Perhaps, she thought, they would never be able to

go back to the way they once were. That thought was even more unbearable than the thought of not being able to love Sorak. In fact, she thought, I *can* love him. It is only that I can never truly possess him, or be possessed by him, the way it is with normal people. But then, she reminded herself, we are not normal people.

If his female aspects prevented him from making love with her, then they would also prevent him from ever making love with any other woman. In that respect, at least, Sorak would be like most villichi. He would remain celibate. Not by choice, perhaps, but by necessity. So she would do the same. In that way, perhaps, their love would be all the more pure. She knew that it would not be easy. It would take time to discipline her mind to this new resolve, just as it had taken time for her feelings toward Sorak to build up her expectations. Perhaps she had no right to any expectations, no right to think of her own desires. That, she realized, was what Saleen had meant when she talked about the vows that they all took.

" . . . above all personal desires and material comfort," she said with bitter irony. She had been but a child when she took those vows. What did she know of their true meaning? It was all so horribly unfair. The question was, what would happen now? Neither she nor Sorak could ever forget what had just passed between them. "Villichi do not marry," Saleen had said. "We do not take mates." Ryana had allowed herself to think she could be different. And it was a curse to be different. She had learned that lesson once before, in childhood, and now, because she had forgotten it, she had painfully learned it once again.

THREE

"There was no reason for you to step in. You only made things worse by interfering."

"I was merely trying to protect you from—"

"I do not require protection from Ryana, or from my own feelings!"

Had any strangers been present to observe this conversation, they would doubtless have assumed that Sorak was a madman. All they would have seen was Sorak sitting on a large, flat rock in the middle of the pool and apparently having a one-sided conversation with himself. They would have heard what Sorak said, for he spoke aloud, but seemingly to no one. The Guardian's remarks were inaudible, for they were spoken only within Sorak's mind. Sorak was capable of carrying on conversations with his other aspects entirely without speech, but he was angry, and he felt that if he tried to keep it all inside, he would explode.

"The girl was being obstinate and selfish," said the Guardian. *"She was not listening to you. She was making no attempt to understand. She was thinking only of her own desire."*

"She was confused," said Sorak. "And she was angry, because she felt I'd kept things from her. The way you spoke to her was needlessly harsh and cruel.

She has always been our friend. And more than just a friend. She cared about us when no one else did."

"The high mistress cared."

"The mistress cared, yes, but that was not the same. She recognized our talents and our condition and felt compelled to help. She understood what we had suffered and took pity on us. She felt an obligation to the Elder Al'Kali. Ryana cared without any cause or condition. It was shameful for you to treat her as you did. And it was shameful for us to have deceived her all these years."

"No one deceived the girl," the Guardian replied. *"To withhold information is not the same thing as deception."*

"Words!" said Sorak angrily. "The fact remains she was deceived. Had she known from the beginning, this never would have happened!"

"Perhaps not," the Guardian replied, *"but you seem to be forgetting something. You, yourself, did not know from the beginning, and when you did know, you feared the others would discover that we were both male and female. You questioned your own masculine identity. It caused you great concern, and so the three of us held back and bolstered your own image of yourself. Then, later, when you and the girl—"*

"Her name is Ryana!"

"When you and Ryana had grown close, there was a part of you that felt afraid to tell her, because you feared how she might react. If there was deception, then you were a part of it yourself."

"Perhaps a part of me was afraid to tell her," Sorak admitted, grudgingly. "But I could have told her now, and much more gently than you did. Now she is hurt and angry and confused, through no fault of her own. We have led her on and caused her to expect something that we could never give."

"*I did not lead anybody on,*" the Guardian replied. "*Villichi do not take mates, and for the most part, remain celibate. How was I to know that she was different? How was I to know what was on her mind?*"

"Liar! You are the telepath among us!"

"*True, but I could not read Ryana's mind when you were out, and when I spoke to her myself, you always cautioned me to be properly respectful, to treat her as our friend. One does not read a friend's thoughts unless one is invited.*"

"You always have some ready answer," Sorak said, sourly. "But then, should I be surprised, when you know my thoughts as well as I know them myself?"

"*Sometimes I know them better.*"

"Sometimes I wish I could drag you out and throttle you!"

"*If an apology will help, then I shall apologize.*"

"I do not need your apologies!"

"*I meant to the girl, not to you,*" the Guardian said. "*As usual, you think only of yourself.*"

Sorak winced. "And, as usual, you strike right to the bone."

"*We are what we are, Sorak,*" the Guardian said. "*I could no more lie with the girl than you could lie with a man. Kivara . . . well, Kivara has no shame.*"

"*I heard that,*" said another voice. Had it spoken aloud, it would have spoken with Sorak's lips and throat, and sounded male. But it had spoken within Sorak's mind, and therefore sounded very female. It was a young voice, and a saucy one.

"Stay out of this, Kivara," Sorak said.

"*Why should I? Does this not concern us all?*"

"*It should concern you least of all, since you apparently have no decisive inclinations, one way or the other,*" the Guardian said wryly.

"*How can I, when I have had no experience in such*

things?" Kivara countered. *"If I leave it all to you and the Watcher, we shall always remain ignorant in this regard. The girl is comely, and has always treated us well. Could it have been so bad?"*

The Watcher, as usual, said nothing, but Sorak felt her apprehension. The Watcher hardly ever spoke, but she was always there, alert, taking everything in. Unlike the others, who slumbered from time to time, the Watcher never slept. Sorak always felt her quiet presence.

"Enough!" he said. "I can see no way to resolve this problem except to remain celibate. It seems a small enough price to pay to avoid this noisome discord."

"It may be a greater price to pay than you think," Kivara said.

"Sorak has decided," said a new voice, cutting through the discussion like an icy wind. Kivara instantly "ducked under," submerging herself deep within the recesses of Sorak's mind. Even the Guardian fell silent. They all did when the Shade spoke. Sorak took a deep breath, trembling as if with a chill as he felt the Shade's grim presence, but the dark persona spoke no more and slithered back into Sorak's subconscious.

Sorak suddenly found himself alone again, or as alone as it was ever possible for him to be. He was no longer sitting on the flat rock in the pool, but standing on the pathway leading back to the convent. He did not remember how he got there. The Ranger must have set his feet back upon the path while he was arguing with the others. It was typical of the way the Ranger did things. He did not have the time or the patience for arguments or social intercourse. The Ranger was nothing if not entirely pragmatic.

"Yes," said Sorak to himself, as he realized that he

had once again, in the intensity of his dispute with the others, managed to forget his body. It happened occasionally, though with considerably less frequency than it once did. "It was past time I started moving."

* * * * *

He heard the high mistress say, "Enter," and he opened the door of her private chambers. She looked up from her loom as he came in and smiled. "Sorak. Come in. I was watching you train with Tamura this morning. She tells me that you are going to be taking over the training of the novices. You should feel honored. It appears that she has chosen her successor."

"I fear that I shall not be lightening Sister Tamura's burden, Mistress," Sorak said. "That is why I came to see you."

Varanna raised her eyebrows. "Oh?"

"Mistress . . ." Sorak hesitated. "I feel the time has come for me to leave the convent."

Varanna nodded. "Ah. I see."

"Do not misunderstand. It is not that I am unhappy here, nor that I am ungrateful—"

Varanna raised her hand. "You need not explain," she said. "I have been expecting this. Come, sit beside me."

Sorak sat down on a bench next to the loom. "I have been very happy here, Mistress," he began, "and you have done more for me than words alone can say. Yet I feel the time has come for me to go."

"Does Ryana have anything to do with your decision?"

He looked down at the floor. "She has spoken with you?"

"Only to request a period of solitary meditation in

the temple tower," said Varanna. "She seemed very distraught. I did not ask her why, but I think I can guess."

"It is all my fault. I was aware of how she felt—how I felt—and I should have done something to discourage her long before this. I should have tried to make her understand, but a part of me still nursed the hope that . . . " He shook his head and sighed. "I suppose it makes no difference now. I have caused her pain without intending to, and she would be better off if I were to leave.

"Besides, Ryana is not the only reason I must go. I have grown up thinking of you all as my family, but the fact remains that I know nothing of my real family. I know nothing of my parents or where I came from. I do not even know my real name. The desire to know these things has grown over the years until I can think of little else. I long to know who I truly am, Mistress. Or, perhaps I should say who I was before I became what I am now. I can remember nothing of my past beyond the point where the pyreen elder found me in the desert. Sometimes, in dreams, I seem to hear my mother's voice singing to me, but I can never see her face. And I have not even the slightest memory of my father. Had I ever even seen him? Had he ever even known about me? I go to sleep each night wondering who my parents were. Do they still live? Are they together? Were they cast out, as I was? So many questions, and not a single answer."

"Have you considered that the answers, if you should find them, may be painful ones?" Varanna asked him.

"I am no stranger to pain, Mistress," Sorak replied. "And better the pain of an answer that settles things than the torment of an unrelenting question."

Varanna nodded. "I cannot dispute that. Nor, as I said, does this come as a surprise. You are free to go, of course. You took no vows to hold you here."

"I owe you much, Mistress. It is a debt that I shall never be able to repay."

"You owe me nothing, Sorak."

"Nevertheless, you shall always have my eternal gratitude and my deepest affection."

"I could ask for no greater reward. Have you thought where you will go from here?"

Sorak shook his head. "Not really. I had hoped, perhaps, you could tell me how to find Elder Al'Kali. Perhaps she could tell me where it was she found me, and I could begin my search from there. Still, the trail is old by ten long years, and I have not seen her in all that time. Perhaps she is no longer alive."

"Perhaps. She is one of the oldest of her race," Varanna said, "but the pyreen are long-lived. Finding her will not be easy, however. The druid peace-bringers are wanderers, and they do not often reveal themselves in their true form. Still, I think I know something that may help you. Each year, she makes a pilgrimage to the summit of the Dragon's Tooth. It was there she heard your call, ten years ago."

"But I do not remember where it was," said Sorak. "Or how I called to her."

"The memory is still within you, as is the ability," Varanna replied. "And you have skills now that you did not possess before. Reach down deep within yourself, and you shall find the way. As for the time, when next the moons are full, it shall be exactly ten years to the day since Elder Al'Kali brought you here."

"Then it would be best if I were to leave at once," said Sorak.

"What of Ryana? She has requested a period of solitary meditation. I have granted her request and must abide by it. She cannot be disturbed until she decides to leave the tower."

"If I am to reach the Dragon's Tooth in time, then I cannot delay. And I think it will be easier this way. Tell her. . ." He moistened his lips. "Tell her that I never meant to hurt her. But the name you gave me is a fitting one. Sorak is the nomad who must always walk alone."

"Before you leave . . . " Varanna said, getting to her feet. "Wait here a moment."

She left the room and returned a few moments later with a long, narrow, cloth-wrapped parcel in her arms. She laid it down on the table.

"This was given to me as a gift many years ago, in token of some small service I performed while on a pilgrimage," she said, as she carefully unwrapped it. "I have never had occasion to use it. I think that it will suit you much better than it has ever suited me."

She removed the final layer of cloth wrapping and revealed a sword, nestled in a leather scabbard.

"I would like you to take it, in remembrance," Varanna said, holding it out to him. "It is only fitting that it should be yours. It is an ancient elvish blade."

By its size, it was a long sword, but unlike a long sword, it had a curved blade that flared out slightly at the tip, rather like a cross between a sabre and a falchion, except that its point was leaf-shaped. The hilt was wrapped with silver wire, with a pommel and cross guards made of bronze.

Sorak unsheathed the sword and gasped as he saw the intricate, wavy marks of folding on the blade. "But . . . this is a *steel* blade!"

"And of the rarest sort," Varanna said, though steel

itself was rare on Athas, where most weapons were fashioned from obsidian, bone, and stone. "The art for making such steel has been lost for many centuries. It is much stronger than ordinary steel and holds a better edge. In the right hands, it would be a very formidable weapon."

"It is truly a magnificent gift," said Sorak. "I shall keep it with me always." He tried a few practice swings with the sword. "It is balanced well, but the shape of the blade is an uncommon one. I thought elves carried long swords."

"This is a special sword," Varanna replied, "the only one of its kind. There are ancient elvish runes etched upon the blade. You should be able to read them, if I have not wasted my time in teaching you the language of your ancestors."

Sorak held the sword up, cradled in his palms, and read the legend on the blade. "Strong in spirit, true in temper, forged in faith." He nodded. "A noble sentiment, indeed."

"More than a sentiment," Varanna said. "A creed for the ancient elves. Live by it, and the sword shall never fail you."

"I shall not forget," said Sorak, as he sheathed the blade. "Nor shall I forget everything that you have done for me."

"When all are gathered together in the hall for supper, I shall announce that you are leaving," said Varanna. "Then everyone will have a chance to say good-bye to you."

"No, I think I would prefer simply to leave quietly," said Sorak. "It will be difficult enough to leave without having to say good-bye to everyone."

Varanna nodded. "I understand. I shall say your farewells for you. But at least you can say good-bye to me." She held out her arms.

Sorak embraced her. "You have been like a mother to me," he said, "the only mother I have ever known. Leaving you is hardest of all."

"And you, Sorak, have been like the son I never could have borne," Varanna replied, her eyes moist. "You will always have a place in my heart, and our gates shall always remain open to you. May you find that which you seek."

* * * * *

"The mistress sent word that you are leaving us," the gatekeeper said. "I shall miss you, Sorak. And I shall miss letting you out at night, too, Tigra." The elderly gatekeeper reached out with a wrinkled hand to ruffle the fur on the tigone's head. The beast gave a purr and licked her hand.

"I shall miss you, too, Sister Dyona," Sorak said. "You were the first to admit me through the gates, and now, ten years later, you are the last to see me go."

The old woman smiled. "Has it really been ten years? It seems as if it were only yesterday. But then, at my age, time passes quickly and years turn into fleeting moments. Farewell, Sorak. Come, embrace me."

He gave her a hug and kissed her wrinkled cheek. "Farewell, Sister."

He stepped through the gates and headed down the path with a quick, purposeful stride. Behind him, the chime was sounding, calling the sisters to supper in the meeting hall. He thought of the long wooden tables crowded with women, laughing and talking, the younger ones occasionally throwing food at one another playfully until the table wardens would snap at them to desist, the bowls of food being passed around, the warm, comforting sense of community and family that he was now leaving behind, perhaps forever.

He thought of Ryana, sitting alone in the meditation chamber at the top of the temple tower, the small room to which he himself had retreated when he needed time to be alone. Her food would be brought to her and slid through a small aperture in the bottom of the heavy wooden door. No one would speak to her, no one would disturb her. She would be left to the privacy of her thoughts until she chose to come out. And when she did come out, she would find him gone.

As Sorak strode away from the convent, he wondered, what must she be thinking? They had grown up together. She had always been very special to him, much more so than any of the others. As Ryana herself had said, she had been the first to extend a hand to him in friendship, and their trust had grown into something that was more than friendship. Much, much more.

For years, she had been a sister to him, not a sister in the same sense as all the women at the convent called each other "sister," but a sibling. Right from the beginning, they had formed a bond, a bond that would always be there, no matter where they were or how much distance separated them. But they were not true siblings, and they each knew it, and it was that knowledge that precluded true sibling love. As they had grown older and started to feel the sexual stirrings of approaching adulthood, those feelings had become stronger, deeper, and more intimate. It was something Sorak had been aware of, though he had always avoided confronting it.

"*Because you always knew it was something that could never be,*" the Guardian said within his mind.

"*Perhaps I did,*" said Sorak inwardly, "*but I allowed myself to hope, and in hoping for something that could never be, I betrayed her.*"

"*How did you betray her?*" asked the Guardian. "*You never promised her anything. You never made any vows to her.*"

"*Nevertheless, it feels like a betrayal,*" Sorak said.

"*What is the purpose of dwelling on this matter?*" asked Eyron, a bored voice that sounded faintly irritable in Sorak's mind. "*The decision was made to leave, and we have left. The girl has been left behind. The thing is done, and the matter has been settled.*"

"*The matter of Ryana's feelings still remains,*" said Sorak.

"*What of it?*" Eyron asked, dryly. "*Her feelings are her own concern and her own responsibility. Nothing you can do will change that.*"

"*Perhaps not, Eyron,*" Sorak said, "*but in becoming a part of her life, I bear at least some responsibility for the effect that I have had on her.*"

"*Nonsense. She has free will,*" said Eyron. "*You did not force her to fall in love with you. That was her choice.*"

"*Had she known you, Eyron, perhaps she might not have made that choice,*" replied Sorak harshly.

"*Had she known me, she would not have suffered under any misapprehensions,*" Eyron said, "*for I would have told her the truth from the beginning.*"

"*Indeed?*" said Sorak. "*And what is the truth, as you perceive it?*"

"*That you are infatuated with her, that Kivara is curious to explore new sensations, that the Guardian feels threatened by her, and the Watcher feels threatened by every-*"

thing. The Ranger could not have been less concerned, one way or another, for love has no pragmatic aspects, and the Shade would have frightened the wits out of her."

"What of the others?" Sorak asked.

"Screech is little better than the great, dumb beast that trails at our heels, and Lyric would never have been capable of taking her seriously, for Lyric takes nothing seriously. And I will not presume to speak for Kether, since Kether does not condescend to speak with me."

"Little wonder," said Kivara.

"No one asked you," Eyron said.

"Enough!" Sorak said out loud, exasperated. "Give me some peace!"

A moment later, he began to sing. The words rang out bright and clear as he walked along the trail, singing an old halfling song about a young maiden and a hunter experiencing love for the first time. It was Sorak's voice that sang, but it was Lyric and not Sorak who sang the words. Sorak did not know them. Rather, he did not consciously remember them. It was a song his mother often sang to him when she had held him cradled in her arms. As Lyric sang, the Ranger guided their feet along the path leading through the valley toward the mountains. The Guardian gently drew Sorak down into a slumber and cradled him in solitude, isolating him not only from the others, but from the outside world, as well.

Tigra sensed the difference in him, but the beast was not surprised by this. It had never known Sorak to be any other way. The Ranger walked with a long and easy stride, Sorak's light leather pack and water skin slung over his shoulders, the sword hanging at his waist. He wore the only clothing that he had, a pair of woven, brown cloth breeches tucked into high, lace-up leather moccasins, a loose-fitting brown tunic with a leather belt around his waist, and a long, brown, hooded cloak that came down almost to his ankles, for warmth against the chill of the mountain air. The only other things he carried were a wooden staff, a bone stiletto knife tucked into his moccasin, his steel sword, and a hunting blade in a soft, leather sheath at his belt.

At the convent, the diet had been strictly vegetarian. On occasion, there was need for skins and leather, and at such times, animals were taken, but always sparingly, with great solemnity and ceremony. The hides would be dressed out and used, and the meat would be salted and cut up into jerky for distribution to the needy by whichever priestess next left on a pilgrimage. Sorak had been taught a reverence for life, and he followed and respected the villichi customs, but elves were hunters who ate meat, and halflings were carnivorous to the extent of feasting on their enemies, so the tribe of one had found its own compromise. On those occasions when Sorak had gone out into the forest on his own, the Ranger hunted game while Sorak slept. Only then did the tribe eat their fill of a raw and still warm kill. The tribe did so now.

When Sorak next became aware of himself, some time had passed and night had fallen. He was sitting by a campfire he did not remember building, and his belly felt full. He knew that he had killed and eaten, or rather, that the Ranger had, but he did not feel ill at ease over the idea. The thought of eating raw, freshly killed meat did not appeal to him in the slightest, but he understood that it was in his blood and that there was no getting away from his own nature. He would remain a vegetarian, but if his other aspects chose to be carnivorous, that was their choice. Either way, the needs of the body they all shared were seen to, one way or another.

He looked up at the stars and at the silhouetted mountains, trying to orient himself so that he could determine how far the Ranger had traveled while he had been asleep. He got up and stepped away from the firelight, scanning his surroundings. Elves had better night vision than humans, and Sorak's night vision, as a result, was quite acute. In the darkness, his eyes seemed lambent like a cat's, and he had no difficulty in making out the terrain around him.

The ground sloped away, down to a valley far below. He had climbed almost to the summit of the crest, and in the distance, he could just make out the tower of the temple, poking up over the scrub. He wondered if Ryana was still in there, and then quickly pushed the thought from his mind. Eyron had been right, he thought. There was little point in dwelling on it now. He had left the convent, probably never to return, and what had happened there belonged to part of his life now in the past. He had to look to the future.

In the distance, beyond the crest of the mountains encircling the secluded valley, he could see the higher peaks of the Ringing Mountains like shadows cast against the sky. The Dragon's Tooth loomed prominently over them all, ominous and foreboding.

Its name came from its appearance. Rising from the higher mountain ranges, it was wide at its base, but narrowed sharply as it rose until its faces were almost completely vertical. Near its summit, it angled up even more sharply, so that its faces were not only vertical, but curved along one side, like a gigantic tooth or fang scratching at the sky. Far removed from the civilized cities of the tablelands, a trek across the

desert and up into the mountains to even reach the
lower slopes of the forbidding peak would have been
arduous in itself. The deadly hazards one would
encounter on the ascent discouraged most adventurers from climbing the Dragon's Tooth. Of those few
who had attempted it, all had failed, and most had
not survived.

Sorak did not know if he would have to climb the
mountain. At least once before, his call had reached
the pyreen where she stood atop the summit of the
peak, and he had been all the way out in the desert,
some miles from even the foothills of the Ringing
Mountains. Yet, since then, he had never been able to
summon up his psionic powers to any such extent. He
had no idea how he might have done it. The Guardian,
who was the telepath among them, had not made the
call. Neither had any of the others. Or at least, they
could not recall having made it. With the body they
all shared pushed to its last extremity, they had all
been either senseless or delirious at the time. Perhaps,
in their delirium and desperation, they had all somehow united in the effort, or one of them had tapped
hidden reserves. Or, perhaps, someone *else* had made
the call, one of the deeply buried core identities that
none of them knew about.

There was, Sorak had learned, a very deeply buried
"infant core," one he could not access on any conscious level. Huddled and cocooned somewhere deep
within his psyche, this infant core had once been his
infant self, but whatever pain and trauma had caused
his fragmentation had also caused this infant core's
retreat deep into his subconscious, where it remained
in some state of frozen stasis, its development arrested
and its senses numbed. Not even the Guardian could
reach it, although she was aware of it. There was

something—or perhaps some*one*—shielding it somehow. And that shielding, whatever it was, suggested that there could well be other core identities within him that were not so deeply buried, but were buried just the same, constituting levels between his infant core and his more-developed aspects.

There are so many things about myself I do not know, thought Sorak. How could I possibly have hoped to . . . With a deliberate effort, he pushed the thought away once more, before his mind became preoccupied with Ryana once again. He purposely turned so that he could no longer see the convent. It was time now to look ahead. But to what?

Beyond seeking out the pyreen, he had no idea what lay ahead of him. Would she be able to recall the place where she had found him? And if she did, what of it? He could attempt to retrace his steps, but to what end? Elves, at least those who did not dwell in the cities, were nomadic. Halflings lived semi-nomadically around a tribal grounds, and certainly didn't live on the flat lands. Whether elf or halfling, the tribe that had cast Sorak out would be long gone by now. How could he possibly hope to pick up a trail that was ten years old?

The answer was, of course, he couldn't. At least, not in any conventional way. But with his psionic abilities, there was a chance he might be able to pick up some sort of psychic impression that may have been left behind, imprinted on the landscape, some telltale aberration that might provide a clue. Failing that, he would simply have to strike out on his own, in whatever direction fate took him.

Mistress Varanna had warned him that the answers he sought would be difficult, if not impossible, to find. It was likely he would spend the remainder of his life looking for them. But at least he would be actively seeking those answers instead of merely wondering about them. And along the way, he might discover a purpose for his existence. At the convent, he had led a sheltered life, one of training and contemplation, but it had been necessary to teach him how to live with his own unique nature. He owed the Elder Al'Kali a debt of gratitude for having the foresight to take him there. He only hoped that he would find her, so that he could properly express that gratitude. Soon, the twin moons of Athas would be full. And then, perhaps, he would begin to know his fate.

FOUR

As the days passed and Sorak traveled, alternating with the Ranger in dominance over his body, he drew closer to the Dragon's Tooth. It was now less than a day's journey away. The trek had been relatively uneventful. At this high elevation, he did not encounter any other travelers and there was not much wildlife above the scrub line of the mountain ridge. Once he had passed that point, the terrain became extremely rocky and desolate.

His body was in peak physical condition, but it needed rest, and even though Sorak could withdraw—"duck under"—when he grew tired, letting the Ranger take over, the body they all shared had limited reserves of energy. He camped for several hours each night so that his body could rest, and by alternating which persona was in control, Sorak was able to make excellent time. The few times he had encountered any animals that could be dangerous, Screech had come to the fore to communicate with them, and any threat was nullified.

Sorak did not fully understand Screech, not in the same way he understood the Guardian, the Ranger, Eyron, Lyric, Kivara, and the others. There were times when he did not understand Kivara all that well,

either, but that was because Kivara was young and
made no real attempt to understand herself. With
Screech, it was different. Screech was not like any of
the others. He was more like Tigra. He did not speak
in any true sense, but he could understand the others
and make himself be understood, albeit on a somewhat primitive level. It was the same as the psionic
communication Sorak had with Tigra, and he would
not have had that communication with the tigone
were it not for Screech.

The others all had their own distinct personas, but
Screech had an ability the others seemed to lack. He
could either take over entirely or effect a blend of his
persona with that of Sorak, resulting in a curious sort
of overlay in which both were present and "out" at
the same time. It was Screech who had effected the
affinity with Tigra, but while the tigone had a bond
with Screech, it felt a bond with Sorak as well, whom
it knew as being separate from Screech, yet still a part
of him. The beast did not concern itself with the com-
plexity of such relationships; it simply accepted Sorak
for what he was.

On the fifth day of the journey, a pride of tigones
came very close to Sorak's camp at night. Sorak,
through the Watcher's vigilance, had been aware of
the pride trailing him for quite some time. Under
ordinary circumstances, encountering a traveler
alone, they would undoubtedly have attacked at
once, but they were confused both by Tigra's presence
and by the psychic signature of Screech, which they
detected with their own psionic powers. Here was
something that was completely unfamiliar, totally
unprecedented, and they had no idea what to make of
it. On one hand, what they saw appeared to be a
human, yet he smelled of both elf and halfling, and he

projected Screech as a tigone signature. Plus, there was a tigone accompanying the strange creature. This disturbed the beasts and puzzled them, and they had trailed Sorak for the better part of an entire day, venturing closer only at night, after he had lit his campfire.

He made no moves toward them, either hostile or defensive, but Screech established contact with them, psionically projecting both a nonthreatening recognition and a subtle dominance. Tigra kept nearby, clearly indicating to the pride its rapport and relationship to Sorak. They approached cautiously and hesitantly, the braver ones—the young males—venturing ahead of the others with tentative sniffs, psionic probes, and challenge patterns of behavior, but Sorak and Screech both projected a calm security, an utter lack of fear, and a disregard of the challenge postures taken by the beasts.

Tigones being essentially large cats, after all, curiosity soon overcame their caution and they came into his camp to smell him and Tigra and get acquainted. They wound up settling down around the fire, yawning and stretching, and just before Sorak went to sleep, he saw Tigra trotting off into the bushes with one of the young females. He smiled and briefly envied his companion its ability to engage in an uncomplicated mating with a female of its own kind. It was an experience that he would never know. And with that sad thought, he went to sleep, surrounded by nine huge, predatory beasts who had accepted him as one of them.

For part of the next day, he traveled with the pride, but as he climbed high up into the mountains, heading toward the lower slopes of the Dragon's Tooth, the huge, psionic cats went their separate way. Sorak wondered for a moment if Tigra would go with them and take its place among its own kind, but the tigone stayed by his side. The female Tigra had mated with the previous night lingered briefly, giving voice to a few plaintive roars, but Tigra paid her no mind.

"Are you sure, old friend?" Sorak said aloud, looking down at the beast by his side.

"Friend," came back the tigone's psionic reply. *"Protect."*

With a dejected air, the female turned and ran after her pride.

"All right, Tigra," Sorak said. "You and me."

It was very cold now, and Sorak bundled his cloak around him. As the dark sun rose higher in the sky, the temperatures down on the desert tablelands far below them were scorching, but at the foot of the Dragon's Tooth, the wind whistled around them with a bitter chill. Sorak looked up at the towering, curved spire high above him and wondered how anyone could possibly make that climb. The pyreens were shapechangers, and so possessed certain unique advantages, but nevertheless, Elder Al'Kali was among the oldest of her tribe. She had lived for over a thousand years. If, at her awesomely advanced age, she still possessed the energy to shapeshift and scale such daunting heights, he marveled at what she must have been like in her prime.

"I would have to be a crystal spider to make that climb," said Sorak, as he stared up at the cloud-shrouded summit of the peak. He glanced down at Tigra. "And you, old friend, could certainly never make it." He sighed. "The twin moons should be full tonight. If she is there, then I shall have to call to her. But how?"

"Screech," Tigra replied.

"Screech?" Sorak shook his head. "I do not think Screech could have made the call alone."

"*Perhaps Kether,*" said the Guardian, within his mind.

Sorak breathed in deeply, exhaled, and bit his lower lip. "But I do not know how to summon Kether."

"*Nor do I,*" the Guardian replied, "*and nor do any of the others. But perhaps if the need is present, and we all give way, Kether will manifest.*"

"And if he does not?"

"*Then I shall have to do my best and hope it is sufficient to the task,*" the Guardian replied. "*We are much closer to the summit of the peak now than we were out in the desert. The call will not have to travel nearly so far.*"

"That is true," said Sorak. "The Elder Al'Kali may hear you . . . if, indeed, she is still alive to make her pilgrimage. In either case, we shall have to get out of this wind."

He was about to start walking in search of shelter but discovered that the Ranger had already set his feet in motion. The terrain was barren and rocky, and it was quite steep. He had to lean forward as he walked. The icy wind whipped at his hair and cloak and the rough ground made for slow progress, but by late afternoon, he had found a niche where a depression in the rocky mountainside was protected somewhat from the elements by several large boulders that had fallen from the heights above. He squeezed into the niche and set his pack down, then took a few sips of water from his bag, squirting some into Tigra's mouth, as well. The tigone was more in its element here than he was, but even the great cats seldom strayed very far above the scrub ridge. It was cruel, inhospitable country, offering almost nothing in the way of game or forage. One thing was certain. He would not be able to remain here for very long.

"Why do we even have to remain here at all?" asked Eyron.

"We must wait for the Elder Al'Kali," Sorak said.

"For what purpose?" Eyron replied dryly. *"To dig up a past that no longer bears any relevance? What will you gain from knowing the answers to these pointless questions you keep fretting about?"*

"A sense of self, perhaps."

"I see. And you do not now have a sense of self? The ten years you have spent at the villichi convent have taught you nothing?"

"The villichi could not have taught me that which they never knew," said Sorak.

"So you do not know who your parents are. So you do not know the name that you were given at birth. Are these things so important?"

"They are to me, if not to you."

"And if you were to learn these things, what would they change? You have never gone by any other name than Sorak. Your true name, whatever it may be, would now sit upon you like an ill-fitting cloak. You have never known your parents. For all you know, they may no longer be alive. Even if they were, they would be strangers to you."

"Perhaps, but if they still live, then I could seek them out. I am still their son. In that sense, we could never truly be strangers to one another."

"Have you considered the possibility that they may have been the ones to cast you out? You may have been unwanted, a living reminder of their folly and indiscretion. They may have regretted what had occurred between them. You would be a painful memory come home to roost."

"But if they were in love—"

"That is merely your assumption, nothing more. Lacking any evidence to the contrary, it is just wishful thinking.

Elves and halflings have always been mortal enemies. Your father's tribe may have attacked your mother's, and you may be the offspring of the pillage."

"I suppose that is possible," said Sorak uncertainly.

"Imagine a mother forced to bear the child of a hated enemy, one who had degraded and abused her. A child that could never be accepted by her tribe. A child that would be a constant reminder of her pain and humiliation. What could a mother feel for such a child?"

"I do not know," said Sorak.

"Enough, Eyron," said the Guardian. *"Leave him alone."*

"I merely wish him to see all aspects of the question," Eyron replied.

"And, as usual, you dwell upon the negative ones," the Guardian said. *"You have made your point. What you have said is, indeed, possible. It is also possible that a mother could love such a child, and hold him blameless for any violence that may have been committed upon her . . . assuming that it happened that way, and none of us have any way of knowing that. If she felt nothing for the child but loathing, why then did she keep it for so long? Sorak merely seeks the truth."*

"If Sorak seeks the truth, then he should know that the truth may not be pleasant," Eyron said.

"I know that," Sorak said.

"Then why stir up the murky waters of the past?" asked Eyron. *"What does it matter? With each passing day, your life begins anew. It is yours to make of what you will."*

"Ours, you mean," said Sorak. "And perhaps therein lies the key to this debate. I am not afraid to learn the truth, Eyron, whether it brings happiness or pain. What about you?"

"I? Why should I be afraid?"

"That is a question only you can answer," Sorak said. "The questions you have posed have already occurred to me. If they had not, I am sure you would have found some subtle way to make me think of them." He smiled wryly. "Perhaps you already have, and are now merely seeking to drive home the point, to build on the uncertainty already present in my mind. Well, I shall not shrink from the task that I have set myself, even if it takes the rest of my life to see it through. Perhaps, Eyron, you find a certain measure of security in our ignorance of our past. Not I. If I am ever to know where I am going in this life, then I shall first have to learn where I have been. And who I was."

"And what of who you are?" asked Eyron.

"That is something I shall never truly know until I discover who I was and where I came from," Sorak said.

"That which you are, that which we all are," Eyron said, *"was born out on the desert tablelands."*

"No, that was where we almost died," said Sorak. "And if I do not find the child who lived before, then he truly will have died, and some part of all of us shall die, as well. Now heed the Guardian and let me be. I must clear my mind and attempt to summon Kether."

Of all the entities making up the tribe, Kether was the most mysterious, and the one Sorak understood the least. With all the others, he could see how parts of his fragmented persona had developed from the seedlings of character traits into distinct, individual identities with personas of their own. The high mistress had helped him understand how the female side of him, that female side that was present in every male, had fragmented and developed into the three individual female personas of the tribe. The Guardian encompassed his empathic, protective, and nurturing aspects. Kivara had developed from his sensual nature, which explained her passion and her curiosity and her apparent lack of concern for any sort of morality. The Watcher encompassed his alert, intuitive self and desire for security.

Among his male aspects, the Ranger represented an outgrowth of his pragmatic nature and his motivating force, as well as the inherited characteristics of his elf and halfling forebears. Lyric was his humorous, creative side, the playful child within him who took nothing very seriously and found innocent joy in everything around him. Eyron was the cynic and the pessimist, his negative aspect grown into a world-weary realist who weighed the pros and cons of everything and was wary of romantic optimism. Screech was an outgrowth of his halfling affinity toward beasts and other, lower creatures, a simple and uncomplicated aspect of his own animal nature. And the Shade was the dark, grim side of his subconscious, which manifested rarely, but with a frightening, primitive, and shockingly overwhelming force. There were at least three or four others who were deeply buried, such as his infant core. Sorak did not really know these personalities at all, but it was a lack of knowledge based on ignorance and not, as was the case with Kether, an inability to comprehend.

Perhaps, as the high mistress had suggested, Kether was an evocation of his higher, spiritual self. To Sorak, however, Kether did not seem to spring from any part of him at all. Kether had never spoken with the high mistress, so her only knowledge of him came from what Sorak had told her of his own infrequent contacts. With most of the others, what Sorak experienced was awareness and communication. With Kether, it was more like a visitation from some other-worldly being.

Kether had knowledge of things that Sorak could not account for in any rational way. They were things he could not possibly have known. And Kether was old, or at least he seemed very old. There was an ancientness about him, a sense of separateness more profound that anything Sorak had felt with any of the others. It was as if, when he had fragmented into a tribe of one, some sort of mystical gate had been opened in his mind and Kether had come through from some other level of existence.

Kether knew of things that happened before Sorak was ever born. He spoke of something called the Green Age and claimed to have been alive then, thousands of years ago. In the few times Sorak had been in contact with Kether, the mysterious, ethereal entity had not revealed very much, but what Kether had revealed were things completely outside Sorak's knowledge and experience.

Eyron pretended an indifference to Kether because Kether did not "condescend" to speak with him. In truth, though, Sorak felt that Eyron feared him. Perhaps fear was not quite the proper word. Eyron was in awe of Kether because Eyron could not explain where Kether came from, nor could he understand precisely what he was. Kivara, on the other hand, simply never mentioned him. Perhaps she did not know him. The Ranger seldom commented on anything, so Sorak had no way of knowing how the Ranger felt about him. The Watcher was aware of Kether, but she, too, said nothing. And it was hard to get a straight answer out of Lyric about anything. Of all the others who made up the tribe, only the

Guardian had revealed any knowledge about Kether, but even she knew little. With her empathic abilities, she was able to ascertain that Kether was good, and possessed a purity of essence the like of which she had never encountered in any other being. But when Kether came, the Guardian went "under," as did all the others, and her awareness at such times was limited only to the knowledge of his presence.

What was Kether, exactly? Sorak had no way of knowing. He felt that Kether was a spirit, the shade of some being who had lived far in the past, or perhaps a representation of all his past lives. There was, the high mistress had told him, a continuity throughout the many generations of life that most people were not aware of on any conscious level, but it was still there, nevertheless. Perhaps Kether was a manifestation of this continuity. Or perhaps Kether was some other sort of being entirely, a spirit being who was able to cross over from another world to possess him.

"Questions," Sorak mumbled to himself as he huddled in his cloak, drawing it around him tightly as the wind whistled through the niche where he had taken shelter. "Nothing but questions, never any answers. Who am I? *What* am I? And what is to become of me?"

Tigra huddled closer to him, sensing his need for warmth. He ruffled the huge beast's massive head and stroked it gently. "Who knows, Tigra? Perhaps I shall simply freeze up here in these rocks and that will be an end of it."

"*You shall not freeze,*" said the Guardian. "*It would have been foolish to come all this way only to fail. Clear your mind, Sorak. Still your thoughts. Perhaps Kether will come.*"

Yes, thought Sorak, but from where? From within

me somewhere? From within my own fragmented mind, or from somewhere else, some place that I can neither see nor feel nor comprehend?

He inhaled deeply, then slowly exhaled, repeating the process several times as he tried to still himself and settle into a state of serene, thoughtless drifting. He concentrated on his breathing and relaxed his muscles and listened only to the wind and the sound of his own breaths. As he had been trained in the villichi convent, he gradually settled down into a calm, meditative state, shutting his eyes and breathing regularly and deeply. . . .

* * * * *

"Sorak?"

His eyelids flickered open. The first thing he became aware of was that night had fallen and the twin moons hung full in the sky. The second thing he noticed was that he was no longer cold. The wind had not abated, though it no longer blew so fiercely. Even so, he felt very warm. And finally, he saw the figure standing just outside the niche where he was huddled, leaning back against the rock. It was a slight figure in a hooded cloak, an old woman with long white hair trailing down her chest and shoulders.

"For the second time, you called to me, and I have come. Only this time, I find not a child, but a full-grown elfling."

"Elder Al'Kali?" Sorak said, getting slowly and a bit unsteadily to his feet.

"There is no need to be so formal," she said. "You may call me Lyra."

"Lyra," he said. "I . . . called to you?"

"Your powers have not diminished," she said. "In

fact, they have grown even stronger. I was right to take you to the villichi convent. It seems they have taught you well."

He shook his head, feeling a bit dazed. "I do not remember. . . . It seemed that but a moment ago, it was still daylight and . . . " Then he realized what must have happened. He had lost a period of time, as had happened many times before when any of the others would fully manifest. However, in this case, neither he nor any of the others had any memory of what had happened during those missing hours. Though he felt slightly cramped from sitting there for so long, he was suffused with warmth and a sense of deep, inner tranquility. Kether. Kether had come, to manifest and make the call that neither he nor any of the others could have made, the call that reached Lyra Al'Kali at the summit of the Dragon's Tooth, as it had ten years before.

"Come," said Lyra, holding out her hand to him. "There is a dry gulch running down the mountain-side a short distance due west of here. Follow its course until you reach a briny pond, where it ends. Make your camp there and build a fire. It will be dawn soon, and I have my devotions to perform. I shall meet you there shortly after sunrise."

She turned and started climbing up into the rocks, heading toward the summit. The wind whipped at her cloak as she ascended with firm, purposeful steps. Her cloak seemed to billow out like wings, and then she suddenly took flight. The metamorphosis had taken place in an instant, faster than the eye could fol-low, and Sorak watched with astonishment as the pterrax rose high into the sky, its large, leathery wings spread out as it rode the wind currents. Within moments, he lost sight of it.

* * * * *

The campfire had burned down to embers. It was just past dawn when Sorak awoke by the shore of the small mountain lake. He felt sated, and knew the Ranger had hunted while he slept. There was no sign of the kill. The Ranger was always careful not to confront Sorak with evidence of flesh-eating, knowing his aversion to it, so Sorak had no idea what had nourished his body. He preferred it that way. His hair felt damp, so he knew that the Ranger, or perhaps one of the others, had washed in a freshwater pool beside the briny lake. The lake was at a significantly lower elevation than the lower slopes of the Dragon's Tooth, so the morning was pleasantly cool, a welcome change from the biting cold of the previous night.

As Sorak rose to a sitting position, he saw a rasclinn come trotting along the lake shore toward him. Tigra's ears pricked up at the scent of the doglike creature, its silvery hide gleaming in the morning sun. The animal was no danger to Sorak, its diet being exclusively vegetarian. Its amazingly efficient system enabled it to extract trace metals from almost any type of plant, even poisonous ones, to which the rasclinn was immune. This gave its hide an extremely tough, almost metallic texture, a hide highly prized by hunters, who sold it for armor. Rasclinn were usually small, standing no more than three feet at the shoulder and weighing no more than about fifty pounds. However, this one was a larger specimen, and when it spotted Sorak, it trotted eagerly toward him instead of running off in the opposite direction. The tigone made no move toward it, and a moment later, Sorak saw why. He blinked and saw Lyra getting up from all fours, brushing her hands off on her cloak.

"These old bones are creaking more and more these days," she said with a sigh as she approached Sorak's camp. "And they feel the chill more with each passing year." She settled down on the ground next to the burning embers of the campfire, tossed a few pieces of wood on, and warmed herself by the flames. Her ancient face was as wrinkled as old parchment, but her eyes still sparkled with vitality. "I don't suppose you have any Tyrian brandy with you?"

"I have only water," Sorak said, "but you are welcome to it. The waters of the lake are fresh and cool, and I have refilled my bag from it."

"Then water shall do nicely," Lyra said, accepting the water bag and squirting a stream into her mouth. "Ahh. Traveling is thirsty work. And since I am always traveling, I am always thirsty. But some Tyrian brandy would have been very welcome after that cold trek."

"What is Tyrian brandy?"

She raised her eyebrows with surprise. "Ah, but of course. You have lived a sheltered life in the villichi convent. As I recall, the villichi make a most excellent wine out of bloodcurrants."

"I have tried it," said Sorak, "but it was not to my liking. I found it much too sweet for my taste."

"Well, then, you may like Tyrian brandy. It is not sweet, but tart, and wonderfully smooth. But see that you approach it with caution the first few times you try it. More than a goblet will make your head spin, and you will likely wake up the next morning with a frightful headache and an empty purse."

"I am no stranger to headaches," Sorak said, "and I do not even own a purse."

Lyra smiled. "You will have much to learn, if you should ever venture down into the cities."

"I have much to learn, in any case," said Sorak. "And that is why I have sought you out. I had hoped that you could set my feet upon the path to knowledge."

She nodded. "You have left the convent then to find your own way in the world. That is as it should be. The convent was a good training ground for you, but the school of life has much to teach, as well. What knowledge do you seek?"

"Knowledge of myself," said Sorak. "I have always felt a lack from not knowing who my parents were, or where I came from. I do not even know my true name. I feel that I must know these things before I can discover a purpose in my life. I had hoped that you could help me, since it was you who found me and brought me to the convent."

"You thought that I could tell you these things?" she asked.

"Perhaps not," Sorak replied, "but I thought that if I had said anything when first you found me, you might remember. If not, perhaps you could tell me where you found me, and I might start my quest from there."

Lyra shook her head. "You were near death when I found you in the desert," she said, "and you spoke not a single word. As for where I found you, I can no longer remember. I had followed your call, and I had not marked the spot. One stretch of desert looks much like any other. I cannot see how that would be of help to you, in any case. How long has it been, ten years? Any trail would have long since been eradicated, even psychic impressions left behind would have been blurred, unless they were extremely powerful, such as those sometimes imprinted on the land by some great battle."

"So then you cannot help me?" Sorak said, feeling disappointment welling up inside him.

"I did not say that," Lyra replied. "I cannot provide you with the answers that you seek, but I may be able to help you. That is, assuming you will accept my advice."

"Of course I shall accept it," Sorak said. "Without you, I would have had no life. I owe you a debt that I shall never be able to repay."

"Perhaps you can repay it, and help yourself at the same time," said Lyra. "You know the purpose of the peace-bringers? You have been educated in the Druid Way?"

Sorak nodded.

"Good. Then you have been taught about the defilers and the sorcerer-kings who drain the life out of our world. You have been taught about the dragons. What do you know of the avangion?"

"A legend," Sorak said, with a shrug. "A myth to keep hope alive for the downtrodden."

"That is what many people believe," said Lyra, "yet the story is much more than a legend. The avangion is real. It lives. Or, I should say, he lives, for the avangion is still a man."

"You mean that someone has actually begun the metamorphosis?" asked Sorak, with surprise. "Who?"

"No one knows who he is," Lyra replied, "and no one knows where he may be found. At least, no one I have ever met has claimed to know the hermit wizard's whereabouts, or even his true name. He is known only as the Sage, for knowledge of his true name would give power to his enemies, which include all the sorcerer-kings. However, there are those who are aware of his existence, and who receive communications from him from time to time, for it

gives hope to their cause. The Veiled Alliance is one
such group, the pyreens are another. And the high
mistress of the villichi is aware of him, as well. And
now you know."

"Mistress Varanna knew?" Sorak said. "But she
never spoke to me of this. And what has this hermit
wizard to do with me?"

"Varanna gave you Galdra, did she not?"

Sorak frowned. "Galdra?"

"Your sword," said Lyra.

Sorak picked up the elvish sword and scabbard
lying by his side. "This? She made no mention of its
having a name."

"It bears writing on its blade, does it not?" said
Lyra. "There are ancient elvish runes that spell out the
legend: 'Strong in spirit, true in temper, forged in
faith?' "

"Yes," said Sorak. "I said it was a noble sentiment,
and the mistress replied that it was more than that, it
was a creed. That so long as I lived by it, the blade
would always serve me well."

"And so it shall, unless, of course, it was not given
to you, and you stole it."

"I am not a thief," said Sorak, his pride offended.

"I did not think you were," said Lyra with a smile.
"But it is good to see that you have pride. That means
you are strong in spirit. And so long as your spirit
remains strong, Galdra will be true in temper. Its
blade is forged in faith, the faith of whomever wields
it. So long as your faith is true, Galdra's blade shall
never fail you, and its edge shall cut through whatever obstacle it may encounter."

Sorak slowly pulled the sword partway out of the
scabbard. "Why did the mistress not tell me any of
these things?"

"Perhaps she meant for me to tell you," Lyra said.

"Why?"

"Because it was I who had given her the sword," said Lyra. "And she knew that by giving it to you, she would be sending me a message."

Sorak shook his head. "I do not understand. This sword was yours? I thought it was an elvish blade."

"It was, a long, long time ago," said Lyra. "And the sword was never truly mine. It was given to me in trust, and in time, I gave it to Varanna for safe keeping."

"She said it was given to her as a token of some service she had performed," said Sorak.

"So it was," said Lyra, with a smile. "And now she has performed it."

"You speak in riddles."

Lyra chuckled. "Forgive me," she said. "I did not mean to confuse you. I shall start at the beginning. There was a time, many centuries ago, when the elves were very different from the way they are today. These days, the elves of Athas are scattered far and wide, with no unity among the different tribes, and they have fallen into decadence. Or perhaps been driven into it. The nomadic tribes are frequently engaged in smuggling and thievery, while those who reside in the cities are merchant traders of questionable reputation, likely as not to cheat their customers or sell them stolen goods. You will hear the expression, 'As crafty as an elf,' or 'With no more honor than an elf,' but there was a time when the elves were a proud and honorable people. They were skilled artisans and warriors, with a rich culture all their own, and rather than being scattered bands of wanderers who live from day to day and hand to mouth, they were strong tribes who were unified under one king.

In my youth, I knew such a king. His name was
Alaron, and he was the very last of his line.

"Alaron had no less than a dozen wives, yet he
could sire a son with none of them. He had been
cursed by Rajaat, the most powerful of the defilers,
with a spell that made him sterile. Rajaat sought to
destroy the kingdom of the elvish tribes, for they
were a threat to him. He worked first to destroy the
royal line of succession, then to sow discord among
the tribes about whose right it would be to sit upon
the throne when Alaron's rule had passed. To enlist
the aid of elves among those tribes, he used bribery
when he could, and magic when bribery would fail,
and in the end, he succeeded in driving the tribes
apart into warring factions. The kingdom fell, and
Alaron was forced to flee into the forest, where he
expired of his wounds. I found him, as I found you,
half-dead. Unlike you, however, he was beyond my
help. Before he died, he gave his sword to me, a
sword famed among the elvish tribes as Galdra, the
sword of kings. He knew it would not serve him anymore, for he had lost his faith, and he was dying.

"He bid me take it," she said, "and keep it safe, so
that it should never fall into the hands of the defilers,
for the blade would shatter if they tried to use it.
Alaron did not want the symbol of the elvish royal
house destroyed. 'I was cursed never to have a son,'
he said, 'and a proud tradition dies with me. The
elves are now a beaten people. Take Galdra and keep
it safe. My life span is but the blink of an eye to a
pyreen such as you. Perhaps, someday, you will succeed where I have failed, and find an elf worthy of
this blade. If not, then hide it from the defilers. I can at
least deny them this.' And with those words, he died.

"Alaron always was my friend," Lyra continued,

"and I could not deny him. I hid the blade, and as the years passed, I moved it from one place of concealment to another, never being satisfied that it was truly safe. Then, one day, after many years had passed, I met a young villichi priestess on a pilgrimage, and that priestess was Varanna. I had been surprised and injured by a young dragon, which mistook me for a human, and I was too weak to properly heal myself. Varanna stopped to help me, and I sensed the goodness in her heart, and saw that fate prepared her to be high mistress. I realized that nowhere would the blade I had been entrusted with be kept as safe as in the villichi convent. I gave it to Varanna, and told her what it was, and what it represented, and she has kept it all these years."

Sorak glanced down at the sword, then looked up at Lyra with a puzzled expression. "But . . . why, then, did she give it to me?"

"Because she knew I would approve," said Lyra, with a smile. "Varanna understood why I had brought you to her. Ten years ago, when I heard your call, I felt your power, and when I found you, I sensed what you were . . . and what you could be. The sword has been a special bond between Varanna and me, but it was held only in trust."

"For me?" said Sorak, gazing at her with a puzzled expression. "But I am not of the elvish royal house. If the line died out with Alaron, as you say, then I could not possibly have any claim to this blade. And I am not even a full-blooded elf."

"Nevertheless, there is elvish blood flowing through your veins," said Lyra, "and Alaron knew that Galdra could never pass to his successor, for the line would die with him. His only hope was that someone worthy of the blade would come along one day. Varanna believed that you were worthy, and I perceive the potential that you have within you, but you have yet to prove that worth. Not to me and not to Varanna, but to yourself and to the blade. You seek answers to the question of your origin. I cannot provide those answers, but I know who can. Only the preserver magic of the Sage would be strong enough and pure enough to serve your needs. But first you shall have to seek him out, and in your quest for him, you shall serve his needs, and mine, and that of your forebears."

"How?"

"By aligning yourself with him against all defilers," said Lyra. "The Sage is very powerful, but he has many enemies, which is why he must remain hidden in seclusion. The path of metamorphosis into an avangion is long and arduous, and it entails much pain and suffering. Each stage of the transformation requires rituals that take years to perform. Distraction is the enemy of every mage, and there is no distraction quite so profound as being sought after by those who wish to take your life. The Sage is the most hunted wizard in all of Athas, for he represents a threat to the power of the defilers. And yet he is the most vulnerable, for if he were to direct his energies against the defilers, it would interfere with the transformation process. Remember, also, that defilers can accumulate their power much more quickly than those who follow the Path of the Preserver, and while the Sage works to complete his metamorphosis, the powers aligned against him grow ever stronger."

"I still do not see my part in all this," Sorak said.

"Your part has already been written by the fates, Sorak," Lyra replied. "You were raised by the villichi in the Way of the Druid, to follow the Path of the Preserver. In itself, that places you in opposition to defilers. In searching for the Sage, you must also align yourself with him, for that is the only way that you shall ever find him. But be warned that it shall not be an easy quest, and it will be dangerous. Those who seek to find the Sage and kill him will also seek you, just as they seek the members of the Veiled Alliance and all preservers who are aligned against them."

"So then my part is to support the Veiled Alliance and all those who take a stand against defiler magic while I seek this hermit wizard," Sorak said. "You are saying that to find him, I must somehow make him aware of the fact that I am seeking him, and prove myself to him by deeds against his enemies."

Lyra nodded. "Remember that, for many years now, all the sorcerer-kings, their templars, and their minions have been searching for the Sage, and they have employed both magic and subterfuge in their efforts."

"So proving myself will not be easy," Sorak said with a nod. "I understand."

"There is, of course, another choice," said Lyra. "It all depends on you. Your life is yours to direct in the manner that you will. Perhaps there is a way that you may find the answers to your questions without needing to consult the Sage. Or, perhaps, knowing what you risk, you may no longer feel those questions bear so much importance. When you leave here, you may choose to follow a different path and take no part in the conflict for the soul of Athas. That is entirely up to you, and if you should make that choice, I shall respect it. All you need do in that event is return Galdra to me, and you will be free to do whatever you desire."

Sorak picked up the sword, holding the scabbard across his palms as he gazed down at it. "No," he said. "If not for you, I would have died out in the desert. And if not for Mistress Varanna, I would have had no home these past ten years. And if not for these questions that have plagued me all my life, I would have possessed, perhaps, some peace of mind. I shall keep the blade, and undertake this quest." He smiled, wryly. "Besides, I have nothing better to do."

Lyra chuckled. "I never doubted for a moment that you would answer that way."

"But how should I begin my search?" asked Sorak.

"Make your way to the nearest city," Lyra said. "That would be Tyr, which lies to the west in a valley at the foothills of these mountains. When you reach the lower elevations, you will find trails leading to the city, and you shall be able to see it from the ridge. The city of Tyr was once ruled by the sorcerer-king, Kalak, but he was killed and his chief templar, Tithian, attempted to succeed him. Now, Tithian has disappeared, and in his place, Tyr is being ruled by a Council of Advisors, whose leaders have the support of the people. It is, however, an unstable government, and the defilers who are still in Tyr will surely seek to topple it. Also, word has reached the other cities that Tyr no longer has a sorcerer-king, and that Tithian and the rest of Kalak's templars are no longer in power. Tyr may be ripe for an invasion. It will be a place of intrigue, with many factions vying to gain power, and new arrivals will be considered with suspicion. Be wary. Remember, you have led a sheltered life among the villichi sisters. A city such as Tyr offers numerous temptations and is rife with criminals of all description. Trust no one, look for hidden motives behind every friendly offer. And above all, watch your back."

"I shall," said Sorak. "What must I do when I reach Tyr?"

"You must try to make contact with the Veiled Alliance," Lyra said. "This will not be easy. Kalak is dead, Tithian is gone, and the power of the templars has been broken, but those who make up the Veiled Alliance have seen the power shift too many times to come out into the open. They will be on their guard. Remember, they will have no reason to trust you. For all they know, you could be a spy sent to infiltrate their covert network. They shall not welcome you with open arms. Expect to be sorely tested."

Sorak sighed. "It all sounds so very different from the life that I have known."

"It *is* very different," Lyra agreed. "But if you seek answers to your questions and a purpose to your life, you must be prepared for new experiences. In many ways, you are better prepared than most, for you have trained and schooled in the arts of combat and psionics. But you will find that it is a very different matter to put that training to good use in the outside world. Tread softly and think carefully."

"I shall," said Sorak. "Will I be seeing you again?"

Lyra smiled. "Perhaps. If not, then you know where you may find me—each year at this time. And if I should fail to make my yearly pilgrimage, then you will know I have passed on."

"I want to thank you for your help, and for your kindness to me," Sorak said. "I owe you my life. That is something I shall never forget. If there is ever anything that I can do for you—"

"Succeed in your quest and follow the Path of the Preserver," Lyra said. "That is all I ask. Do that, and I shall be well repaid."

"I only wish there were something more I could do," said Sorak. He turned and reached for his pack, opened it, and rummaged around inside. "I know it is not much, a small thing, really, but save for Galdra, it is the only thing I have of value. There was a girl back at the convent, someone very special to me, and . . . well, when she used to brush her hair, I would take the stray strands from her brush to plait into a cord. She never knew, and I had thought to . . . well, that is not important. It is all I really have to give, and I would be honored if you would accept it."

He found the cord plaited from Ryana's hair and took it from the pack, then turned to offer it to Lyra. "Consider it a token of my . . . " His voice trailed off. The pyreen was no longer there. He glanced around quickly, but there was no sign of her. And then he looked out over the lake and saw a small wind funnel skimming over the water's surface, receding rapidly into the distance.

"Keep it, Sorak," Lyra called back to him, psionically. *"I know what it means to you. The offer in itself is a gift that I shall always treasure."*

And then she was gone.

Sorak glanced down at the thin, tightly plaited cord he'd braided from stray locks of Ryana's hair. She belonged to his past now. He had wanted to give something to Lyra, and this was all he had that he truly valued. All he had left of the life that he had left behind, and of his dreams about what might have been. Galdra, the sword of elvish kings, represented what yet might be. One talisman for the past, one for the future. It was fitting.

He tied the plaited cord around his neck.

FIVE

The old castle ruins stood on a scrubby ridge in the lower foothills, a thousand feet above the valley and the city of Tyr. As Sorak made his way down the mountain trail, heading toward the ridge where the ruins stood, he could see the sprawling city in the valley below. To the west, beyond the city, lay the Great Sand Wastes of the desert, crossed by caravan routes that connected Tyr with the other cities of the tablelands. From Tyr, one route led toward the merchant village of Altaruk, across the desert to the southwest, at the tip of the Estuary of the Forked Tongue. To the west of Altaruk, the route then curved along the southern shore of the estuary, toward the city of Balic.

Another trade route led directly east from Tyr, branching off near a spring at the midpoint of the tablelands. One branch led north to the city of Urik, which lay near the vast depression known as the Dragon's Bowl, then east, to the cities of Raam and Draj, beyond which lay the Sea of Silt. The other branch led south, back toward the Estuary of the Forked Tongue, where it branched off yet again, with one branch leading southeast, to Altaruk, and the other east, along the estuary's northern shore, until it took a sharp turn to the north, through a verdant

section at the northeastern boundary of the Great
Ivory Plain, toward the Barrier Mountains and the
cities of Gulg and Nibenay.

This much Sorak knew, but what he did not know
would fill a book. In fact, it was from a book that he
had learned the little he knew so far. He had found
the book inside his pack, wrapped up in cloth tied
with a piece of twine. His first thought had been that
one of the others of the tribe had slipped it in there
without his awareness, but that seemed unlikely,
since he did not own any books, nor were any of the
others likely to have taken one from the convent
library. The personas each had their own idiosyncra-
cies, but none of them were thieves. At least, not so
far as he knew. Then it occurred to him that the only
one who would have had a chance to slip the parcel
down inside his pack was Sister Dyona, the old gatekeeper. She must have done it when they embraced,
as he was leaving. This suspicion was confirmed
when he unwrapped the parcel and found the book,
together with a note from the gatekeeper. It read:

A small gift to help guide you on your journey.
A more subtle weapon than your sword, but no
less powerful, in its own way. Use it wisely.
                              Affectionately, Dyona

There was no writing on the worn, hidebound
cover of the book, but on the first of its parchment leaf
pages was written the title, *The Wanderer's Journal*. The
author, presumably the Wanderer of the title, was not
identified in any other way. Sorak had never been
much interested in reading. His lessons every day
back at the convent had given him a distaste for it,
and after struggling through old scholarly texts on

psionics and the long, rambling, poetic passages of
the ancient druidic and elvish writings, he could not
understand why anyone would want to read in his
spare time. He had always studied his lessons duti-
fully, but much preferred spending his hours in
weapons practice or out in the woods with Tigra and
Ryana, or on extended field trips with the older sisters
of the convent. Whether in the mountains or the foothills or the empty stretches of desert far to the south
of Tyr, Sorak preferred learning firsthand about
Athasian flora and fauna.

Now, he realized that he was heading out into a
world about which he knew very little, and he understood the value of Dyona's gift. The journal opened
with the words:

> I live in a world of fire and sand. The crimson
> sun scorches the life from anything that crawls
> or flies, and storms of sand scour the foliage
> from the barren ground. Lightning strikes from
> the cloudless sky, and peals of thunder roll
> unexplained across the vast tablelands. Even
> the wind, dry and searing as a kiln, can kill a
> man with thirst.
>
> This is a land of blood and dust, where tribes
> of feral elves sweep out of the salt plains to
> plunder lonely caravans, mysterious singing
> winds call men to slow suffocation in a Sea of
> Silt, and legions of slaves clash over a few
> bushels of moldering grain. The dragon despoils
> entire cities, while selfish kings squander their
> armies raising gaudy palaces and garish tombs.
>
> This is my home, Athas. It is an arid and
> bleak place, a wasteland with a handful of aus-
> tere cities clinging precariously to a few

scattered oases. It is a brutal and savage land,
beset by political strife and monstrous abomina-
tions, where life is grim and short.

This was writing of a different sort from the scholarly works he had been exposed to at the convent.
Most of the scrolls and dusty tomes in the meticu-
lously cataloged convent library were surviving writings from ancient elvish and druidic lore, and were
set down in a dense and florid style that he found
laborious and tiresome. The other writings in the
library were those compiled by the sisterhood, relat-
ing primarily to psionics and Athasian flora and
fauna, and many of these were little more than ency-
clopedic lists, which made for reading that was infor-
mative, but not very entertaining.

The Wanderer's Journal was different. It owed little,
if anything, to the flowery and high-flown traditions
of the ancient bards. Except for the rather colorful
opening passages, the book was written in a simple,
unpretentious style. Reading it was almost like having a casual conversation with the Wanderer himself.
The journal contained much information with which
Sorak was already familiar from his studies at the
convent. It also contained the Wanderer's personal
observations of Athasian geography, the diverse races
of Athas and their social structures, detailed reports
on life in various Athasian villages and cities, and
commentary on Athasian politics. The latter, although
somewhat dated, nevertheless provided Sorak with a
glimpse of Athasian life, about which he knew practically nothing.

Clearly, the Wanderer had traveled far and wide
across the world, and had seen and experienced
many things, all of which he commented on with firm

and well-considered opinions. For the first time, Sorak realized that reading could be more than a plodding study of archaic texts and dusty scrolls. The Wanderer seemed endlessly fascinated by the world he lived in, and he brought his enthusiasm for the subject to his writings.

Each night when he stopped to rest, Sorak opened the journal and read by his campfire for a while before he went to sleep. Reading the words of the Wanderer was almost like having a friendly and loquacious guide for his journey. Tonight, he planned to camp inside some castle ruins on a ridge. The crumbling walls would provide some measure of protection from the strong desert winds that struck the foothills. In the morning, he would proceed to Tyr. If he got an early start, he thought he would be able to reach the city by late afternoon or early evening. Just what he would do when he got there, however, was something he had not yet decided.

Somehow, he had to make contact with the Veiled Alliance. But how? Lyra had given him no clues. She had no clues to give him. The pyreens generally avoided the cities. They found them decadent and oppressive, and as preservers, they would be far from welcome. Every city held strongholds of subversive defilers, which forced the Veiled Alliance to function underground. Aside from that, any magic-user, whether preserver or defiler, was at risk in an Athasian city.

This was a fact Sorak had learned back at the convent, and the point of the lesson had been strongly driven home by an incident described in *The Wanderer's Journal*. The Wanderer had witnessed a "witch" being beaten to death by an angry crowd in a marketplace, and no one had raised a hand to help her. The incident had taken place in Tyr, and in describing it, the Wanderer wrote, "Magic has left the world of Athas a deadly desert. Its people blame all magicians for its ruin, defilers and preservers alike—and not only blame, but despise them. For protection from nearly universal hatred, the good wizards of Athas and their allies have formed secret societies, collectively known as the Veiled Alliance."

According to the Wanderer, the Veiled Alliance had no central leadership. Each city had its own chapter, and on occasion, similar groups formed in some of the larger villages, as well. These chapters all functioned independently, though there was occasional contact between groups in nearby cities. Each chapter of the Veiled Alliance was divided into cells, with the number of people in each cell usually quite small, anywhere from three to six members. The first rank cells had secret lines of communication to the chapter leadership, to other first rank cells, and to the next lower ranking cells. The second rank cells each maintained communication only with the first rank cell directly above them, and with the third rank cells directly below them, but not with any of the other first, second, or third rank cells. This organizational pattern provided that, if the security of any one cell was breached, the security of other cells would not be compromised. The structure also allowed one or more cells to be "cut off" at any given time.

In the cities, the Wanderer explained, the powerful defilers who constituted the ruling elite—the sorcerer-kings and the nobles under their protection—had templars and soldiers to maintain their security and enforce their oppressive rule. Any magic-user, whether defiler or preserver, who was not under such protection would be wise to maintain anonymity;

exposure could, and usually did, mean death.

Sorak had no idea how he would proceed once he reached Tyr. How did one make contact with a secret organization? From what Lyra had told him, it seemed that he would have to do something to draw their attention to him so that they would be encouraged to make contact. He had a feeling that contact was liable to be rather dangerous. He also realized that trying to make contact with the Veiled Alliance would probably take time, certainly more than merely a day or two, and that posed a problem in itself. He had no money.

The villichi never carried any money. At the convent, there was no need for it. They grew their own food and made everything they needed from scratch. On their pilgrimages, the sisters lived off the land for the most part, except when they ventured into villages and cities. In the villages, they were usually fed by the people, who rarely objected because the sisters always ate very sparingly and consumed no meat. And if there was no villichi child present in the village, they moved on after only a brief stay.

In the cities, they were made to feel less welcome, for they were aligned with the preservers. But since they took no part in politics, they were not perceived as a threat by the ruling classes. Villichi were also well known for their fighting prowess and their psionic abilities, and it was considered wise not to antagonize them. At best, they received a passively hostile reception from the people. An innkeeper might set aside a small, unobtrusive table in a corner and provide a bowl of gruel, with perhaps a few chunks of stale bread. It would be done grudgingly, however, for even if the innkeeper was in sympathy with the preservers, it would not do to be observed treating one with courtesy and kindness.

Sorak was not villichi and could not expect even that kind of cursory treatment. If he had to remain in the city for any significant length of time, he would require money. That meant he would probably have to find some sort of work for which he would be paid. Having never even set foot in a city before, he had no idea what sort of work that might be or how to go about finding it.

His thoughts were suddenly interrupted by the Watcher. *"There are men inside the ruins,"* she said.

Sorak stopped. He was still some distance up the trail from the ridge where the ruins stood, but now he saw what the Watcher had already detected through his own senses. There was a thin, barely perceptible trail of smoke rising from behind the crumbling walls. Someone had built a campfire, the smoke of which was quickly dissipated by the wind. However, it was blowing in his direction, and he could now smell the faint aroma of burning dung, and an unfamiliar odor mixed with the stink of beasts and cooking flesh. . . . He realized it was the scent of man.

Both elves and halflings possessed senses more acute than those of humans, and Sorak's were unusually so, in part because he was both elf and halfling, and in part because the Watcher was preternaturally alert to the evidence of those senses.

Unlike beasts, rational creatures could be distracted by their thoughts and, unless they truly paid attention, might miss things reported to them by their senses. No one man could remain in a constant state of alertness, aware of every single piece of information reported by his senses. Such a constant state of concentration would be exhausting, and would leave room for nothing else. However, Sorak was not one man. He was a tribe of one, and the role of the Watcher in that tribe was to do nothing else but pay attention to everything reported by the senses of the body they all shared. The Watcher missed nothing, whether it was significant or not. In this case, the Watcher felt the information was significant enough to alert Sorak to what his senses had already detected, but his own consciousness had not. And now that his alertness had been triggered by the Watcher, Sorak's senses seemed suddenly to become much more acute.

The scent of man. But how did he *know* it was the scent of man without ever having met a man before? The Watcher knew, which obviously meant that at some point in his past, beyond the reach of conscious memory, he had smelled this scent before and known it for what it was. He did not know why, but for some reason, this scent had an association that was unpleasant and disturbing. The corners of his mouth turned down.

"Tigra," he said softly. "Get out of sight."

The tigone obediently bounded off into the underbrush.

Sorak approached with caution. So far, he could not see them, but as he drew closer, their scent became stronger. . . the smell of human males, and something else, almost like the scent of human males, but different in some subtle way. And there was the scent of beasts, as well. . . crodlu—large, bipedal lizards with thick, massive legs, and long, thin forelimbs. Sorak could see them now, tied up to a stand of scrub just beyond the outer walls of the ruins. They stood erect on their heavily muscled legs, their long necks stretched out to their full length as their beaklike jaws tore leaves and small branches from the scrub. He counted six of them, and saw that each of the creatures had a saddle strapped to its broad back, which meant the beasts had been tamed for use as war mounts.

As they sensed his approach, they reacted with loud snorts and pawed at the ground, but Screech came to the fore and snorted back at them, which calmed them down. They went back to munching on the foliage.

"Something is disturbing the crodlu," a male voice said from just beyond the wall.

"Probably just some animal," one of the others said. "Anyway, they're quiet now."

"Perhaps I should go check on them."

"Relax, Silok. You worry too much. There's not a soul around for miles. If someone were trying to sneak up on us, the crodlu would be making a great deal more noise."

Sorak came up close to the wall, pressing his back up against it as he listened.

One of the men grunted with contentment from his meal, then belched loudly. "You think the caravan will leave tomorrow?"

"Perhaps, but it will likely take more time to fill the wagons and organize for the return trip. Never fear, Kivor, we shall have no trouble spotting the caravan from here when it leaves the city. There will be plenty of time for us to ride down and alert the others."

"I wish they would hurry up about it," the one called Silok said irritably. "Damn those lazy merchants. We've been up here for three days now, and who knows how much longer we may have to wait? I'm growing sick of this place."

"What sickens me is that Rokan and the others are having themselves a fine old time in Tyr, drinking and carousing with the ladies while we sit up here in these miserable ruins and freeze our asses off each night."

"Zorkan's right," said one of the others. "I see no reason why we can't take turns going down into the city. Why should it require six of us to keep watch for the caravan?"

"Because that way we can work in shifts, and some of us can sleep or go to empty our bowels or hunt game. Or would you prefer to sit up here all alone, Vitor? There is greater safety in numbers. We do not know these hills."

"Nor do I want to know them," Vitor replied sourly. "The sooner we are quit of this place, the better I shall like it. The cursed bugs up here are eating me alive."

As the men spoke, Sorak withdrew inside his mind, and the Guardian came to the fore, using her telepathic ability to read their thoughts.

These men are bandits, she realized at once. Marauders from the Nibenay region. But then, what are they doing here? Nibenay is clear across the desert, at the foot of the Barrier Mountains. She probed more deeply, opening herself to all their thoughts. At once, she recoiled from the contact. These were ugly, crude, and vicious minds, preoccupied with the basest thoughts and instincts. With a sense of revulsion, she forced herself to extend her telepathic awareness out toward them again.

She tried to push past their vile thoughts of greed and lust, the images of violent acts these cruel men had committed and cherished in memory. As she sorted through the brutal thoughts and impulses of their minds, she came to loathe them.

These men were parasites, predators of the worst kind, without faith or scruples. They had left their base camp in the Mekillot Mountains and gone east, then followed a trade caravan from Altaruk. Some of them had joined the caravan, posing as traders. They now waited down in the city, waited for the caravan to begin its journey back to Altaruk bearing weapons to be sold in Gulg and profits from the merchant houses of Tyr. Before the caravan could reach Altaruk, however, the marauders planned to attack it. These men camped inside the ruins were the lookouts. When the caravan started out from Tyr, their task was to ride down to where the rest of their band was waiting in the desert and alert them to prepare the ambush.

But why had they come all this way? If their goal was merely to attack the caravan and pillage it, then why not simply strike the caravan near Altaruk or Gulg, both of which were much nearer to the Mekillot Mountains, where these marauders made their home? Why travel so far? The Guardian probed deeper.

One of the men, a brute named Digon, seemed to be in charge of this group. She focused her psionic probe on him. Once again, she had to fight down her revulsion as she came into deeper contact with his mind; the images within it were repellent and disgusting. At last she found what she was seeking.

There was more to this than simple banditry. Of those who had joined the caravan from Altaruk, some would strike from within when the trap was sprung, but others were in Tyr as spies. There was a fairly new government in Tyr. Word had reached Nibenay that Tithian was gone and his templars had been deposed. Tyr was now ruled solely by a Council of Advisors, and apparently this government was not a stable one.

There was a secret alliance between these marauders and a powerful aristocrat in Nibenay. Digon did not know the identity of this noble. It seemed only their leader, a man named Rokan, knew this noble and had regular contact with him. He had made an agreement with the aristocrat, in return for certain considerations, to send some of his marauders to infiltrate several of the merchant houses in Tyr and gather information about the state of the government. Robbing the caravan added the incentive of greater profit to the enterprise and enhanced the nobility of Nibenay, since it denied valuable trade goods to their rivals in Gulg.

While the Guardian digested this information, she kept examining the thoughts of the marauders. For the most part, they were irritated by the dull task of keeping a lookout for the caravan and grumbled about how their comrades who had joined the caravan were enjoying themselves in Tyr, drinking and debauching, while they were forced to keep watch from the windswept ridge. They wondered impatiently how long it would take for the return trip to be organized and underway, and they looked forward to taking out their frustrations on the hapless traders and travelers who made up the caravan. Eventually, however, all of these concerns were laid aside as they settled down to a game of dice.

The Guardian pulled back with a sense of great relief and ducked under, allowing Sorak to come back to the fore, with knowledge of all the information she had acquired through her probes. Only a few moments had passed, and Sorak barely noticed the time that he had been away. However, he now had a great deal of information to ponder, and he wondered what he should do about it.

"Why should you do anything?" asked Eyron. *"What are these men to you? Nothing. What difference does it make to us if they attack the caravan?"*

"It may make a great deal of difference," Sorak replied inaudibly. *"If I warn the caravan of the impending attack,*

they can make preparations for it and avoid being taken by
surprise. Lives will be saved, and the merchants will avoid
sustaining losses. They would be indebted to me for this
information. And the government would benefit from
knowing about these spies from Nibenay."

"*Assuming they believed you and did not suspect you*
were a spy, yourself," Eyron replied.

"*As a stranger, I would be suspect, anyway,*" said
Sorak. "*I know no one in the city, and I have no money. Yet*
here I have stumbled upon an opportunity to ingratiate
myself to powerful interests in Tyr and perhaps gain some
sort of reward, as well. It is an opportunity that seems to
good to pass up."

"Gith's blood!" someone cried out. "I smell halfling!"

The wind had shifted, but Sorak had not thought
the humans would have been able to catch his scent.

"I knew something was bothering the crodlu!" one
of the others cried.

There were sounds of commotion beyond the wall
as the bandits jumped to their feet and snatched up
their weapons. Sorak realized it would be pointless to
run. The trail was open in both directions and he
would present an easy target for their bows, or they
could mount up and ride him down with their crodlu
before he had gone a hundred yards. There was nothing to do but stand and face them.

Sorak quickly moved away from the wall so he
would not be hemmed in by them if they came from
either side, which was precisely what they did. Three
of them came around the wall from the right, three
from the left. Two of the bandits were armed with
crossbows; two carried obsidian-tipped spears and
round, leather-covered, wooden shields; one carried a
stone axe and a wooden shield; the last was armed

with an obsidian broadsword and a shield. They all wore obsidian daggers at their belts and in their boots, and all six wore lightweight, leather breast-plates. Five of them were human males, but the sixth marauder was a half-elf.

"Stand where you are!" called out the one named Digon, as the two archers leveled their crossbows at Sorak.

"He's no halfling," said the one named Silok. "Your nose is off, Aivar. This man is human."

"I tell you, I smell halfling on him," the half-elf insisted. He took another sniff. "And elf, as well, by thunder!"

"A half-breed?" Digon said, with a frown. "Impossible. Elves and halflings do not mate."

"Look at his ears," said Vitor.

"Never mind his ears," said Zorkan. "Look at that sword!"

Sorak stood perfectly still through this exchange, making no motion toward his weapons.

"If you move so much as a muscle, my archers will shoot you down where you stand," said Digon. "What are you?"

"Merely a pilgrim," Sorak replied in an even voice.

"With a blade like that?" said Digon. He smiled and shook his head. "No, I do not think so. How much have you heard?"

"I heard men talking," Sorak said, "and I saw the smoke from your fire. Before that, I had thought to camp here myself this evening, but it seems you have already claimed the spot. I shall not begrudge you. I can find another place."

"Why take any chances?" Vitor asked. "We should just kill him and have done with it."

"Hold your tongue," said Digon. "We shall find out

what he has heard, and if he is alone. Drop your staff, pilgrim, and put down your pack."

Sorak did as he was told.

"Good," said Digon. "Now, let me see that sword. But slowly, mind, else my archers become nervous."

Sorak slowly unsheathed the elvish blade. The sight of Galdra provoked immediate reactions of astonishment from the marauders.

"Steel!" said Vitor.

"Look at that blade!" said Zorkan. "I have never seen the like of it!"

"Silence!" Digon shouted, with a quick glance at the others. Then he turned back to Sorak once again. "That is quite a sword for a mere pilgrim," he said.

"Even pilgrims require protection," Sorak replied.

"That blade is too much protection for the likes of you," said Digon. "Toss it on the ground, before you."

Sorak tossed the blade to the ground, just in front of him.

"There's a good boy," said Digon, with a smile. "And now those daggers."

Sorak slowly reached for the hunting blade in his belt. At the same time, the clump of crodlu tied up beneath the stand of scrub suddenly began to snort and bellow in alarm, pawing at the ground and straining at their ropes. As the marauders turned to see what was disturbing them, Tigra came bounding out of the underbrush, charging toward them with a roar.

"Look out, a tigone!" Aivar cried.

Zorkan turned and aimed his crossbow, but before he could shoot, Sorak's hunting knife buried itself to the hilt in his throat. Sorak rolled as soon he had thrown the blade, and as he came up, he drew the bone stiletto from his boot and in one smooth motion hurled it at the second bowman. It struck the half-elf in the chest, penetrating his heart, and Aivar was dead before he hit the ground. By that time, Sorak had already snatched up Galdra from where it lay on the ground in front of him, and he came up ready to face his remaining opponents. Kivor was closest. The marauder raised his axe, but he was not quick enough. Sorak's blade plunged through his chest and came out his back. Kivor gurgled horribly as blood spurted from his mouth and his axe fell to the ground. Sorak pushed him off his sword with his foot, kicking his dying body back into Digon. The leader of the marauder group fell with his dead comrade on top of him.

Vitor screamed as Tigra leaped and brought him down. Silok raised his spear to throw it at the tigone, but saw Sorak coming at him fast with his sword raised and turned to meet the blow, bringing up his shield. Galdra came whistling down, slicing through both the shield and Silok's arm. The marauder screamed as he saw his severed arm drop to the ground together with the split pieces of the shield. Blood sprayed out in a fountain from where his arm ended in a stump. Sorak swung his sword again and Silok's head came off his shoulders and landed at his feet. As Silok's body collapsed, Sorak spun around to see Digon charging him, bringing down his broadsword in an overhead blow. He brought Galdra up just in time to block it, and as the obsidian blade struck the elven steel, it shattered to pieces.

The marauder's eyes grew wide as he backed away, holding his shield up before him. He dropped the broken blade and clawed for the dagger in his belt. However, before his fingers could close around the hilt, the knife suddenly flew from its sheath and sailed through the air to land on the ground about twenty feet away. An instant later, Digon felt the shield wrenched from his grasp, as if by invisible hands, and it, too, went flying. He saw his opponent simply standing there, holding his sword down by his side, and he turned to run.

"Tigra," Sorak said.

The tigone bounded after the marauder.

"Make him stop, but do not harm him."

Tigra cut off the marauder and crouched before him, snarling. Digon froze, staring at the huge beast in terror.

"If you move, Tigra will kill you," Sorak said.

"No, please!" the marauder pleaded. "I beg you, spare my life!"

"As you would have spared mine?" said Sorak. "Tigra, fetch."

The tigone took the marauder's forearm between its teeth and brought him back to Sorak. Digon's face was absolutely white with fear.

"Spare me, please! I beg you! I will do anything you say!"

"Yes, I think you will," said Sorak as he sheathed his sword.

He turned and retrieved his pack, daggers, and staff, then walked back toward the ruins, where the marauders had made their camp. Tigra followed, pulling Digon along by his arm. The marauder whimpered with fear.

The campfire was burning low. Sorak bent down, picked up several pieces of wood, and tossed them on the fire. He quickly examined the campsite, then put down his staff and pack and sat down on the ground, beside the fire. "Sit down," he said to the marauder.

Tigra released Digon's arm, and the marauder

slowly sat down across from Sorak, with the campfire between them. He swallowed hard, his gaze going from the fearsome beast beside him, to Sorak, and back again. He could not believe what had just happened. There had been six of them against one, and now he was the only one left alive. One of his men had been killed by the tigone, but this "pilgrim" had dispatched the other four himself, and with a speed and effortlessness that seemed impossible. He had never felt so afraid in his entire life.

"I have money," Digon said. "Silver coins and merchant scrip. Spare me and you are welcome to it all."

"I could take it all in any case," said Sorak.

"So you could," said the marauder glumly. "But listen, I still have things to bargain with."

"What things?" asked Sorak.

"Information," Digon said. "Passed on to the right people, this information could net you a reward far greater than what my purse contains."

"You mean information about how your bandit friends plan to attack the caravan?" said Sorak. "Or are you referring to the men your leader sent to Tyr to spy for Nibenay?"

Digon's jaw went slack with astonishment. "Gith's blood! How in thunder did you know that?" And then he recalled how his dagger had been yanked from its scabbard and how his shield had been wrenched out of his grasp, as if by unseen hands. "Of course," he said. "I should have known by the way you command the tigone." He sighed and stared morosely into the flames. "Just my luck to encounter a master of the Way. That means I have nothing left to bargain with. My life is forfeit."

"Perhaps not," said Sorak.

The marauder glanced up at him sharply, hope flaring in his eyes. "What do you mean?"

"Your leader . . . Rokan," Sorak said, and as he spoke, he ducked under, and the Guardian probed the thief's mind. An image of his leader came to Digon's mind, and she perceived it.

"What of him?" Digon asked, uneasily.

"Who are the men he chose to spy for Nibenay?"

As he heard the question, Digon thought of the men picked for the mission and the Guardian saw all their faces in the mind of the marauder. And with their faces, came their names.

The marauder saw the way Sorak was looking at him intently, and he swallowed hard. "I could hide nothing from you. You know already, do you not?"

"Yes. I know."

Digon sighed. "What more would you have of me?"

"When your friends attack the caravan, where is the ambush to take place?" And no sooner had the Guardian asked the question than she perceived the answer in the marauder's mind. Without even waiting for his reply, she then asked, "How many are they?" And that answer, too, was instantly forthcoming. Digon could not resist thinking of it. "What are their arms?"

"Stop it!" the marauder cried. "At least give me time to answer! Leave me some shred of self-respect!"

"Self-respect?" said Sorak. "In a man such as you?"

The corners of Digon's mouth twisted down and he looked away, avoiding Sorak's gaze.

"Go," said Sorak.

The marauder stared at him with disbelief, uncertain that he heard correctly. "What?"

"I said, go."

"You are releasing me?" Then he glanced uneasily

at Tigra.

"The tigone shall not harm you," Sorak said. "Nor shall I. You are free to leave, though you deserve to die."

Scarcely able to believe his good fortune, Digon slowly got to his feet, as if expecting Sorak to change his mind at any moment.

"Before you go," said Sorak, "consider what would happen if you were to ride out and attempt to warn your friends waiting in the desert, or went down to Tyr and sought out Rokan. A long journey made for nothing, spies exposed, and plans for plunder gone awry, all because of you."

Digon bit down on his lower lip. "They would kill me. But . . . why do you spare my life?"

"Because I can," Sorak replied. "And because you can do a service for me."

"Name it."

"I seek contact with the Veiled Alliance," Sorak said.

Digon shook his head. "I have but heard of them," he said. "I know nothing that could help you."

"I know that," Sorak said. "But you can go down to the city and help prepare my way. Ask questions. See what you can learn. And if they should contact you, then tell them about me. Steer clear of your marauder friends, however. That would be in your own best interest."

"You need not remind me," Digon said.

"You will do it?"

Digon gave a small snort. "You know I will. It would be pointless trying to deceive one who can read your very thoughts. What you ask entails risk, but that risk is nothing compared to what Rokan would do to me, and it is a small enough price to pay for the gift of my life. When I speak of you, what name shall I give?"

"I am called Sorak."

"A nomad who walks alone? Then Aivar was wrong. You are an elf?"

"I am an elfling."

"So he was right. You are a half-breed. But it is unheard of for halflings and elves to mate. How did that come about?"

"That does not concern you."

"Sorry. I did not mean to offend. May I take my crodlu?"

"Yes, but leave the others."

Digon nodded. "They should fetch a good price in the marketplace. What about weapons? Will you leave me with none?"

"I shall leave you with your purse," said Sorak. "You can use it to purchase new weapons in the city."

Digon nodded. Sorak followed him out beyond the wall. As the marauder headed toward the stand of scrub where the crodlu were tied up, he hesitated by the bodies of his comrades. He bent down over one of them, and Sorak saw him retrieve a purse.

"Leave it," Sorak said. "Your own should be sufficient to your needs."

"If I am to make inquiries on your behalf, I shall have to frequent taverns," Digon said. "That will take money. And I shall be poorer for the purchase of new weapons, without which I would be a fool to undertake your errand."

What the man said made sense, thought Sorak. "Did they all carry purses?" he said, indicating the corpses.

"In expectation of a visit to the city, we all brought silver, yes," Digon said sourly. "We six did not expect to be chosen for this lousy duty."

"Take half, then, and leave the rest to me," said Sorak.

Digon nodded and proceeded to relieve the bodies of their purses. He brought three to Sorak and kept the rest himself. "All right?" he said.

Sorak weighed the purses. They were full of jingling coins. "Very well," he said. "You may go. But take care that you do not betray me. If it should occur to you, remember I have touched your mind. That will make it easier for me to find you."

"Believe me, I shall give you no cause to look," said the marauder. "If my path never crosses yours again, I shall count myself well blessed."

He untied one of the crodlu, climbed up on the lizard's back and spurred it to a gallop down the trail leading to the valley. Sorak watched him go, then called Tigra to dig holes for burying the corpses. He couldn't care less whether they were decently buried, but he did not wish to tempt any of the tribe. Halflings ate human flesh.

SIX

Seen from the ridge overlooking the valley, the walled city of Tyr resembled the body of a legless spider. The main portion of the city made up the spider's abdomen, while the head contained the king's palace and the templars' quarter. Roughly in the center of the main part of the city, overlooking the stadium and the arena, stood Kalak's ziggurat, a huge, square-stepped tower constructed of massive blocks of mortared stone. The Wanderer wrote that it had taken thousands of slaves laboring from dawn to dusk for over twenty years to construct the massive edifice. It rose high over the city, dominating the slums and marketplaces all around it, and was visible for miles beyond the city's outer walls.

At the opposite end of the stadium, separated from the main part of the city by a thick, high wall, stood the Golden Tower, the palace where the sorcerer-king, Kalak, had resided. Surrounded by lush gardens and colonnaded walkways, the Golden Tower was ringed by the templars' quarter, where the servants of the king had dwelt in luxury, isolated from the people under their authority.

There were three large gates that gave entrance to the well-fortified city. The Grand Gate faced the mountains and gave access to the sprawling palace compound. The Stadium Gate, located between the templars' quarter and the tradesmen's district, led to the stadium and the arena. The Caravan Gate, at the opposite end of the city from the palace, was the main entrance to the city. It opened onto the largest and busiest street in Tyr, Caravan Way, which led through the merchant district to the central market square, near the foot of Kalak's ziggurat.

The Grand Gate was the closest to the trail coming down out of the foothills, but Sorak did not expect to be admitted through the palace gate. He chose to ride around the city's outer wall, past the outlying farms and fields, to the Caravan Gate. He rode one of the crodlu belonging to the slain marauders and led the others in a string behind him. He had not needed to rope them all together, for they would easily have followed Screech, but Sorak saw no purpose to be served in drawing attention to his unique psionic powers. At least, not yet. And he prudently kept his blade concealed beneath his cloak.

The guards at the gate questioned him briefly before passing him through. He told them he was a simple herdsman who raised and trained crodlu out in the tablelands, and that he had brought in this string to sell in the marketplace.

The guards were primarily interested in Tigra, having never seen a tame tigone before. Tigra was not exactly tame, but Sorak did not tell them that. He explained that he had raised Tigra from a cub and that the beast was bonded to him and a great help in tending the crodlu herd. Then he demonstrated his control over the beast with a few simple commands, which Tigra promptly obeyed, and by encouraging the guards to pet him. One of the braver souls ven-

tured to do just that, and when Tigra suffered the
caress without taking his arm off, the others seemed
well satisfied. They were always eager to admit
traders to the city, for the profits of anything sold in
the marketplaces of Tyr were subject to a tax that
went into the city's coffers, from which the guards
were paid their salary. However, they warned Sorak
that he would be liable for any damage that his tigone
caused, either to life or property.

As he passed through the massive gates, he rode
along Caravan Way, the widest street in the main part
of the city. The other streets he saw leading off the
main avenue were little more than narrow alleyways
winding through the tightly clustered buildings. As
he led the crodlu through the street, he was assailed
by a bewildering agglomeration of sights and sounds
and smells. In the forests of the Ringing Mountains,
there had been no shortage of stimulation for the
senses, but his first impression of the city brought him
close to confusion and panic.

"*So many people!*" said Kivara excitedly. "*And so
much noise!*"

"*They swarm like ants,*" Eyron said with astonishment. "*How can so many live together in so small a
space?*"

In the stretch of one city block, Sorak saw humans,
elves, half-elves, even a few dwarves and half-giants.
Some drove wagons or pushed wooden carts, others
carried baskets on their heads or heavy loads on their
backs, all bustling in a steady stream of traffic heading both to and from the central market square. The
marketplace itself extended all the way out to the city
gates, with tents and stalls with awnings set up along
both sides of the busy street. Nobles reclined in the
comfort of their shaded litters, ignoring the filthy

beggars who sat in the dust and held out their hands
in supplication. Armed soldiers mingled with the
crowd, on the watch for thieves and pickpockets.
Food vendors chanted their offerings to passersby
and merchants with goods of every description held
up their wares and cried out to entice customers.

Sorak had never experienced such an overlay of
odors. Long accustomed to catching the subtlest of
scents on the cool, crisp mountain breezes, he was
overwhelmed by the smell of all the bodies mingling
around him, the musky scents of herd animals and
beasts of burden, and the heavy aromas of basted and
spiced meats cooking over braziers in the food stalls.
This was a far cry from the peaceful and spiritual
atmosphere of the villichi convent and the bucolic
serenity of the Ringing Mountains.

He felt the Watcher's anxiety as she tried to assimilate it all. His pulse raced with Kivara's exultation at
the novelty of the experience. He sensed Lyric's childlike awe, Eyron's apprehension, and the Ranger's
steadfast determination to remain alert and avoid
being distracted by all the tumult and confusion. As
he rode through the crowded street, glancing all
around him at one fascinating sight after another, he
felt the Guardian's reassuring presence, striving to
maintain a balance within the tribe in the face of so
much that was new to them.

"I had no idea it would be like this," he said to her.
"How can anyone think straight with so many distrac-
tions? How can anyone stand living with so much noise?"

"One probably becomes accustomed to it after a while,"
the Guardian replied.

"I do not think I ever shall," said Sorak. He shook his
head. "Do you suppose this goes on all the time?"

"I imagine it dies down at night," the Guardian

replied. "*Perhaps it is quieter in other sections of the city. I do not know, Sorak. I am a newcomer here, too.*"

Sorak smiled inwardly at her jest, then hushed Kivara, who wanted him to stop at every stall and tent they passed. "*I, too, am curious, Kivara,*" he said. "*There is much to see here, but now is not the time. Be patient.*"

He had no difficulty making his way through the crowd. Mounted on a crodlu and leading a string of four others behind him, he could not only see well above the crowd, but his approach caused them to part before him with alacrity. Crodlu were known for occasionally snapping and taking a piece out of an arm or leg. Their chuffing, bleating, snorting sounds helped part the traffic, and more than a few of the people that he passed stared up at him curiously.

"*Why do they look at me so?*" he wondered.

"*Because they have never seen an elfling before,*" the Guardian said.

"*Am I truly so different?*"

"*If we were on foot, then we might not be so readily noticed,*" the Guardian replied, "*but mounted on a crodlu, we stand out among the crowd. They cannot help but notice. Even the half-elves we have seen are taller than the average human, and longer of limb. We possess normal human proportions, yet our features are different.*"

"*I have never felt so out of place,*" said Sorak. "*I had looked forward to visiting a city, but I do not think I would want to live like this.*"

Before long, he came to an open square at the center of the merchant district, where the beast traders had set up their pens. The odor of manure mingled with the smell of sweat and the musky scent of pelts from beasts of almost every description. One of the pens was filled with z'tals, upright lizards sold primarily for meat, though their flexible scales were often used for razors or small knives. They hopped about, trying to leap over the wall of their enclosure, but they were unable to jump high enough. Stupidly, they kept hopping en masse from one end of the pen to the other, emitting high-pitched, yipping sounds.

Another pen held jankx. The small, furry mammals lived in burrow communities out in the desert and were valued for their meat and for their pelts. Their enclosure had a stout wooden floor to prevent the jankx from digging their way out. Puzzled, they kept scratching at the wood with their paws, unable to comprehend why this curious "soil" would not loosen.

Farther on, Sorak saw larger pens that were used to contain kanks. The large, docile insects moved about sluggishly in their overcrowded confines, the clicking of their mandibles providing a percussive accompaniment to the yelps and cries of all the other beasts. Their exoskeltons were often used for armor, but it was not armor of high quality, for it was brittle and had to be replaced quite frequently. Kanks were more prized for the thick, green honey they excreted, which was nourishing and widely used as sweetener in food and drink.

Beyond the kank pens were large corrals that held erdlus, flightless, gray- and red-scaled birds that stood as high as seven feet and weighed up to two hundred pounds. Erdlu eggs were a staple of Athasian diet. The skittish birds milled about inside their corrals, their long, powerful legs pawing at the ground. Their snaky necks craned around in all directions, and shrill, high-pitched cries came from their wedge-shaped beaks, especially when Sorak approached with Tigra. The tigone's presence sent them running around in circles, shrieking with alarm.

At the far end of the square, nearest the ziggurat, was an open area that held no pens, for the beasts sold there were too large to be contained by them. Inix lizards grew to a length of sixteen feet and weighed up to two tons. No pen would have held them, and so they were chained to massive blocks of stone that functioned as anchors to keep them from wandering about. Their backs were protected by hard, thick shells and armored scales, capable of bearing a great deal of weight. They were often used in caravans to transport riders in howdahs strapped to their large backs, and the nobility frequently used them as vehicles to get around the city, allowing a servant to drive the beast with an obsidian-tipped prod while they relaxed in their shaded and luxurious howdahs.

On the other side of the open square, well away from all the other beasts, Sorak saw several mekillots. The largest of Athasian lizards, mekillots were used as caravan beasts, easily capable of pulling the heaviest of wagons, or as war lizards, bearing armored howdahs. Only wealthy merchant houses or standing armies could afford to buy them since mekillots were expensive to maintain and were quite vicious. Anyone who strayed within reach of their long tongues was liable to wind up a meal. There was only one way to control them, and that was to employ psionicists as handlers. Obviously, any merchant who dealt in mekillots needed to employ a number of psionicists to keep the gigantic lizards under control, for they could easily break through any enclosure or snap the strongest chains.

Of the beast traders in the square, only the one who dealt in inix lizards had crodlu to sell, and Sorak saw that he only had two of them, placed in a separate pen. He approached the trader, a human who sized him up quickly and decided he wanted to do business.

"I see you brought in some crodlu," said the trader, as Sorak dismounted in front of him. And then he saw Tigra. "Great dragon! A tigone!"

"Tigra will not harm you," Sorak said. "I have raised the tigone from a tiny cub, and it always does my bidding."

"I did not know they could be tamed," the trader said with interest. "It must require great patience. But then, a herdsman who raises crodlu in the tablelands would have no shortage of that commodity, would he?"

Sorak smiled.

If the trader was curious about Sorak's ancestry, he said nothing. He had his mind on business. Sorak ducked under to allow the Guardian to come to the fore, and she instantly perceived that the trader was going to try to cheat them.

"Are you interested in making me an offer on these crodlu?" she asked.

"Perhaps," the trader said. "But as you see, I already have two, and demand for crodlu is not great these days."

"Ah," the Guardian said. "Well, in that case, you would have little interest in adding to your stock. I shall not waste your time. Perhaps one of the other traders might be interested in making me an offer."

"Well, now, let us not be hasty," said the trader quickly. "I did not say I was not interested, merely that the market conditions for crodlu are not as favorable as they might be. However, who is to say that these conditions may not change? I am in the market every day, unlike a herdsman, who does not have the luxury of waiting for demand to rise. I might take the gamble of increasing my current stock, if the price was right."

"What would you consider a fair price?" asked the Guardian, and at once, she saw in his mind what the current market conditions for crodlu were. They were far from unfavorable. Quite the opposite, in fact. He already had a standing order from the Tyrian legion for a dozen crodlu, but he could not fill it. With the two he already had and Sorak's five, he would need only five more, and the legion would take the seven even if he could not fill the entire order. He stood to lose nothing on the trade.

The trader named a figure that was half of what the going price was. The Guardian immediately made a counter proposal, tripling the amount that he had named. They began to haggle in earnest. The trader offered to barter for the crodlu with some of his inix stock, of which he had a surfeit, but the Guardian declined and said that only cash would do. With her ability to read the trader's mind, the Guardian had the man at a hopeless disadvantage, and he did not even suspect it. It did not take long. The Guardian eventually accepted an amount that was only slightly under the going rate for crodlu, allowing the trader that small satisfaction. After all, the crodlu had cost Sorak nothing, and he walked away with a purse full of silver coins to add to the money he took from the slain marauders.

"*I wonder if this will be enough?*" he said.

"*We shall have no way of knowing until we find out what things cost here,*" the Guardian replied.

"*We may be in the city for some time before we can make contact with the Veiled Alliance,*" Eyron said. "*Sooner or later, this money shall run out, and then we will have no means of getting more."*

"Then we shall have to find the means," said Sorak, out loud. One or two people passing by gave him a curious glance, and he realized he would have to watch the tendency to speak out loud when he was talking to the tribe. He could not expect these people to understand.

He recalled a conversation with Mistress Varanna. "Here at the convent," she had said, "there is greater tolerance for those who are, in some significant way, different. That is because we all know what it means to be different ourselves. Yet even villichi are not immune to fear or prejudice. When you first came here, there was strong resistance to the idea of a male being accepted in the convent, and an elfling male, at that."

"But once the sisters knew me, they were able to accept me," Sorak had replied.

"Yes, that is true, and it may well be true for many in the outside world, as well. But you will find less tolerance there, Sorak. We villichi know what it means to be a tribe of one because it has happened before among us. Out there, people have no knowledge of it. If they knew, they would not understand, and it would frighten them. When people are frightened, they feel threatened, and when they feel threatened, they become frightening."

"So then . . . am I always to keep my true nature a secret from everyone except the sisters?" he had asked.

"Perhaps not always," Varanna had replied. "But there are things in all of us that are best kept private, at least until such time as we encounter someone from whom we would wish to hide nothing, someone whom we would not hesitate to trust with that which is our deepest and most intimate essence. And that is the sort of trust that is only built with time. It is good to value truth and pursue it, but certain truths are not meant for everyone. Remember that."

Sorak remembered. He remembered that he was in a brand new world and that he did not know these people. And they did not know him. Outwardly, there was already enough about him that was different, and as he walked through the crowded street, people could not help but notice. They saw a tall stranger in the garb of a herdsman, dressed all in brown, with thick, shoulder-length black hair and exotic-looking features. They saw the tigone trotting by his side like a tame pet. Some met his penetrating gaze and quickly looked away, not really knowing why. They pointed at him as he passed, and whispered among themselves.

He stopped at one of the food stalls and asked the vendor for a small bowl of cooked vegetables and several large pieces of raw z'tal meat.

"Raw?" asked the vendor.

"For my friend," said Sorak, glancing down at Tigra. The vendor looked over the waist-high partition of his stall and saw the tigone lying on the ground at Sorak's feet. He gave out a yelp and jumped back, knocking over some of his pots.

"There is no need for alarm," Sorak reassured the vendor. "Tigra will not harm you."

The vendor swallowed hard. "If you say so, stranger. How . . . how many pieces of raw meat will you require?"

Sorak selected a few choice cuts and gave them to Tigra, then paid the vendor and took his bowl of vegetables. He had taken no more than two or three mouthfuls when he heard the clinking of carapace and armor behind him and turned to see a squad of soldiers standing several feet away, their swords unsheathed. Several held pikes, which they pointed down at Tigra.

"Is that your beast?" their officer demanded. His voice was stern and forceful, but still betrayed uneasiness.

"Yes," said Sorak.

"Wild animals are not permitted within the city," said the officer.

Sorak continued eating. "What about all those wild animals back in the market square?" he asked.

"They are kept in pens, under control," the officer replied.

"The inix are not kept in pens," Sorak reminded him, "nor are the mekillots, and they are far more dangerous than my tigone."

"They all have handlers," said the officer.

"As does this tigone," Sorak said. "Tigra belongs to me. I am the handler."

"The beast poses a threat to the citizens of Tyr."

"My tigone threatens no one," Sorak protested. "You will note that Tigra remains calm despite your hostile attitude and the weapons you point in my direction. That sort of thing usually upsets the beast."

The soldiers behind the officer glanced at one another nervously.

"It is illegal for the beast to be within the city walls," the officer replied.

Sorak ducked under and allowed the Guardian to slip to the fore. She probed the soldier's mind. "There is no law that specifically prohibits tigones in the city," she said with Sorak's voice.

"Are you telling me I do not know what the law is?"

"No, I have no doubt you know what the law is,"

the Guardian replied. "And you also know I have not broken it. However, if you wish to take me before the Council of Advisors to clarify this matter, I have no objection. I have important information to present to them, in any case."

The officer suddenly seemed uncertain of his ground. His eyes narrowed. "You have business with the council?"

"Yes. In fact, I was on my way there and merely stopped to have something to eat. Perhaps you would be so kind as to escort me?"

The Guardian saw doubt in the soldier's mind. Perhaps, he was thinking, it would be wise not to antagonize this curious-looking stranger. He might be important. He hardly looks important, but he seems very sure of himself.

The Guardian decided to add to his uncertainty.

"Of course," she said, "if you have more important matters to attend to, I would not wish to keep you from them. What is your name, Captain, so I may be sure to commend you to the council for your diligence?" And as she spoke, she allowed Sorak's cloak to fall open slightly so the officer could see the sword.

His gaze flicked quickly toward the blade, noting the silver wire-wrapped hilt and the bronze crossguards, the finely made leather scabbard and its unusual shape. His eyes met Sorak's once again, and the expression on his face was no longer quite so stern. "The name is Captain Zalcor. And if you wish to be escorted to the council chambers, I have no other pressing business at the moment."

"Excellent," said the Guardian. She handed back the empty bowl to the vendor, who had listened with fascination to the entire exchange. "Thank you. Whenever you are ready, Captain Zalcor."

* * * * *

Sadira slammed her ebony fist down on the long and heavy table in the small council chamber, upsetting several water goblets. "That is enough, Timor!" she said angrily, her amber eyes flaring beneath her blond hair. "I am tired of hearing the same thing over and over again! We cannot and will not go back to the way things were, however much you templars may protest!"

"With all due respect, I was not protesting," the senior templar replied smoothly, drumming his bejeweled fingers softly on the tabletop. "I was merely pointing out that all the problems we are now experiencing are attributable directly to one thing and one thing only—the end of slavery in Tyr. You can hardly hold the templars responsible for that, as it was your idea to free the slaves, not ours."

"Slavery will be brought back to Tyr over my dead body!" the bald mul Rikus said, rising from his chair to glare menacingly at the senior templar.

"Sit down, Rikus, please," Sadira said. "These constant quarrels are getting us nowhere. We need solutions, not more problems."

With a scowl, the massive former gladiator resumed his seat at the head of table, beside Sadira.

"As for accepting blame in this matter," Sadira continued, "the blame lies not with the edict outlawing slavery in Tyr, but with the regime that instituted slavery in the first place. When the people were oppressed, they had no hope. Yet now that they are free, they have no livelihood. We may have given them their freedom, but that is not enough. We must help them find their rightful place in Tyrian society."

"The templars have never tried to hinder you in

that regard," Timor replied. "In fact, we have cooperated with this new government to the fullest extent of our abilities. However, you cannot expect to overturn a long-standing institution without encountering some difficulties. You will remember that I cautioned you about this. I warned you that freeing the slaves would wreak havoc with the merchants and disrupt law and order in the city, but your thoughts were on your lofty principles, rather than pragmatic considerations. Now you reap the results of your ill-considered actions."

"What we reap are the results of centuries of oppression by Kalak and his templars," Rikus said angrily. He pointed at the senior templar. "You and the parasites who make up the nobility have grown fat on the blood of slaves. I find it hard to sympathize with you for wishing you had all your slaves back."

"Much as I hate to contradict one of the heroes of the revolution," Timor said sarcastically, "the fact is that I, personally, have no wish for my former slaves to be slaves again. My household slaves have always been well cared for, and they have all chosen to stay on as my servants rather than plunge into the maelstrom of uncertainty you have created for the other former slaves of Tyr."

"They have *chosen* to stay on with you?" asked Rikus, frowning.

"And why not? I pay good wages, as the new edict demands. The added expense is easily offset by what I charge them for their room and board."

"In other words, nothing has changed for them," said Rikus with disgust. "You pay their wages with one hand, then collect the money back for rent with the other. They are still no better than slaves."

"I beg to disagree," protested Timor, raising

his eyebrows. "They are merely experiencing the economics of freedom. As slaves, they were my property, and I was obliged to care for them. As freemen, they are free to come and go as they choose, and I am obliged only to pay them for the work they perform. I am not obliged to house them, and there is nothing to prevent them from seeking cheaper accommodations in the warrens. However, they seem to prefer the comfort and safety of the templars' quarter to the crime-ridden and pestilential conditions they would encounter elsewhere in the city. Since I am offering them superior accommodations, I feel it is not unreasonable that I charge for them accordingly. In fact, I am being more than fair. I do not charge them any more than what they can afford to pay."

"Trust a templar to find a loophole in the law," Rikus said contemptuously.

"Enough," Sadira said firmly. "While I cannot condone Timor's self-serving rationalizations, they nevertheless underscore a valid point. We had not given enough thought to how the city would be affected by outlawing slavery, and we are now paying the price for that oversight. The question now before the council is how to remedy the situation. Granting homesteading rights to the former slaves in Kalak's fields outside the city has not addressed the problem adequately. Many are not taking advantage of the opportunity, but even if they did, there would not be enough fertile land for all of them. And among those who have established homesteads, we have already seen disputes over water rights and boundaries and rights of way.

"We still have scores of former slaves in the city who are beggars on the street. Riots in the warrens, as well as in the elven market, have become common, and they are spreading to other sections of the city. The mobs are growing large enough to intimidate the soldiers, and if these uprisings continue, fewer traders will come to the city. They have already started joining caravans to Urik, instead. We have survived one war with Urik only to be plunged into another—a war of trade. If our treasury dwindles further while Urik's grows, it shall not be long before they are strong enough to attack us once again."

"The way things have been going, they may not have to," Timor said wryly. "The people will simply open up the gates and let them in."

"Never!" Rikus said. "Not after all they have suffered to see the end of Kalak's tyranny!"

"For the moment, perhaps, you enjoy the people's support," said Timor, "but do not count on it overmuch. The people have short memories, and the mob is fickle. The heroes who killed Kalak will very soon become the council members who have brought the city to ruin, and the mob that once cheered you will start howling for your heads."

"And I bet you would like that, wouldn't you?" asked Rikus through gritted teeth.

"I?" said Timor. "You mistake me, Councilman. I bear you no malice or ill will. Remember that I, too, sit upon the council, and if the mob starts howling for your head, they shall call for mine, as well. I might also add that it would hardly be in my best interests if this government should fail and Tyr falls prey to Urik. As one of Kalak's former templars, I would be among the very first to be executed by King Hamanu."

"Thus far, we have heard a litany of things we have done wrong," Sadira said. "We have yet to hear any suggestions from the templars as to what we can do right."

The other council members nodded and muttered in agreement. None of them appeared to have any constructive suggestions to offer, and they would just as soon see that burden fall on the templars.

"As it happens, I do have a few modest proposals," Timor replied.

"I can well imagine what they are," Rikus muttered.

"Let him speak, Rikus," said Councilman Kor. "We cannot judge these proposals until we hear them."

"Thank you," Timor said, bowing his head slightly. "My first proposal is that we institute a tariff on all farm produce brought into the city."

"What? *More* taxes?" Rikus said with disbelief. "*That* is your solution? We need to stimulate trade, not drive farmers away from our markets!"

"To stimulate trade, we must first take steps to stop unfair competition," Timor said. "Former slaves who homestead outside our city walls and grow crops to feed the citizenry will be exempt from this tariff. In this way, they will be able to market their produce more cheaply than the farmers who bring in produce from the outlying areas. It will ensure a ready market for the homesteaders and add incentive for others to take part in the program. And the profits the homesteaders make will enable them to employ laborers, which will cut down on the ranks of beggars in the city."

"What about the farmers who bring produce to our markets from the outlying areas?" asked Sadira.

"They shall have to settle for a lesser profit," Timor said, "or else market their produce elsewhere."

"They can simply choose to lower their prices enough to compete with locally grown produce," Councilman Dargo said.

"If the tariff is sufficiently high, they shall find themselves unable to compete with the homesteaders," Timor replied. "Besides, why should we concern ourselves with them? They have been growing fat from their profits in our marketplaces, and in the absence of local competition, they have been able to control the prices, which has driven up the cost of food here in the city. The tariff would not only stimulate crop production, it would bring about lower prices for produce, and thereby lower the price of meals at food stalls and at the city's inns and taverns. That is something the people would certainly support."

"The idea has merit," said Sadira thoughtfully. "However, you neglect the fact that there is still not enough fertile land to go around."

"There is more than enough to make the city self-sufficient in terms of farm-grown produce," Timor said. "And it is only fitting that those who had the foresight and industriousness to take advantage of the program first receive the greater rewards. For those who have delayed in taking advantage of the program, there will still be jobs as laborers on the homestead farms, once they start to make a profit. Or else they can take advantage of our second proposal, which will create a new program to address the very issue you just raised.

"Under this new program," Timor continued, "loans would be made from the city's treasury, at a modest rate of interest, to anyone who will homestead in the valley for the purpose of raising herds for marketing in Tyr. These loans could be used to purchase beasts in our own markets that would serve to start the herds, and for those taking advantage of the program, there would be a one-time exemption from the market tax. They could then raise z'tals or kanks or crodlu for our army, bring them in to market here in Tyr, and use their profits to pay off their loans in reasonable installments. As with those who participate in the homestead plan, they would be exempted from the tariff and this would assure a ready market for their beasts."

"But what is to prevent them from marketing their beasts elsewhere?" asked another council member.

"Absolutely nothing," Timor replied, "except that it would be more convenient for them to market them in Tyr. The expense of driving their beasts to market elsewhere would eat into their profits, and they would be forced to compete with herdsmen from the outlying areas in the tablelands, who would be seeking other markets to avoid our tariff. And, as with the farmers, these herdsmen have driven up their prices due to lack of competition. This plan would serve to give a profitable livelihood to many of the former slaves, as well as lower the prices for meat animals and such to a more reasonable level. The herdsmen in the program would be making money, and the people of the city would be saving money. Everyone would be well pleased, and the new government would be lauded for the new prosperity."

"Much as I hate to admit it," Rikus said, "these proposals make a lot of sense, at least on the surface. However, what stops free citizens of Tyr from taking part in the programs and shutting out the former slaves?"

"What if they do?" Timor replied. "Our goal is to diminish the ranks of beggars, whether they be former slaves or not. If these programs reduce the number of beggars on our streets, or cut down on thievery by granting livelihoods to those driven to steal out of desperation, no one would complain. And if some of our citizens leave their jobs to take advantage of these programs, then that would leave openings that could be filled by former slaves. The point behind these proposals is that Tyr must become more self-sufficient if our city is to survive. We must import less and export more. And to that end, I make a third proposal, and that is to grant tax credit to anyone who chooses to start a new industry in Tyr that would employ citizens and provide products for export. We have, for example, greater resources in iron than any other city, yet those resources have never been properly exploited."

"But if we made all these loans out of our treasury and granted all these tax credits, that would cut into the city revenues," said Councilman Kor.

"Only for now," Timor said. "Our revenues would fall in the first year, yet the moment the participants in these programs started to turn a profit, the loans would start to be repaid, and revenues would continue to increase, because we would have more and richer taxpayers. That is the beauty of the import tariff. We create, in effect, a new tax that does not affect our citizenry, and we demonstrate our concern for their welfare by exempting them from it. In part, this new tariff will compensate for whatever short-term revenue losses we may incur through the creation of these programs, but in the meantime, the remainder of our tax structure remains unaffected."

"But what about these tax credits you have proposed?" Sadira said.

Timor shrugged. "They are merely one-time credits, and they add incentive to get the programs started. Once they are underway, we shall be seeing increased revenues as a result. Meanwhile, we announce that instead of increasing taxes to deal with our current problems, we have decided to freeze them at their current rate, so as not to place an added burden on our people, and even use available tax revenues to create new jobs. Once those jobs have been created, they increase our revenues without the odious necessity of having to raise taxes. The council will have held firm, demonstrated its concern for the people, and increased tax revenues in a manner that would be all but unnoticeable."

"It sounds dishonest, somehow," Rikus said, scowling.

"Oh, forgive me. I thought we were discussing ways to save our city from destruction," Timor said dryly. "I was unaware that we had elevated this discussion to the morality of Tyr. I fear I did not come prepared to propose measures to address that concern. Besides, I think you will find that is a rather low priority among our citizenry. The people do not want honesty and starvation. They want the semblance of honesty and food. If you tell them the truth, they will lynch you every time."

"Leave it to a templar to shade the truth," said Rikus sourly.

"Trust a templar to know the truth has many shadings," replied Timor with a smile. "If I may continue, I have one final proposal, and it addresses the issue of Tyr's human and demihuman resources."

"Go on," Sadira said.

Timor nodded. "I am sure you will agree that the greatest asset of a city is its people, and that any governing body would be wise to exploit that asset to its fullest potential. Regrettably, we are denied the full value of that asset because some of our citizens choose to hide their light under a basket, or perhaps, to put it more appropriately, they keep it under-ground."

"You are referring to the Veiled Alliance?" asked Councilman Kor.

"Precisely," Timor said. "Now, in the past, the templars and the Veiled Alliance have been at odds politically, as we had served a defiler sorcerer-king and they are all preservers. Or so they claim, at least. Those political differences no longer exist. Kalak is no more, Tithian is gone, and this council has no quarrel with the preservers. There remain, however, certain compelling reasons for the Veiled Alliance to remain veiled, as it were, and chief among those is the antipathy of the people toward magic-users."

"Can you blame them," Rikus said, "when magic has brought our world to ruin?"

"Perhaps," said Timor with a shrug, "but that is an arguable point. There are those who blame so-called 'defiler magic' for the ruin of Athas, and exempt those who call themselves 'preservers,' when the fact is that both use the same magic. And it is debatable whether it was magic that was responsible for turning our world into a desert, or the science practiced by our forebears. For that matter, certain natural conditions over which no one had any control may well have been responsible. However, that is not the issue. Whether rightly or wrongly, most people have come to believe that magic is immoral because it destroys natural resources, and they condemn all magic-users as a result. One can certainly contend that such an attitude is manifestly unfair to the preservers, who make a virtue of following the Druid Way and see themselves as custodians of nature rather than exploiters of it."

"Do my ears deceive me?" said Sadira, with

astonishment. "You are taking up the cause of the pre-servers?"

"I deal not in causes, but in practical considera-tions," Timor said. "We are concerned with filling our treasury and making Tyr more self-sufficient. This will entail developing our farmland and raising crops successfully, which in turn will entail proper water use, the planting of shrubs and trees to prevent ero-sion of the soil, and so forth. Who better qualified to oversee such projects than the preservers who make up the Veiled Alliance? We are also seeking to improve our industry—and magic, judiciously applied, can be of help to us in that area, as well."

"Let me understand," said Rikus. "The templars are actually proposing that the Veiled Alliance, an organization they have sought to destroy for all these years, be given a role in restructuring Tyr?" He shook his head. "I cannot believe it. I must be hearing things."

"The templars sought to destroy the Veiled Alliance in the past because Kalak ordered it. He saw the orga-nization as a threat to him, and we templars acted as the loyal servants of our king. However, Kalak is dead. Our loyalty now lies with the new government of Tyr."

"Whichever way the wind blows, eh?" said Rikus.

"It is a government that may not love us well," said Timor with an arch glance at the former gladiator, "but it has seen fit to include us, however inconve-nient it might seem, largely because to dispense with us would have proved an even greater inconvenience. Just the same, we are grateful for the role we are allowed to play in the future of the city that has always been our home."

"You expect us to believe you bear no malice

toward the Veiled Alliance?" asked Sadira.

"I bear no malice toward anyone," said Timor. "I am a templar, and I seek only to do my duty. In that capacity, I cannot support the existence of any underground organization—however well-intentioned it may claim to be—that functions independently and violently in disregard of our laws. I have always been convinced that the Veiled Alliance is, at heart, a subversive group of malcontents who shelter criminals under the guise of patriotism and high moral imperatives. They would disagree, of course.

"However, in the interest of reducing lawlessness within our city and making its citizenry more productive, I am willing to give them the benefit of the doubt. Kalak is dead, and the reason for their secretive existence in our city no longer exists. Let them prove their stated intent and come forward to take part in helping this government build our city's future. Let them prove to our people that magic can be used as a force for good, and thus gain their support. In return, I propose we offer amnesty to all those who take advantage of this offer."

"And you think they will come forward?" said Sadira skeptically.

"Those who truly believe in what the Veiled Alliance claims to stand for should have no reason to reject such an offer. Still, I expect some of them to refuse. Those who are and have always been criminally inclined shall not come forward, and in refusing to do so, they shall expose themselves for what they truly are. But at least those among them who are well intentioned will have an opportunity to come out of hiding and take part in our society."

"I move that we adopt Timor's proposals," said Councilman Kor.

"I second the motion," said Councilman Hagon, at once.

"Not so fast," said Rikus.

"The motion has already been seconded," said Councilman Kor. "The templars were accused of not contributing any constructive proposals. Well, it seems that they have called our bluff and produced some excellent ones. Procedure now dictates that we put these proposals to a vote."

"That is the accepted procedure," Sadira was forced to admit. "All those in favor?"

There was a show of hands. Only Rikus did not raise his.

"The motion is carried," said Sadira, who had abstained. As director of the council, she would have only voted in the event of a tie. "The council secretary is directed to formulate the proposals as new edicts, which will be presented to this body for approval of the wording prior to being instituted. And now, if there is—"

The council chamberlain rapped his staff on the floor by the entrance to the room. "With the indulgence of the council," he said, "a captain of the city guard has arrived with a visitor who claims to have business with the council."

Sadira frowned. "I am aware of no one who has petitioned to speak before this body today. Who is this visitor?"

"He has given his name as Sorak," said the chamberlain.

"I know no one by that name," Sadira said. She glanced at the other members of the council. "Do any of you know this Sorak?"

The other members all shook their heads and glanced around at one another.

"What is the nature of his business?" asked Sadira.

"He did not say," the chamberlain replied, "only that it was most urgent and that it concerned a matter of utmost importance to the security of the government of Tyr."

"No doubt merely another malcontent seeking to air his grievances," said Councilman Hagon. "Must we waste our time with this?"

"This body exists to serve the people, not deny them a voice in our government," Sadira said.

"Then let him petition to be heard during the proper time, when we conduct the regular forum," said another council member.

"If, indeed, he has news that may affect the security of Tyr, then we should hear him," Rikus said. "I say let him speak."

"Have this visitor brought in, Chamberlain," Sadira said.

"There is . . . something else," the chamberlain replied uneasily.

"Well?" Sadira said. "What is it?"

"He has a tigone with him, and insists that it accompany him."

"A tigone!" Rikus said, rising to his feet.

"The creature appears tame," the chamberlain said. "However, it is, nevertheless, a full-grown tigone."

"A *tame* tigone?" said Sadira. "This is something I would like to see."

"Surely you are not going to allow this!" said Councilman Hagon.

"Have the visitor brought in," Sadira said.

SEVEN

Despite the reassuring presence of the heavily armed soldiers, Sadira, Rikus, and Timor were the only ones who did not react with alarm when Sorak entered the small council chamber with Tigra at his side. Sadira had her magic to protect her; Rikus had faced tigones in the arena, and while he remained tensely alert, he saw that the beast's behavior was not aggressive. As for Timor, the senior templar did not scare easily.

He was a crafty survivor who had faced the hatred of the people under Kalak and the wrath of the mercurial late tyrant and had floated in that maelstrom without once losing his composure. He had weathered the storm of revolution and managed to secure a continuing strong role for the templars in the new government, while at the same time presiding over a subtle campaign designed to bring about change in attitude toward the templars among the people of Tyr. Where once the templars were reviled as oppressors in the service of the tyrant, now they were at least tolerated, and Timor's clever word-of-mouth campaign about templars as victims of Kalak, more so than any other citizens, was starting to take hold.

The templars, it was now said, were born into a

legacy of service to the sorcerer-king and had never been given any choice in directing their own fate. They had no magic of their own—that much, at least, was true—and what powers they had wielded came to them through Kalak. As such, they were ensorcelled, trapped in a life of bondage to the tyrant as effectively as were the slaves who toiled in the brickyards. And, like the slaves, the death of Kalak finally freed them.

Unlike the slaves, however, the templars labored under the burden of the guilt they shared, and so they sought to redeem themselves in service to the new government. The fact that they pursued this redemption while living in their own, luxurious, secluded compound, walled away from the common citizens of Tyr, was something that was never mentioned. Also never mentioned, and unknown by anyone except a handful of Timor's closest and most trusted associates, was the fact that the senior templar was a secret defiler who schemed to topple the revolutionary government and seize power for the templars, with himself as the new king.

As such, the lean, dark templar with the thoughtful gaze and the sepulchral voice listened with intense interest to what Sorak had to say. If what this elfling herdsman claimed was true—that some aristocrat in Nibenay had dispatched spies to Tyr—then clearly the Shadow King of Nibenay had his eye on the city and was anxious to assess its vulnerability. This, thought Timor, could interfere with his own plans.

"Why have you come to us with this information?" asked Sadira when Sorak had finished.

"Because I am but a simple herdsman," Sorak replied, "and I thought the council of Tyr would find this information of some value."

"In other words, you hoped we would reward you for it," Councilman Kor said wryly. "How do we know you are telling us the truth?"

"I have given you names and descriptions," said Sorak, "and I have given you as many details of their plan as I know. I have also told you of the attack the marauders plan on the caravan. You may look into these matters for yourselves. As far as any reward is concerned, I would be content to wait until you have satisfied yourselves that the information I have brought you is correct."

Timor pursed his lips thoughtfully. "It could take time to investigate these allegations," he said.

"I am content to remain in the city in the meantime," Sorak replied.

"And what about your herds?" asked Timor, watching Sorak carefully. "Who will tend them in your absence?"

"I have not left any herds untended," Sorak said, which was absolutely true, as he had no herds to tend. "Remaining in the city will eat into the profits of my sale, but I am willing to sustain a minor short-term loss in anticipation of a long-term gain."

"Where shall we find you if we need to speak with you again?" Sadira asked.

"I am told that cheap accommodations can be found in the warrens, near the elven market," Sorak said. "Perhaps if Captain Zalcor would be kind enough to escort me, I could arrange for a small, inexpensive room, and then he would know where I am to be found."

Sadira nodded. "Captain Zalcor, you will accompany this herdsman to the warrens near the elven market and see that he finds a room." She turned to Sorak. "And so long as you are in the city, herdsman, the council would be gratified if you were to remain where you could be reached. We shall look into this report that you have brought us, and if it is accurate, then you shall be rewarded."

Sorak inclined his head in a respectful bow and turned to leave, accompanied by Zalcor and his soldiers.

"If that elfling is a 'simple herdsman,' as he claims, then Timor's a kank," said Rikus after they had left. "Did you see that sword he wears?"

"Yes, I noted it," Sadira said, nodding. "And I sensed magic in the blade. Without a doubt, he is not what he appears to be, but if there is even a remote chance that what he says is true, we must investigate."

"I agree," said Timor. "We already know that King Hamanu wants this city as his prize. If the Shadow King of Nibenay lusts after it as well, we cannot afford to give an impression of weakness. If spies have been sent to Tyr, they must be apprehended and dealt with severely, in a manner that will serve as an example. And if marauders plan to attack one of the merchant caravans leaving our city, we must send soldiers to reinforce the merchant guard and see that the attack is crushed. We must show that Tyr is safe for trading, and that we know how to protect our interests and look after our security."

"Indeed," agreed Councilman Kor. "We are not so strong that we can afford to overlook potential threats."

"I still say this elfling bears watching," Rikus said. "We know nothing about him, and I, for one, don't believe he's a simple herdsman."

"I agree," said Timor. "For all we know, he may be a clever spy, himself. It would be prudent for us to keep an eye on him. The templars can see to that task easily enough, and we stand ready to assist this council in the investigation of the elfling's claims."

"I move that the templars undertake this investigation with the assistance of the city guard," said Kor.

"I second the motion," said Councilman Dargo.

"All in favor?" said Sadira.

The vote was unanimous.

"Motion carried," said Sadira. She rapped her gavel on the table. "This council meeting is adjourned."

As the members of the council filed out of the chamber, Sadira remained seated, hands steepled before her, eyes staring down with a thoughtful expression. Rikus lingered also, watching as Timor left the chamber. The senior templar was speaking earnestly and in low tones with Kor and Dargo as they walked from the room.

"I don't trust those three," muttered Rikus. "Especially that foul templar. They've got something cooking."

"Their own brand of revolution," said Sadira.

"What?"

"Timor conspires to discredit and depose us, then seize power for the templars," Sadira said.

"You *know* this? You have proof?"

"No, but even if I did, I could not act upon it. It would be the sort of thing that would play right into Timor's hands. The templars could then point to us and say we are no better than the previous regime since we allow no opposition."

"So what are we supposed to do, sit idle while the templars plot against us?"

"No, we must not be idle," said Sadira, "but we must act in subtle ways, using methods as covert and devious as theirs." She sighed heavily. "Casting down a tyrant king and leading a revolution is much easier than running the government that replaces him. Believe me, not a day goes by that I don't wish I could pass the responsibility to someone else."

"But not to Timor!" Rikus said.

Sadira smiled. "No, not to Timor and his templars. Otherwise, it would all have been for nothing." She patted the massive former gladiator on the shoulder. "In battle, there are none to match you, Rikus, but you must now learn to fight in a different sort of arena. And in this new mode of battle, your strength will give you no advantage. We must learn to fight using Timor's weapons, only we must use them better."

"What do you propose?" asked Rikus.

"We must keep an eye on Timor, and take steps to counter his devious machinations. And I think we would do well to keep an eye on this elfling, also."

"My instincts tell me he is not what he seems."

"Your instincts have always been good," Sadira said. "He is obviously no herdsman. He has the build of a fighter, and the carriage of a ranger. There is also something in his gaze . . . something quite unsettling. I could detect magic on his blade, which is unlike any weapon I have ever seen, and he has a tigone for a pet, a beast no one has ever tamed before. No, he is no simple herdsman. The question is, what *is* he?"

"That is something I intend to find out personally," Rikus said with determination.

"No, Rikus. With Timor plotting against us, I need you here," she said. "He is too clever for me to deal with alone. Those proposals of his made a great deal of sense on the surface, and I could not think quickly enough to find any fault with them. Now they have passed, and if, indeed, they do turn things around in

Tyr, Timor shall not hesitate to make the most of it. He is a practiced intriguer, and I lack experience in such things. Here is where I need your help."

"Then what should be done about this Sorak?"

"That is a task you shall have to delegate to someone else," she replied. "Someone who can be trusted. Someone clever enough to shadow this Sorak without revealing himself. Someone who knows how to walk softly, think swiftly, and make decisions on his own. Someone crafty enough to counter whatever Timor may attempt as regards this elfling stranger."

Rikus smiled. "You have just painted a perfect portrait of a very old friend of mine."

"Is this old friend someone you can rely on?" asked Sadira.

"Without any reservations," Rikus said.

"That is enough for me. Will your friend undertake this task for us? It may prove highly dangerous."

"That would merely add spice to it," said Rikus, with a grin.

"How soon can you enlist this person's aid?"

"I'll go at once."

"Do not stay away too long, Rikus," she replied. "I am surrounded by smiling faces here, but few of them belong to friends."

* * * * *

Sorak had never seen anything even remotely like the warrens before. Long accustomed to the peaceful solitude and open spaces of the Ringing Mountains, he had found the market district's noise and crowded conditions shocking enough. He was not prepared for what awaited him in the warrens.

The streets grew narrower and narrower until they

were little more than zigzag dirt paths. These paths
led through a maze of two-, three-, and four-story
buildings constructed from sun-baked brick covered
with a reddish plaster that varied in hue. The colors
were a patchwork of earth-tones, muted reds and
browns, and many of the walls were cracked where
the outer coating had flaked off with time, exposing
the bricks underneath.

The buildings were square or rectangular, with
slightly rounded corners. The front of almost every
building had a covered walkway, with arched sup-
ports made out of plaster-covered brick and a roof of
masonry or wood. Often, the roof would extend along
the entire length of the building front, providing
some shelter from the blistering sun. Some of these
walkways were paved with brick, some had wood-
plank floors, but most had no floors at all. In the
shade of many covered walkways, filthy beggars
crouched, holding out their hands in supplication. In
others, scantily dressed women struck provocative
poses.

All of Sorak's senses were assailed as never before.
The smell was overpowering. The people here simply
threw their waste and refuse into the narrow alleys
between buildings, where it was left to rot and decay
in the intense heat, creating an eye-watering miasma
of oppressive odors. Flies and rodents were everywhere.

As he was escorted through the narrow streets by
Captain Zalcor and a contingent of the city guard,
people rushed to get out of their way. There were
many unusual sights in Tyr, but this was the first time
anyone had ever seen a tigone in the city streets. Even
for the warrens, a squad of city guards escorting an
elfling with a psionic mountain cat by his side made

an unusual procession.

"Well, you said you wanted to find the cheapest accommodations," Captain Zalcor said to Sorak as they halted outside one of the buildings. "This is it. You won't find cheaper rooms anywhere in the city, and when you see them, you'll know why."

Sorak gazed at the three-story inn. Its plaster coating had flaked off in many places so that much old brick and mortar was exposed, and the walls were veined with cracks. The smell here was no less offensive than anywhere else in the warrens, but that wasn't saying much. Scrofulous beggars crouched in the dirt beneath the covered walkway, which ran the length of the building. A number of women with heavily painted faces and lightly clothed bodies lounged by the entrance, gazing with interest at the group.

"I suppose this will do," said Sorak.

"Are you sure?" the captain asked. "The council bid me to escort you to an inn. They did not say it had to be the worst one in the city."

"But it is the cheapest?" Sorak asked.

"It is that," said Captain Zalcor. "Look, I can understand your desire for frugality, but there is such a thing as taking practical virtues a bit too far. I thought that when you saw this place, you would change your mind, but as you seem intent on holding your purse close, regardless of the inconvenience, I should caution you that you may well lose it altogether here. This is a dangerous neighborhood. The elven market is just down the street there, and even I would hesitate to venture there without a squad of guards to back me up."

"I appreciate your concern, Captain," Sorak said. "However, my means are limited, and I do not yet know how long I shall be remaining in the city. I need to hold on to what money I have for as long as possible."

"Then I would suggest you keep one hand firmly on your purse, and the other on your sword hilt," Zalcor said. "And stay away from that place."

Sorak looked in the direction the captain had indicated and saw a large, three-story building where the street ended in a cul-de-sac. This structure had been better maintained than those around it, and had a reasonably fresh coat of brown plaster over its bricks. Unlike most of the other buildings in the area, it had no covered walkway in front of it, but a wall that extended out into the street, creating a paved courtyard that held some desert plants and a small fountain. An arch over a bone gate in the wall provided access to the courtyard, and a paved path led to the building's entrance. Sorak noticed a steady stream of people wandering in and out. Above the gate, mounted on the archway, was a large iron spider, plated silver.

"What is that place?" asked Sorak.

"The Crystal Spider," Zalcor said. "And, trust me, my friend, you do not want to go in there."

Sorak smiled. "You did not seem so concerned about my welfare when we first met."

"In truth, I was more concerned about your pet eating our citizens," replied Zalcor, with a grin. Then his face grew serious. "But if I feel better disposed toward you now, it's because I heard what you said back there in the council chamber."

"You believe me? The members of the council seem to have some reservations," Sorak said.

Zalcor gave a small snort of derision. "They're politicians. Except for Rikus, who was a gladiator, but then again he's a mul, and muls have never been the most trusting sorts. When you've been a soldier for as long as I have, and a commander in the city guard dealing with criminals of all stripes each and every day, you develop an instinct for whether or not someone speaks the truth. You didn't need to come forward with your information. You have no vested interest in the security of Tyr."

"But I do have a vested interest in the reward," said Sorak.

"I do not begrudge you that," said Zalcor. "I was born and raised in Altaruk, and I know something of the marauders of Nibenay. I have a feeling you know how to use that fancy sword of yours. The marauders are formidable fighters, yet you not only survived an encounter with them, but managed to extract information from one of them, as well."

"Some of the council members seem to find that suspect," Sorak said. And then he hastily added, "I could see it in their eyes."

"And what I see in your eyes tells me that you spoke the truth," said Zalcor, "although not the entire truth, I think." He gave Sorak a level stare. "You are no herdsman, my friend. You lack the gait for it, and your skin has not the look of one who spends his time on the windblown plains out in the tablelands."

"All good reasons not to trust me, I should think," said Sorak.

"Perhaps," said Zalcor, "but I am a good judge of character, and my instinct tells me you are not an enemy. I do not know what your game is, but I suspect it has little to do with Tyr itself. And if such is, indeed, the case, then it is none of my concern."

Sorak smiled. "I can see why you have been made an officer," he said. "But tell me, why should I avoid the Crystal Spider? What sort of place is it?"

"A gaming house," said Zalcor. "The most notorious in all of Tyr."

Sorak frowned. "What is a gaming house?"

Zalcor rolled his eyes. "If you do not know, then believe me, it is the last place on Athas you should be. It is a house of recreation, or at least that is what they call it, where games of chance are played for money, and other diversions are offered to those with the means to pay for them."

"Games of chance?"

"Where have you *lived* all this time?" asked Zalcor, with amazement.

"In the Ringing Mountains," Sorak said, seeing no reason why he should tell him.

"The Ringing Mountains? But, there are no villages up there, not even a small settlement, except for . . . " His voice trailed off. He shook his head. "No, that would be impossible. You are male."

"You were telling me about games of chance," said Sorak.

"Forget about it," Zalcor told him. "You might win a few small wagers, but the odds will turn on you, for they always favor the house. Nor are the games always honest ones. If you were a gambler, I would merely caution you, but as you know nothing of such things, then I urge you most strongly to stay out of that damned place. You would lose everything you have, and like as not be knocked on the head or drugged and lose your sword, as well. A blade such as yours would fetch a high price in the elven market. You would stand about as much chance of surviving in there as I would in a den of tigones."

"I see," said Sorak.

Zalcor sighed resignedly. "You are going anyway."

He shook his head. "I can see that. Well, do not say I did not warn you. Remember, that is the elven market district, and the guard does not trouble to patrol there often. We barely have enough men to keep the crime down in the warrens. If you go there, you are on your own."

"I thank you for your advice, Captain," Sorak said. "I shall consider it."

"But you probably won't take it." Zalcor shrugged. "Suit yourself. I just hope you live long enough to collect whatever reward the council decides to give you, for it is probably all you will take home with you from Tyr."

He rejoined his men, and they turned to march back to the central market district. Sorak stared up at the dilapidated inn for a long moment, then gazed down the street, looking toward the gaming house.

"*Why ask for trouble?*" Eyron said. "*You heard what the captain said. We stand to lose everything we have.*"

"On the other hand," said Sorak, "*we might also win.*"

"*Zalcor said the games are not always honest,*" Eyron added.

"*True, he did say that,*" Sorak replied. "*However, we have certain advantages in that regard, do we not, Guardian?*"

"*I could detect dishonesty,*" she said, "*and we will not find the Veiled Alliance by sitting in a room, alone.*"

"*My thoughts, precisely,*" Sorak said. "*And if the city guard does not patrol the elven market district, then what better place to find them?*"

"*I want to go!*" Kivara said. "*It sounds like fun!*"

"*It sounds dangerous, to me,*" said Eyron.

The others kept their peace, leaving Sorak to decide. He thought about it only for a moment, then started walking toward the Crystal Spider.

Approaching the gates, Sorak ignored the beggars, who whined pitifully and held out their hands toward him, and he ignored the women who posed and beckoned to him. Instead, he walked purposefully toward the gaming house, wondering what he would find inside.

The half-elf gatekeeper's eyes grew wide when he saw Tigra. "Stop!" he said, quickly retreating behind the safety of the gate. "You cannot bring that wildcat in here!"

"He will harm no one," Sorak said.

"Am I to take your word?" the gatekeeper replied. "Forget it. The beast stays outside."

"Tigra goes everywhere with me," said Sorak.

"Well, it isn't coming in here!"

"I have money." Sorak jingled his purse.

"You could have the entire city treasury for all I care. You are still not coming in with that creature!"

"What seems to be the trouble, Ankor?" asked a sultry, female voice from the shadows behind the gatekeeper. Sorak saw a cloaked and hooded figure approaching from the inner courtyard.

"No trouble, my lady, merely a herdsman trying to get in with his beast," the half-elf gatekeeper replied.

"Beast? What sort of beast?" The cloaked figure approached the gate and looked through. "Great dragon! Is that a *tigone*?"

"He is my friend," said Sorak, perceiving by the gatekeeper's attitude that this woman was in some position of authority here. "I have raised him from a cub, and he obeys me implicitly. He would not harm anyone, I assure you, unless someone attempts to harm me."

She pulled back her hood and stepped up to the gate to get a better look at Sorak. He, in turn, got a better look at her, and saw that she was a striking, half-elf female, as tall as he was, with long, lustrous, black hair framing her face and cascading down her shoulders, emerald-green eyes, and delicate, sharply pronounced features. Her eyes widened slightly when she saw him, and she gave a tentative sniff, after which her eyes grew wider still.

"Halfling *and* elf?" she said, with astonishment.

"Yes, I am an elfling," said Sorak.

"But . . . elves and halflings are enemies! I have never heard of elves and halflings mating. I did not even know they could!"

"It would seem that I am proof they can," Sorak replied wryly.

"How fascinating! You must tell me more," she said. "Ankor, let him in."

"But . . . my lady . . . " the gatekeeper protested.

"Let him in, I said." Her voice was like a whip crack, and the gatekeeper obeyed at once, keeping the iron gate between himself and Tigra as he swung it open.

"You are certain you can control the tigone?" she asked.

"Quite certain."

"You had best be," she replied, looking at Tigra warily. "Otherwise, I shall have the creature killed and hold you responsible for any damage it may cause to my establishment."

"You are the owner, then?"

"Yes. I am called Krysta."

Sorak smiled. "The crystal spider?"

She smiled back and took his arm as they walked down the paved pathway leading through the court-yard to the entrance of the gaming house. "What are you called, elfling?"

"Sorak."

She raised her delicately arched eyebrows. "And do you?"

"Always walk alone? Not entirely. I have Tigra."

"Tigra," she said, and the beast looked up at her. "It knows its name," she said.

"Tigones are psionic cats," said Sorak. "They are intelligent and quite perceptive. Tigra can read my thoughts."

"How interesting. A shame he cannot speak, for I would ask him what you are thinking now."

"I am thinking that I was cautioned against coming here," said Sorak.

"Indeed? By whom?"

"By a captain in the city guard."

"Would his name, by any chance, be Zalcor?" Krysta asked.

"Yes, you know him?"

She laughed. "I have been arrested by him on numerous occasions in the past. I have known Zalcor since he was a mere guardsman, but he does not condescend to visit me these days."

"Why not?"

"As a captain in the city guard, he must keep up appearances. It would not do to have him paying regular visits to my gaming house, even if those visits were entirely innocent and in the line of duty. People might suspect that I was bribing him. The city guard is also rather overextended these days. It is all they can do to keep the mobs under control in the market district and the warrens. No one of great importance resides in the elven market, so they tend to look the other way in this part of the city. Part of the reason I have my establishment here."

They reached the front entrance, and a footman

opened the thick and heavy wooden doors for them. They came into an elevated entrance alcove, with stone steps leading down to the main floor of the gaming house. The entire first floor of the building was one cavernous room in which people of all descriptions mingled, moving among the gaming tables. There was a long bar at the back, extending the length of the entire room. Behind and in front of the bar were a number of elevated stages, where dancers without a single stitch of clothing gyrated provocatively while musicians played. The pungent odor of exotic smoke hung thickly in the air, and there were excited shouts and woeful cries coming from the tables, where coins were won and lost as quickly as the dice were thrown.

"So, what do you think of my establishment?" asked Krysta, giving Sorak's arm a gentle squeeze.

Sorak felt apprehension among the others of the tribe, all save Kivara, who was thrilled by the palpable energy that permeated the room. "*What sort of games do they play here?*" she asked excitedly. "*I want to try them! I want to try them all!*"

"*Patience,*" Sorak counseled her silently. Then, aloud, he said, "I have never seen anything like it."

"There is a great deal more here than what you see," said Krysta in a tone that promised tantalizing revelations. "Let me show you around."

She removed her cloak and handed it to a footman. Beneath it, she wore barely enough for modesty. She had on a pair of low, black boots made from the shiny hide of a z'tal. Her long legs were bare all the way up to the short, black, wraparound skirt she wore, made from the same skin as the boots and cut slanted, so that it came down to mid-thigh on one side and left the other leg completely bare almost to her waist. A

matching black halter top barely covered her breasts,
leaving her entire back bare. Around her waist, she
wore a belt of gold coins interconnected with fine
links of silver chain, and several necklaces and
amulets adorned her throat, as well as gold circlets
around her wrists and arms. As she handed her cloak
to the footman, she watched Sorak for a reaction. A
flicker of puzzlement and then annoyance passed
over her features briefly when he did not react as
most males did. The footman lingered a moment, but
when he saw that Sorak did not intend to remove his
cloak, he backed away.

Clearly, Krysta enjoyed making an entrance, and
this time she could make it on the arm of an exotic-
looking stranger with a full-grown tigone at his side.
As they descended the stone steps, many of the
patrons turned to point and stare at them, but others
were so intent on their games they didn't even notice.
As they made their way between the tables, patrons
hastily moved back, and not a few of them cried out
and dropped their drinks at the sight of Tigra. Krysta
was enjoying every minute of it as she escorted Sorak
toward the bar.

"May I offer you a drink?" she asked, snapping her
fingers. An elvish female behind the bar instantly
moved toward them.

"Thank you," Sorak said.

"Bring us two goblets of our best spiced mead,
Alora."

"Yes, my lady."

A moment later, she set two tall ceramic goblets on
the bar before them. Krysta took one for herself and
handed the other to Sorak. "To new experiences," she
said with a smile, and raised her goblet, touching it
lightly to his. As she drank, Sorak brought the goblet

up to his lips, sniffed tentatively, and took a taste. He made a face and set the goblet back down on the bar.

Krysta looked surprised. "It does not meet with your approval?"

"I would prefer water."

"Water," Krysta repeated, as if she wasn't sure she heard correctly. She sighed. "My friend would prefer water, Alora."

"Yes, my lady." She took the goblet back, and came back with one filled with cool well water. Sorak sipped it, then took a deep gulp, emptying half of it.

"Is that more to your liking?" Krysta asked mockingly.

"It is not as fresh as mountain spring water, but better than that sticky syrup," Sorak said.

"Spiced mead of the rarest and most expensive vintage, and you call it sticky syrup." Krysta shook her head. "You are different, I will say that for you."

"Forgive me," Sorak said, "I did not wish to offend."

"Oh, you did not offend me," Krysta said. "It is simply that I have never met anyone else quite like you."

"I do not know if there is anyone else quite like me," Sorak replied.

"You may be right," said Krysta. "I have never even heard of such a thing as an elfling before. Tell me of your parents."

"I do not remember them. As a child, I was cast out into the desert and left to die. I have no memory of anything before that."

"And yet you survived," said Krysta. "How?"

"I somehow managed to make my way to the foothills of the Ringing Mountains," Sorak said. "Tigra found me. He was merely a cub then. He had been

separated from his pride, so we were both abandoned, in a sense. Perhaps that is why he formed a
bond with me. We were both lost and alone."

"And he protected you," said Krysta. "But there is
still only so much a tigone cub could do. How did
you manage to survive?"

"I was found by a pyreen, who cared for me and
nursed me back to health," Sorak said.

"A pyreen!" said Krysta. "I have never known anyone who has actually met one of the peace-bringers,
much less been raised by one!"

"Take care, Sorak," said the Guardian. *"This female
asks much, yet offers little in return."*

"You have still told me nothing of yourself," said
Sorak, noting the warning.

"Oh, I am sure my story is nowhere near as interesting as yours," she replied.

"Nevertheless, I would like to hear it," Sorak said.
"How did a young and beautiful half-elf come to be
the proprietor of such a place?"

Krysta smiled. "Would you like me to show you?"

"Show me?"

"After all," she said, "you did not come to a gaming house just to talk, did you?"

She took him by the arm and led him toward one of
the tables. Sorak saw how the people at the table
instantly made room for her. He also saw a number of
large, armed guards spread out around the room,
watching the tables carefully. And the ones nearest
them never took their eyes from Krysta.

The table they approached had a sunken surface,
with sides of polished wood. The flat surface of the
table was covered with smooth, black z'tal skin. At
the table stood a game lord with a wooden stick that
had a curved scoop at the end. As the gamers tossed

dice onto the table, he announced the scores and then retrieved the dice by scooping them back with the wooden stick. Sorak saw that the dice were all different. One was triangular, made in the shape of a pyramid with a flat bottom. Three numbers were painted on each of the four triangular sides, in such a manner that only one would be right-side up when the die fell. Another die was cube-shaped, with one number painted on each side, while two others were shaped like diamonds, one with eight sides and the other with ten. Two more dice were carved into shapes that were almost round, except that they were faceted with flat sides. One of these had twelve sides and the other had twenty.

"I have never played this game before," he said to Krysta.

"Truly?" she replied with surprise.

"This is my first time in a gaming house," he said.

"Well, then we shall have to educate you," said Krysta with a smile. "This game is really very simple. It is called Hawke's Gambit, after the bard who invented it. You will note that each of the dice is different. The number of sides they have determines the wager. Each round of play consists of six passes. On the first, only the triangular die is used. It has four sides, therefore, the wager is four ceramic pieces, which go into the pot. On the second pass, both the triangular and the square dice are thrown. The square die has six sides, so added to the four sides of the first die, the wager on this pass is ten ceramics, or one silver piece. On the third pass, the eight-sided die is added, so that now three are thrown, and the wager is increased to eighteen ceramic pieces, or one silver and eight ceramics. On the fourth pass, the ten-sided die is added, and now four dice are thrown. The wager on this pass is twenty-eight ceramics, or two silver pieces and eight ceramics. The fifth pass adds the twelve-sided die, so that now five dice are thrown, and the wager increases by twelve to a total of forty ceramics, or four silver pieces. And on the final pass, the twenty-sided die is added, so that you throw all six dice together and the wager goes up to six silver pieces. Each time a pass is made, the score is totaled, and the winner takes the pot. If the losers wish a chance to make good their loss, they must risk the amount of the next wager, or else drop out of the round and wait for the next one to begin."

"What happens if several people get the same score?" asked Sorak.

"Then the pot is divided equally by the number of winners who tie for the highest score," Krysta replied. "The sixth and final pass opens up Hawke's Gambit, where the players can wager not only on the outcome of the sixth pass, but on the final tally of the entire round. The house only takes a small percentage of the winning pot at the end of every round. And that is all there is to it. Simple."

"*Simple enough to lose your shirt,*" said Eyron. "*Four ceramics to begin the game, ten for the second pass, eighteen for the third, twenty-eight for the fourth, forty for the fifth, and sixty for the final pass. That's one hundred and sixty ceramics for each round, or sixteen silver pieces. That amounts to almost two gold pieces per round. Small wonder this female can afford to make a belt of them. She strips the breeches off her customers.*"

"Perhaps," said Sorak, answering Eyron in his mind, "*but not all her customers have the ability to control how the dice may fall. This is not all that different from the psionic exercises we had in the villichi convent.*" Aloud, he said to Krysta, "And one may withdraw from a round at any time?"

"Once the wager has been made, a player is committed to the pass," she said, "but a player is free to withdraw from the round prior to the wagering for any subsequent pass."

"*It would seem that a wise player would risk wagering only on the first pass, and unless he wins, withdraw until the beginning of the next round,*" the Guardian said. "*To continue wagering after a loss would only increase the risk.*"

"*Either way, the house stands to lose nothing, and wins on every round by taking a percentage,*" Eyron said. "*Running a gaming house appears to be a very lucrative profession.*"

The game lord announced that a new round was about to begin.

"Would you care to try your luck?" asked Krysta.

"Why not?" said Sorak, and he stepped up to the table.

There were four players, including himself, who elected to game on this round. Krysta stood by his side, watching and holding on to his arm. The game lord cast an uneasy glance at Tigra, lying on the floor at Sorak's feet, but Krysta gave him a nod, and he moistened his lips nervously, then commenced the game.

"Four ceramics to open on the first pass," he announced. "Four ceramics. Ante up into the pot."

Each of the players tossed down four ceramic pieces. The game lord used his scoop to rake them up and then dropped them into the small black cauldron set in front of him.

"First pass, Player One," he said, pushing the pyramid-shaped die toward a tall, thin, intense-looking human male across from Sorak. He had the look of a

merchant, for he was very finely dressed and wore
heavy gold and silver rings on several fingers of both
hands. He picked up the die and blew on it lightly as
he shook it in a loosely clasped fist, then rolled. It
came up a three.

"Player One rolls three," the game lord said, scooping up the die. "First pass, Player Two."

Player Two, a young human female with a hungry
look about her, rolled the die between both palms
while she whispered, "Come on, come on," under her
breath, then cast with a flourish.

"Player Two rolls one," the game lord said, as the
woman winced and made a grimace. "First pass,
Player Three."

Player Three, a heavyset and balding man who per-
spired freely, picked up the die and stared at it
intently, as if willing it to do his bidding. He took a
deep breath and then rolled.

"Player Three rolls two," the game lord announced.
The balding man swore softly. "First pass, Player
Four."

Krysta picked up the die and handed it to Sorak.
"Good luck," she said.

"Best not to make it look too easy," Sorak said, as he
slipped back and allowed the Guardian to come to the
fore. Casually, she rolled the die.

"Player Four rolls three, for a tie," the game lord
said. "First pass winnings, sixteen ceramics, split two
ways, eight to Players One and Four. Second pass, ten
ceramics to open, ante up, please."

"You see? You have doubled your money," Krysta
said with a knowing smile. "Your luck is good tonight.
Why not stay in?"

"Why not?" said Sorak. He put down ten ceramics.
The other three players all stayed in, as well.

On the second pass, Player One rolled a four. Player Two beat him with a six, then Player Three topped them both with a ten. The dice came to Sorak.

"Second pass, Player Four," the game lord said. "You need a ten to tie."

"Roll nine," said Sorak.

"Nine?" said Kivara. *"But we can do no better than a tie on this pass, and nine will lose!"*

"Roll nine," Sorak said again. *"It will keep the score up for the final tally, but still give us a loss to allay any suspicion."*

"Very clever," Eyron said. *"But we shall have to watch the tally closely."*

"I intend to," Sorak said.

The Guardian rolled nine.

"Player Four rolls nine," the game lord announced. "Not enough to tie, the win goes to Player Three, forty ceramics. Third pass, eighteen to open, ante up, please."

"What a shame," said Krysta. "But you were only one point away from a tie, which would have brought you winnings. Try again."

On the third pass, the thin, dark merchant rolled an eleven. The anxious young woman rolled an eight, for her third loss. She bit her lower lip and clenched her fists. The heavyset man also rolled an eight, which gave him two losses and one win. The three dice were passed to Sorak.

"Roll ten," said Sorak.

"No!" Kivara protested. *"We need a win!"*

"Not yet," said Sorak. *"Trust me."*

The Guardian rolled ten.

"Player Four rolls ten," the game lord called out. "Not enough, the win goes to Player One, seventy-two ceramics. Fourth pass, twenty-eight ceramics to open, ante up, please."

"My luck does not seem to be holding," Sorak said.

"But you were still only one point away," said Krysta. "You are not doing badly. But you may quit now, if you wish."

"Not when I am down twenty-four ceramics," Sorak said tensely.

On the fourth pass, Player One rolled sixteen. Player Two rolled ten, for her fourth loss in a row, and she was beginning to look frantic. Player Three rolled a nineteen and looked well pleased with himself.

"We could use a win this time, to give us encouragement to continue in the game," said Sorak. *"Roll twenty."*

The four dice fell and the game lord added the score. "Player Four rolls twenty for a win of one hundred and twelve ceramics. Fifth pass, forty ceramics to open, ante up, please."

"You see?" said Krysta with a smile. "You were down twenty-four, but now you are ahead sixty. And you began with but four ceramics. I told you your luck was good tonight."

"Perhaps it shall get better," Sorak said with a grin as he counted out the coins for the fifth pass.

This time, the thin merchant rolled a seventeen, and snorted with disgust. The anxious young woman rolled the dice between her cupped hands, her eyes closed, her lips moving soundlessly. She rolled a twenty. She took a deep breath and looked uneasily at Player Three, and when he rolled a twenty-four, her face fell. So far, she had lost more heavily than anybody else. The dice were passed to Sorak.

"We are ahead," said Eyron. *"By my calculations, we are leading by three points in the total tally."*

"Which means it would be prudent for us to fall behind a bit on the next pass," Sorak said.

"How far behind?" the Guardian asked.

"Not too far," Sorak said, *"but enough to make for a convincing loss this time. Roll . . . nineteen. That way, at least half the players beat us on this pass."*

The Guardian rolled the dice.

"Player Four rolls nineteen," the game lord said. "The win goes to Player Three for one hundred and sixty ceramics. Sixth and final pass, sixty ceramics to stay in. Ante up, please."

"If you drop out now, you will still be ahead by twenty ceramics," Krysta said. "If you stay in and lose, you will be down by forty, but you stand to win over two hundred."

"The risk would seem well worth it," Sorak said.

All four players stayed in. Sorak had expected the young woman to drop out. There was no way she could win now unless she rolled an almost perfect score, but desperation was written clearly on her face. Her hands trembled as she counted out the coins. When all four players had wagered, the game lord called out, "Hawke's Gambit. Place your bets, please."

"I will wager twenty ceramics," Player One said.

The young woman swallowed hard and bit her lower lip. "I shall wager . . . one hundred and sixty ceramics." It was the precise amount she had bet so far, and by the look on her face, it was clear that she was thinking emotionally and not logically. The odds were very much against her.

"Player One, it will cost you one hundred and forty ceramics to stay in the gambit," said the game lord.

The merchant nodded. "I will match the wager," he said.

Player Three was ahead at this point in terms of the final tally, but only by two points. He thought about it for a moment, then said, "I decline."

"Player Three declines the gambit, and participates only in the final pass," said the game lord. He turned to Sorak. "It is up to you, sir."

"It will cost you one hundred and sixty ceramics to match the wager and participate in the gambit," Krysta said. "Or else you may elect to decline and take part only in the final pass."

Sorak glanced at the young woman, who looked as if she had wagered as much as she could possibly afford. If she lost this final pass, she would also lose the gambit, and her losses would be doubled. She did not look as if she could afford it.

"Player Two has increased the wager," Sorak asked. "Do I have the same option?"

Krysta smiled. "If you wish."

"Then I will wager three gold pieces," he said.

The young woman gasped.

"The wager is three gold pieces, or three hundred ceramics," said the game lord. "Players One and Two, it will cost you an additional one hundred and forty ceramics to stay in."

The young woman looked down and shook her head. "I do not have it," she said.

"Player Two declines the gambit and takes part only in the final pass," the game lord said. He turned to the merchant. "That leaves you, sir."

The merchant gave Sorak a level stare. "I will match the wager," he said.

"Betting is closed," the game lord said. "All players to take part in the final pass; gambit for Players One and Four. Sixth and final pass, Player One."

The merchant picked up all six dice, gave Sorak a long look, and rolled. The score totaled fifty. He looked up at Sorak and smiled. The young woman rolled next, and she came up with a twenty-nine. She sighed when she realized what might have happened. She had still lost, but nowhere near as heavily as she would have if she had participated in the gambit, even at the level she had originally wagered. Player Three rolled next and came up with a thirty, which meant that the merchant still had the top score. His smile broadened.

Sorak quickly calculated the merchant's final tally. On his first pass, he had rolled a three. On his second pass, the merchant rolled a four, then eleven on the third, sixteen on the fourth, and seventeen on the fifth. Adding the fifty that he had just rolled, that gave him a final tally of one hundred and one. As of the last pass, Sorak's own final tally stood at sixty-one, and if he lost the final pass, he would be down forty ceramics, but that was not counting the gambit.

"*Roll forty-one,*" he said to the Guardian.

The Guardian rolled.

"Player Four rolls forty-one," the game lord said. "The win for the final pass goes to Player One, for two hundred and forty ceramics, less the house take of ten percent, which leaves the pot at two hundred and sixteen ceramics. Final tally for Hawke's Gambit: Player One, one hundred and one points, Player Four, one hundred and two points. Gambit to Player Four, for six hundred ceramics or six gold pieces. Congratulations, sir. Next round, four ceramics to open, ante up into the pot."

"One point," said the merchant, through gritted teeth. He slammed his fist down on the side of the table. "One lousy point!"

"Better luck next time," Krysta said to him. She turned to Sorak with a wary smile. "For someone who has never played this game before, you seem to have done rather well. I am curious; could you have stood the loss?"

"Not very well," said Sorak.

She smiled. "You have the instincts of a gambler."

"You think so?" he replied. "Is this the way that you have built your fortune?"

"One of the ways," she replied slyly.

"Indeed? What are the others?"

"I am not sure you would possess the same talent for them as you seem to have for gambling," she replied, with a chuckle.

"Then perhaps I should play to my strength," he said. "This time, I shall buy you a drink, and you can help me celebrate. Then I think I will try this game again."

"You may wish to try that table over there," she said. "It has higher stakes."

"Only if you stand next to me and bring me luck," he said.

She smiled. "I will do my best. Now, about that drink. . . ."

EIGHT

After Sorak won his first round, Krysta moved on to circulate among her other patrons. She wished him luck and made him promise that he would see her again before he left. He remained at the table long enough to win a few more rounds and lose some others, playing in such a manner that despite leaving the table on a loss, he still wound up coming out ahead. Then he moved on to a different table. There were other games to be played; some fairly simple, where the players wagered on a little wooden ball that spun around inside a wheel, others more complicated, where cards were used and the wagering was based on strategy. Sorak decided to stick with the game that he already knew. It all went smoothly, and no one seemed to be aware that he was cheating, though Krysta's eyes were sharp on him the whole night.

Before long, his purse was heavy with his winnings, despite his having converted all the ceramics to silver and gold coins. He had to transfer most of his winnings to his pack because his purse would not hold them all. As he made his way toward the door, Tigra at his side, he suddenly found his way blocked by three half-giants, all armed with heavy clubs of knurled agafari wood.

"The lady would like to speak with you," one of them said.

He ducked under quickly so the Guardian could probe the half-giant's mind. There was not much there. Simple, brutish thoughts and simple, brutish appetites. The half-giant knew nothing about what he had done. He was simply following orders to bring Sorak to "the lady."

A low warning growl rumbled from Tigra's throat. "It's all right, Tigra," he said. He looked up at the half-giant and smiled. "Lead the way," he said.

The guards escorted him toward the back of the room where there was a stairway leading to the upper floors. They went up to the second floor and down a long corridor, then stopped before two heavy wooden doors about halfway down the hall. One of the half-giants knocked, and the door was opened by a half-elf male. Sorak noted that the half-elf was armed with an iron sword and several daggers. The half-giants did not enter with him.

He came into a luxuriously appointed sitting room, with three more half-elf males standing guard inside. All three were armed. At the far end of the sitting room was a curtained archway, flanked by two heavy iron braziers. The half-elf beckoned Sorak through the beaded curtain. Sorak went through with Tigra while the others remained outside in the sitting room. On the other side of the curtained archway was a large room with a heavy, intricately carved wooden desk at the back, placed before an arched window looking out over the gaming hall below. The window was covered with a beaded curtain, so that it would be a simple matter for someone to pull aside a couple of strands and secretly watch the action in the hall below.

There were two chairs placed in front of the desk, and there were two more doors on either side of the room. Krysta sat behind the desk, pouring water from a chilled pitcher into a fluted goblet. She held it out to him.

"Since you do not seem to care for my mead, I took the liberty of having some water sent up," she said. "And I have had some raw z'tal meat brought up for your tigone. Please, sit down."

As he took the chair she indicated, Tigra began to eat noisily from the large bowl placed on the floor beside the chair.

"You broke your promise," Krysta said. "You said that you would see me before you left."

"I had forgotten," Sorak lied.

"Am I so unmemorable, then?" she asked with a wary smile. Without waiting for a reply, she went on. "I understand you did quite well at the tables tonight."

Sorak shrugged. "It must have been beginner's luck."

"Oh, I think luck had very little to do with it," she replied, opening a small, lacquered wooden box and offering it to him. It was full of neatly rolled, black fibrous sticks. Sorak shook his head, and Krysta pulled back the box, taking one for herself. She lit it from a fragrant candle burning on her desk and drew in a deep lungful of the pungent-smelling smoke, then exhaled it through her nostrils. "Did you really think that you could use psionics in my gaming house and get away with it?"

"*She knows we cheated!*" said Kivara, in a frightened tone.

"*How could she know?*" Eyron replied. "*The Guardian would have felt it if someone tried to probe us. She is merely guessing. She hopes to trick us into an admission of guilt."*

"I don't understand," said Sorak with a frown.

"Please," said Krysta, a wry grimace on her face. "Do not insult my intelligence by playing the innocent. I pay a great deal of money to employ the finest game lords in the city. Each of them is expert at computing odds, and at watching how the dice roll. The more clumsy attempts—such as when someone palms our dice and substitutes weighted ones—my game lords can spot at once. And they can usually tell within three or four passes if the dice are receiving a psionic assist. You were very good. It took them three whole rounds before they were certain you were cheating."

Sorak cursed himself for being careless. It had never even occurred to him that his cheating could be exposed by such ordinary means. He had been on guard against psionic probes when he should have been reading the thoughts of the game lords, as well. The problem was that the Guardian could only exert one psionic ability at a time, and the game had moved so quickly there had been little opportunity to make telepathic probes, even if it had occurred to him to try.

"You knew I was cheating, yet you allowed me to play on," he said. "Why?"

"I was curious about you," she replied. "Also, I did not wish to risk an unpleasant incident. You carry a formidable-looking sword, and I did not want to have any trouble with your tigone. I had no wish to see my guards or any of my patrons injured."

"I see," said Sorak. "However, you still allowed me in here with both my tigone and my sword." He glanced back at the curtained archway. "I suppose those guards are out there listening, ready to burst in at any moment."

"If necessary," she replied. "However, I do not think it will be necessary."

As she spoke, Tigra made a groaning sort of growl, tried to get up, then keeled over with a rumbling sigh.

"Tigra!" Sorak jumped up out of his chair and knelt by the fallen tigone's side. The bowl was completely empty. "The meat!" he said as realization dawned. "You poisoned it!" His hand went to his sword.

"Stay your sword hand, Sorak," Krysta said calmly, "or my guards will have arrows in your back before you can even draw your blade."

He glanced back over his shoulder and saw several crossbows protruding through the beaded curtain. They were aimed directly at his back.

"Your psionic powers may turn aside one arrow," she said, "but not several at once. Your pet has not been harmed. I could easily have poisoned it, but I had no wish to kill the beast. The meat was simply laced with sleeping powder, enough to drug at least four grown men. The tigone should suffer no ill effects except, perhaps, an unsettled stomach. Now please, sit down."

Sorak resumed his seat. "You want me to surrender my winnings? Take them." He dropped his pack down on her desk, then tossed his purse beside it.

"I do not really care about the money," she said, with a dismissive wave of her hand. "It represents no loss to me, only to the players you cheated. They would have lost, in any case. They always do. It is a rare gambler who knows enough to quit while he's ahead. Had you played against the house, it would have been a different matter, but I noticed you were wise enough to avoid those games."

"Merely because I was not familiar with them," Sorak said.

She made a dubious face. "You expect me to believe that?"

Sorak shrugged. "Whether you believe it or not, it happens to be the truth. I have never been to a gaming house before, and I am beginning to regret that I did not heed Zalcor's warning. If you do not care about the money, then what is it you want of me?"

As he asked the question, he ducked under and allowed the Guardian to come briefly to the fore so that she could look into Krysta's mind. What she found there came as an interesting surprise.

"I want some answers, to begin with," replied Krysta. "We can start with who you really are, and why you came here. You are no simple herdsman, that much is certain."

"No," said Sorak. "But the rest of what I told you was essentially the truth. As a child, I was cast out into the desert and left to die. I was found by a pyreen elder who nursed me back to health and brought me to the villichi convent. Until I came to Tyr, I had spent my entire life there."

"Ridiculous," said Krysta. "You shall have to do better than that. Everyone knows the villichi are a female sect. There are no male villichi."

"I did not say I was born villichi," Sorak replied calmly. "Merely that I was raised in their convent."

"The villichi would never accept a male among them."

"They accepted me. They took me in because I had great psionic talent and because I was an outcast. The villichi know what it means to be shunned for being different. The pyreen elder asked that I be given shelter at the convent, and because the villichi honor the pyreen, the high mistress granted her request."

Krysta thoughtfully pursed her lips. "The villichi

follow the Path of the Preserver and the Way of the Druid, as do the pyreen. That much, at least, is true. But I find the rest of your story difficult to accept."

"Why should it matter to you one way or the other?" Sorak said. "Unless, of course, your interest goes beyond mere curiosity and the matter of my cheating in your gaming house. Why not ask Councilman Rikus to join us so that he can ask his questions for himself? He must be growing tired of standing with his ear pressed up against that door."

Krysta's eyes grew wide. Before she could reply, Rikus opened one of the side doors and stepped into the room.

"I was right," he said. "You never were a mere herdsman. So you were schooled in the Way by the villichi? And doubtless taught by them to fight, as well. That makes you very dangerous."

"Perhaps, but only to my enemies," Sorak replied.

"Indeed," said Rikus. "And how do you regard me?"

"As one who suspects my motives," Sorak said with a smile.

Rikus grinned mirthlessly. "Well then, if you can read my thoughts, you know what my next question is."

Sorak briefly ducked under again so that the Guardian could read the former gladiator's thoughts. They were guarded, but it took less than an instant for the Guardian to perceive what the councilman was thinking, and to see that the mul could be trusted.

"It was pure chance that I came here," Sorak replied. "I could not have known you planned to enlist Krysta's aid in having me watched since you had not decided it until after I left the council chamber. It was only chance that brought us both to the same place. Or perhaps it was fate taking a hand."

Rikus grunted. "Perhaps," he said. "But I still have my doubts about the rest of what you told us."

"What I told the council was the truth," said Sorak. "However, I am sure you will discover that for yourself."

"I intend to," Rikus said. "Still, I find it difficult believing your only motive for coming to us was a reward."

"I do not know how long I shall have to remain in Tyr," Sorak replied. "In the forest and the desert, I can live off the land. In the city, I require money."

"I see," said Rikus. "And if you were to receive your reward tonight, would you be leaving in the morning?"

"If given a choice, I would prefer to stay," said Sorak.

"Somehow, I thought as much," Rikus said. "But why? What business do you have in Tyr?"

"I came to make contact with the Veiled Alliance."

Rikus looked surprised at his candor; then he frowned. "Are you a sorcerer, as well?"

"No," Sorak replied. "I seek the Sage."

"The Sage?" said Krysta. She snorted with derision. "You mean the legend of the so-called 'hermit wizard' who is becoming an avangion? That story is nothing but a myth."

"You are wrong," Sorak replied. "The Sage lives, and I must find him."

"And you think the Veiled Alliance can help you?" Rikus asked.

"I have reason to believe there are those in the Veiled Alliance who may possess information that will help me in my quest."

A quick psionic probe of Rikus's and Krysta's

thoughts revealed that neither of them had any connection with the Veiled Alliance. Krysta had no strong feelings about them, one way or the other. She was a survivor who looked out for herself first. Rikus had an innate distrust of magic-users, whether defiler or preserver, though this uncertainty was tempered by his experience with the sorceress, Sadira. His concern about the Veiled Alliance was tied in with his concerns about the government of Tyr, of which he was a vital part. He saw the Alliance as a potentially disruptive influence, but he had far greater concerns about the templars, to whom the Alliance was unequivocally opposed.

"Assuming the Sage truly exists, why do you seek him?" Rikus asked.

Sorak saw no harm in telling him the truth. "I seek to know my origins," he replied. "I do not know who my parents were. I remember nothing of my life before the pyreen elder found me in the desert. I do not know into what tribe I was born, or even which race it was. I know one of my parents was a halfling and the other was an elf, but I do not know which was which. I do not know what became of them. I have been plagued by these questions all my life."

"And you believe the Sage can help you find the answers?" asked Rikus. He frowned. "Would not any sorcerer do as well?"

"The pyreen told me that only the Sage possesses preserver magic strong enough to part the veils of forgotten memory and time," said Sorak. "And I could never seek help from a defiler. I may not have been born villichi, but I was raised among them. Their beliefs are my own. I am sworn to follow the Way of Druid and the Path of the Preserver."

"You are, at least, forthright enough to admit you

seek contact with the Veiled Alliance," Rikus said. "Or perhaps you are merely being naive. In either case, I cannot help you. As a member of the council, I could hardly assist you in making contact with an underground group that functions outside the laws of the city, even if I had any information that would be of use to you."

"If you did, I would already possess it," said Sorak with a smile.

Rikus grimaced. "Yes, I suppose you would. Well, so long as you keep out of trouble, you can stay. I cannot say I am at ease about your presence here, but Tyr is a free city now, and you have not broken any laws."

"What I did tonight was not a crime?" asked Sorak.

"No crime has been officially reported to me," Rikus said with a quick glance at Krysta. Then, turning back to Sorak, he added, "I advise you to make sure that it remains that way. When the templars have completed their investigation, you shall receive your reward. In the meantime, it seems you have acquired sufficient means to pay for your lodging and your board while you remain in Tyr. What you do about the Veiled Alliance is your own concern. Just see to it that it does not become mine."

He turned and left the room.

"It would seem you have impressed him favorably," said Krysta.

"He has a peculiar way of showing it," Sorak replied.

She smiled. "That is Rikus for you," she said. "One does not learn charm fighting in the arena."

"Where did you learn it, then?" asked Sorak.

"There is not much point in trying to keep anything from you, is there?" she replied. "Yes, I fought in the arena. As for my charm, I came by it naturally, I suppose. A female must use whatever weapons she can in this world, especially if she is a lowly half-breed. A full-blooded elf would consider me contaminated by my human blood, and a human male might desire me, but only to satisfy his appetites. He would never accept me as an equal."

"I know what it means to be different," Sorak said. "I have seen the way people look upon me in the streets."

"Yes, we are two of a kind," she said in a low voice. "And if you know my thoughts. . ."

Sorak did not need to be a telepath to see what was on her mind. "I am flattered," he said, "but I have sworn a vow of celibacy."

"Vows can be broken."

"Then they are not vows," said Sorak, "merely self-deluding resolutions."

"I see," said Krysta. "Well, it is a pity. You have no idea what you're missing. Still, a man who makes a vow and keeps it is a man worthy of respect. If you cannot accept me as a lover, then perhaps you can accept me as a friend."

"A friend who has been charged to watch me so that she might report on my movements to the council?" Sorak asked.

"No worse than a friend who came to my establishment under false pretenses so that he could cheat at my gaming tables," Krysta countered. "Or a friend from whom I can hope to have no secrets because he can perceive my every thought."

"Your point is well taken," Sorak said, not bothering to correct her mistaken assumption. In fact, the Guardian could read her mind only when he ducked under and she made a deliberate effort. "It does not seem to be a very promising beginning to a friendship, does it?"

"Let us see if we cannot make amends," said Krysta. "Have you secured lodgings in the city?"

"Not yet, but I was going to take a room at the inn at the far end of the street."

"That pestilential hole? If you are not murdered in your sleep, you will be devoured by the vermin. I will offer you one of the rooms on the upper floor, which I reserve for my special patrons. You may have your meals as well, or take them elsewhere if you like, but you will not find better food than my kitchens prepare. And your tigone is welcome to stay with you, though you will be charged for any damage it may cause."

"Your offer is very generous," said Sorak. "But what must I do to make amends on my part?"

"In return, during the time that you are on the premises, frequent the tables and play as many of the games as possible. The card games, in particular. Professional gamblers find it easier to cheat at those. The house will stake you in your play, and you may keep half of your winnings."

"I see," said Sorak. "In other words, it is all right for your patrons to be cheated, so long as it is only you who cheats them."

"I am not in this business to lose money," Krysta said. "I do not mind if my patrons win occasionally, but I do not wish to see anyone win too much. And if they do, it is probably because they have found some way to cheat successfully. The odds always favor the house, but from time to time, magic-users, cardsharps, and psionicists can be a problem. I can always use some help in that regard."

"And at the same time, it would be easier for you to keep an eye on me for Rikus," Sorak said with a smile.

"True," she replied, "but if you have nothing to

hide, why should that concern you? Rikus only cares
about the security of Tyr and the stability of the government. So long as you do nothing to threaten that,
he does not really care what else you do."

"But you must realize that my aim is to make contact with the Veiled Alliance," Sorak said. "Once my
business with them is concluded, I shall be on my
way. I have no desire to remain in Tyr any longer than
is necessary."

"The best place for you to make contact with the
Veiled Alliance is right here in the elven market,"
Krysta replied. "I can help you to the point of making
some discreet inquiries, but beyond that, you will be
on your own. I do not wish to involve myself. As for
the duration of your stay, that is entirely up to you.
However, for as long as you remain here, why not
take advantage of a situation that can serve both our
interests? So, what is your answer?"

"I accept," said Sorak.

"Good. I shall have a room prepared for you, and I
will summon my half-giants to carry your pet there. It
will sleep until at least tomorrow morning, I should
think. However, you will find that keeping a wild
beast in the city will present certain difficulties. Can
you control it to the extent that it does not damage the
premises or attack any of my staff?"

"I will make sure of that," said Sorak.

"You are certain?"

"Absolutely."

"It is not merely a matter of the tigone being psionic
and obeying because it has a bond with you, is it?"
Krysta said, watching him with interest. "You possess
the power to communicate with beasts."

"Yes."

"You can make them do your will?"

"Most of them," said Sorak.

"Fascinating," Krysta said. "Then that makes for at least three psionic powers you possess," she said. "How many others?"

Sorak did not reply.

Krysta stared at him for a long moment, then nodded and said, "Very well, I shall not pry. I will have your room prepared for you. In the meantime, perhaps you would care to join me at my table for some supper?"

The dining room of the Crystal Spider was on the first floor, through an archway and down a corridor near the back of the main room. A thick brick wall separated it from the gaming hall and kept out most of the noise. What faint sounds might have managed to filter through were masked by the musicians, who played softly on ryl pipes while the patrons ate. The tables and chairs were made of polished, dark agafari wood, and the floor was hand-laid ceramic tile. Heavy support columns held up the beamed and plastered ceiling, and there were numerous small, arched niches in the walls for candles. The atmosphere in the dining room was subdued and refined, for only the wealthiest of patrons could afford its prices.

Even though it was quite late, the dining room was full. Outside, merely a stone's throw away, beggars huddled in the street, pulling their filthy cloaks around them against the night chill, or burrowing in the refuse in an effort to keep warm and find some scraps to eat. Here, behind a stout wall, the wealthy citizens of Tyr supped on the finest cuisine between rounds of gaming, in which they casually wagered sums that would have kept those poor beggars fed for months.

Krysta's private table was located in a secluded alcove that lay up a short flight of steps and through an archway with a beaded curtain. Sorak noticed that all the serving women were young and uniformly lovely. Krysta apparently had no concerns about suffering in comparison with any of them. Every head turned when she walked into the room on Sorak's arm and led him to her private alcove.

"What may I tempt you with?" she asked him when they sat down. "My cooks are the finest in the city. I can recommend the braised z'tal with wine sauce, or baked cloud ray with spiced erdland eggs in jelly. If you would care for something simpler, we have the finest mekillot steaks in all of Tyr."

"Could I have some vegetables?"

"Vegetables?" said Krysta, her eyes widening with surprise.

"I do not eat meat," Sorak replied.

"The mekillot steak sounds tempting," said Kivara, and her hunger for meat activated Sorak's salivary glands.

"I have never tasted cloud ray," Eyron added, filling Sorak with curiosity about the experience.

Sorak resolutely ignored them.

"How can you not eat meat?" asked Krysta with astonishment. "Both elves and halflings are hunters who eat flesh."

"It is simply my choice," said Sorak, trying not to think about the carnivorous members of the tribe, who preferred their meat raw and freshly killed, with the blood still warm. "I was raised in the ways of the villichi, who are vegetarian."

Krysta sighed. "I stock my larder with the finest meats and delicacies money can buy, and all you want are vegetables."

"And some bread and water, please."

Krysta shook her head with resignation. "As you wish." She gave the order to the serving girl, asking for some steamed vegetables for Sorak and braised z'tal for herself. Their goblets were filled, hers with mead and Sorak's with chilled water, and a basket of fresh-baked bread was brought to them, still warm from the ovens.

"So," she asked after toasting him with her goblet, "what was it like, being the only male in a convent full of women?"

"I felt like an outsider, at first," Sorak replied, "but the sisters soon came to accept me."

"The sisters," Krysta said with a knowing smile. "How quaint. Is that really how you thought of them?"

"That is how they refer to one another," he replied. "And it is more than merely a polite form of address. We were all like family. I shall miss them."

"You mean you do not plan on going back?"

Sorak shook his head. "I know I would always be welcome there, but no. Though I have lived with them, and trained with them, and grown up in the Way, I am not villichi. The time has come for me to find my own way in the world, and I do not think I shall return."

"So then you do not think of yourself as one of them?" asked Krysta.

"No," he said. "I do not belong there. For that matter, I do not know if I belong anywhere. The halflings could never accept me because I am part elf, and the elves could never accept me because I am part halfling. I do not even know if there is another such as I."

"It must feel very lonely," Krysta said, her foot touching his under the table. He drew his foot away.

"I know something of what it feels like not to be accepted," she continued. "Though, of course, there are many half-elves in the city, as there are half-dwarves and half-giants. You may have noticed that most of the people working here are half-breeds. I hire them first because there are many places in the city where they could not be hired, and the work that they can find, scarce as work is in Tyr these days, pays the lowliest of wages. Outside the city, there would be little they could do. Work on a farm, perhaps, or become herdsmen. Many become bandits, for they have no other choice. No tribe would accept them, and they become hard and embittered."

"But you seem to have done well for yourself," said Sorak.

"Yes," said Krysta. "Much like you, I recall little of my childhood. I was sold into slavery and grew up working in the arena, picking up body parts and spreading sand to cover up spilled blood. Between the games, I worked in the kitchens, where I first learned about preparing food. In time, I became a gladiator myself and trained with the others."

"That was how you met Rikus?" Sorak asked.

"Yes. He had a partner who took an interest in me. She saw in me a younger version of herself, and so both she and Rikus became my protectors. Otherwise, things could have been much worse. Gladiators are a hard and ruthless lot, and a pretty, young half-elf girl would have been used harshly if she had no one to look after her. One day, I was purchased by a noble, who used his influence with Kalak's templars to buy me as a plaything for himself. He was an old man, and his appetites were not so great. It was not difficult to please him, and it was easier by far than life in the arena, which was hard and brutal and often very short.

I stayed with him for several years and learned much about the ways of the nobility. I learned how they lived, and what they liked, and how they preferred to spend their idle time, of which they had a surfeit."

She crossed her legs under the table and, in doing so, her foot came briefly into contact with Sorak's leg. She went on as if she hadn't noticed.

"One night, while I was in bed with my master, the exertion proved too much for him, and he collapsed upon me. I thought that he had swooned, but when I rolled him off me, I discovered he was dead. It was late, and the servants in the mansion were all asleep. I took what money I could find in his quarters and escaped. I managed to make my way to the elven market, where I took a small room at an inn. I worked in the kitchen of the inn during the day, and at night, I went to the gaming houses. I had learned gaming at my former master's house, watching him play with his friends, and I learned that while some games were mostly ruled by chance, others could have the chances of winning greatly increased by use of clever strategy. I paid close attention, and learned well."

"And you built the Crystal Spider with your winnings?"

"Not entirely," she said. "It would have been dangerous to try keeping all that money with me, and there was no place I could have hidden it that would have been truly safe. I had a friend in a merchant house, and I invested, buying shares in caravan goods and thereby participating in the profits. And what profits I made, I kept reinvesting. I invested cautiously and wisely so that I never had all my money in the same venture. That way, the risk was minimized. Eventually, I had enough to open up my own establishment. By then, I was well known to the merchant houses, and a number of them saw potential profits in the venture and chose to help finance the Crystal Spider."

"So then you have partners," Sorak said.

"Yes," she replied, "but most of the money it took to build this house was mine, and so I retain control. However, there are two merchant houses that have strong interests in the success of my establishment. And if what you told Rikus was true, they will doubtless want to meet you and perhaps contribute to the reward the council promised you."

"It was true," said Sorak, "but I must confess to being puzzled as to how the council is acting in the matter. Neither you nor Rikus seems to trust the templars, and yet, it is they who have been charged with investigating what I reported to the council."

"The templars can be trusted to look after their own interests," Krysta said. "Where it concerns the security of the city, their own interests are involved most intimately. If Tyr were to fall under the domination of another city, such as Nibenay, the templars would be among the very first to fall, as they would pose the greatest threat. You may rest assured that their investigation will be a thorough and honest one. They do not wish to see Tyr fall under anyone's dominion save their own."

"So then the new government is threatened not only from without, but from within," said Sorak.

"Very much so," Krysta replied. "The templars once served Kalak, who was a defiler, and Tithian was the senior templar. When Kalak was slain, Tithian became the king, and if you ask me, he was not much better, but at least he was held in check somewhat by the new council under first Agis, then Rikus and Sadira. Now Tithian is gone, and the council rules the city. The templars sit upon the council, in the person of Timor, and they have strong allies, both in the council and among the nobility. Councilman Kor is Timor's staunchest supporter, for he believes the templars will win out in the power struggle and is therefore already feathering his nest. And the nobles have little love for the new government, which freed their slaves."

"What about the merchant classes?" Sorak asked.

"The merchant houses are keeping to a strict neutrality," said Krysta. "Whoever governs Tyr, they shall still have to do their business, and they deem it wisest to offend neither of the factions."

Their food was brought to them, and Sorak found himself unconsciously licking his lips over the aroma of braised z'tal that rose from Krysta's plate.

"*Kivara!*" he said. "*Stop it!*"

"*Must we eat like desert rats?*" she asked petulantly. "*I am starving for some flesh!*"

"*After all,*" added Eyron, "*it is not as though you have not eaten meat before.*"

"*I have not eaten meat,*" protested Sorak. "*You have eaten meat. There is a difference.*"

"*Somehow, it escapes me,*" Eyron said. "*The flesh I eat nourishes your body.*"

"*Leave him alone,*" the Guardian said, interceding. "*He does not disturb or argue with you when you make your kill. He has a right to choose what will sustain him.*"

"*This paltry roughage would not even sustain a rasclinn,*" Kivara grumbled.

Sorak ignored the exchange and simply ate his vegetables. Beneath the table, Krysta's foot brushed up against his leg. He tried to move his leg back to avoid the contact, but it remained exactly where it was. Puzzled, he tried to move it once again, with no more result.

"*Kivara,*" he growled inwardly, "*what are you doing?*"

"*Nothing,*" she replied with a tone of innocence.

Krysta began gently rubbing her foot against his calf.

"*You are only encouraging her,*" he said. "*Stop it.*"

"*Why? It feels nice.*"

"*You are interfering with me,*" he said angrily. "*I will not have it!*"

"*Some braised z'tal would go nicely with these vegetables,*" she replied.

"*Kivara!*" said the Guardian. "*You are shameless, and this is not the way we function!*"

"*Oh, very well,*" Kivara said in a sulking tone.

Sorak pulled his leg back.

"What were you thinking just now?" asked Krysta.

"That if we are going to be spending time together, we had better be certain that we understand each other," Sorak replied. "I cannot give you what you desire."

"Cannot, or will not?" she asked, with a mocking smile.

"Is there a difference?"

"There is to me," she said. "Would you welcome my advances if it were not for your vow?"

"I am certain that part of me would," he replied, with a wry inner grimace at Kivara, "but part of me would feel an obligation to another."

Krysta raised her eyebrows. "Another? So then there *has* been a woman in your life?"

"Not in the way that you might think," said Sorak. "She is someone I grew up with. A villichi priestess."

"Ah," said Krysta with a smile. "I see. Passion can

be no less intense for being chaste. Or was it chaste?"

"It was. And I would prefer not to discuss it any further."

"Very well," said Krysta. "I shall respect your vow, despite the challenge posed by tempting you to forsake it. But tell me, if you had not taken a vow of celibacy, would you still refuse me because of this young priestess?"

"It is not that simple," Sorak said. "But if I were free to respond to you in the way you wish, I would not hesitate to do so."

"A most diplomatic answer," Krysta said, "and not entirely satisfying. But I suppose that it shall have to do." She glanced down at the table and shook her head. "It is almost funny. I cannot count the men who have desired me, but the one I want the most, I cannot have."

"Perhaps that is why you want him," Sorak said.

She smiled. "Perhaps. Would you care for some dessert?"

NINE

Timor stood on the balcony on the third floor of his palatial estate in the templars' quarter, gazing out at the sun's rays gleaming off the Golden Tower. Kalak's palace had stood empty ever since Tithian had disappeared. No one resided there, not even the slaves who had kept it clean, tended the lush gardens, and seen to Kalak's slightest whim. The slaves had all been freed, and the Golden Palace now stood merely as a monument to the days when the city had a king, rather than a democratic council. It was such a waste.

Tithian would not be coming back. Timor was certain of it. By rights, he was next in line. Tithian had ascended to the Golden Throne because he had been Kalak's senior templar. Tithian himself had appointed Timor senior templar, and now that Tithian was gone, Timor felt the right of succession should have passed to him. Except that Tithian had not been declared dead. His fate remained unknown. The council ruled in his absence, but there had never been any formal move to settle the question of a new king for Tyr. Sadira and Rikus had seen to that. They had always been conspicuously silent on the subject of Tithian's disappearance.

Timor had not pressed the issue. He knew the time

was not yet right. Both Rikus and Sadira had a great deal of support among the people of the city, and most of the council members, sensitive to the prevailing winds, had supported them, as well. However, the overwhelming popular support they had enjoyed as the heroes of the revolution was beginning to erode. They had slain the tyrant and they had freed the slaves, and with each passing week, they had consolidated the power of the council, passing edicts in Tithian's absence that granted more freedom to the people of the city and would make it more and more difficult for Tyr to return to a monarchial form of government. That was, of course, their plan. Bit by bit, they intended to legislate the monarchy out of existence. They were waging another revolution, one that was much more subtle, but no less effective. The longer Rikus and Sadira remained in power as the dominant voices on the council, the more difficult it would be for Timor to supplant Tithian as the king of Tyr.

Difficult, thought Timor, but not impossible. Time worked for him, as well as for Sadira. Since the new government had been instituted, Sadira had consolidated her power on the council; in that, she had been quite successful. But while she was a clever female, she had no experience in government, and she had made one very big mistake. In her rush to free the slaves of Tyr, she had failed to take into account the devastating impact that would have on the city's treasury and trade.

There was not enough work for all of the new citizens, and as a result, the ranks of the city's beggars and thieves had swelled dramatically. Wages had fallen as more people competed for fewer jobs, and there were frequent mob brawls in the warrens and the elven market, even in the city's merchant district. Mobs of beggars attacked recently freed slaves, whose presence in the streets threatened their own livelihood. Bands of thugs roamed the city at night and even during the day, attacking citizens and robbing them. In the warrens, in the elven market, and in the merchant district, vigilante groups had been formed to dispense summary street justice to protect their neighborhoods. The city guard lacked the manpower and the resources to deal with all of the unrest, and they were frequently attacked themselves.

Already, there had been several large fires in the warrens as the angry and frustrated poor people of the city vented their rage on their own neighborhoods. The fires had all been brought under control eventually, but entire city blocks had burned to the ground, and many of the merchants who had their businesses there had left the city in disgust. With each caravan that departed for Altaruk or Gulg or South Ledopolus, there were wagonloads of people who had decided to leave the city and make a new start elsewhere, despite the uncertainty they faced. All this worked in Timor's favor.

During Kalak's reign, the templars had been hated by the people of the city, who had seen them, quite correctly, as oppressors enforcing the will of the tyrant. But with Kalak's death and Tithian's ascension to the throne, that attitude had gradually begun to change. While Tithian had struggled to consolidate his own power, Sadira and Agis, another hero of the revolution, had moved quickly to ram some of their progressive new edicts through the council, and Tithian had been forced to approve them. Timor had seen to it that the templars went along with the new edicts, and that they assisted as much as possible in their implementation. He had made certain his templars were conspicuous throughout the city, keeping order and mediating disputes, functioning as diplomatic liaisons between the people and the council and the city guard. He had waged a subtle campaign of public relations to change the image of the templars from that of oppressors enforcing Kalak's will to that of Kalak's helpless victims, trapped in the thrall of the king and forced to do his bidding.

Day by day, the attitude of the people toward the templars became more and more favorable, while their attitude toward the council grew worse and worse. The heroes of the revolution were starting to be looked on as the inept managers of a city on its way to ruin under their stewardship. People were starting to talk among themselves, recalling the days of Kalak's reign, when things had run more smoothly, when the templars had been in control. Perhaps, they said, Kalak was a tyrant, an insane defiler obsessed with his mad lust for power, but the templars were the ones who really ran things, and the city had fared much better under their efficiency. Timor had spared no expense to start this whispering campaign, but it was paying off. The people were no longer whispering. They were now openly speaking out against the council and blaming them for all the city's woes.

Soon, thought Timor. The time was not yet right, but soon. Sadira's days were numbered, as well as those of that hulking mul who sat at her right hand. There remained but one more link that would complete the chain of the events that he had set in motion. There still remained one potential threat to the templars' plan to seize power—the Veiled Alliance.

With Kalak dead, the templars had no magic anymore. He had channeled his power through them, but

they were not sorcerers themselves. Except for Timor.
For years, he had steadfastly pursued the craft in
secret, developing his own power. Nevertheless, his
own ability, while not insignificant by any means,
was still a far cry from the power that Kalak had
wielded. He could not and would never be able to
empower his fellow templars. He would have to be a
sorcerer-king himself to do that. That meant the
Veiled Alliance was still a serious threat. Timor was
confident of his defiling abilities, but he was not fool
enough to think that he could stand against the Veiled
Alliance by himself.

His plan was to induce them to come out into the
open. With Kalak dead, Tithian gone, and defiler
magic outlawed in the city, there was no longer any
excuse for the Veiled Alliance to remain an underground society. They had once been criminals, but
Kor—at Timor's urging—had already proposed an
edict that would serve as a blanket pardon for the
Veiled Alliance, providing that *all* of them came forward and took part in helping to rebuild the city. As
he had said during the last council meeting, who better than the members of the Veiled Alliance, who followed the Path of the Preserver, to oversee the new
farm program that would feed the city and revitalize
the desert tablelands? He had already seen to it that
his remarks in council were reported to the people of
the city, and he had placards posted everywhere, calling upon the Veiled Alliance to come forward and
take part in "the greening of Tyr."

Once all the members of the secret group were
identified, then he could make his move. The plan
was already in place. In one night, in one fell swoop,
the templars and their agents would eliminate the
Veiled Alliance while the city was distracted by a

massive, widespread riot that would be triggered at Timor's signal. Fires would be started throughout the city, though not, of course, in the nobles' quarter or the templars' quarter, which would be heavily protected. Only isolated, controlled incidents of looting and burning would occur there, merely for the sake of appearances. Timor planned to have his own mansion burned to the ground—after most of his possessions had been discreetly removed—so that he could claim kinship with the populace in that he had been one of the victims. The mobs would be incited to a looting rampage in the merchant district. In one night, the Night of the Scourging, the templars would seize power and declare a state of martial law.

In the interest of public safety, Timor would move into the palace and appoint himself dictator until law and order could once more be restored. The meetings of the council would have to be suspended indefinitely, since many of its members—Sadira, Rikus, and all those loyal to them—would have been killed during the rioting. To punish those who had destroyed the city and brought down the government, rioters and looters would be arrested by the city guard and condemned to slavery, so that they might rebuild what they had helped destroy. And to keep the peace and prevent the recurrence of such massive suffering, Timor would "succumb to the pleas of the populace" and have himself crowned king.

It was a lovely plan, and it covered all contingencies, but before it could be implemented, the threat of the Veiled Alliance had to be removed. That meant they had to be forced out into the open. Timor's informers had heard rumors that some members of the Veiled Alliance were in favor of disclosure, so they could take their rightful place in Tyrian society and

work with the new democratic council to help rebuild
Tyr. However, certain highly placed members of the
Alliance power structure were resistant. They did not
trust the templars, and they did not trust Sadira, who
was known to have practiced defiler magic in the
past, although she had forsworn it.

Somehow, thought Timor, those preservers had to
be identified and neutralized. The question was,
how? And now there was this new threat, reported by
this so-called "herdsman," Sorak. If Nibenay had,
indeed, sent spies to Tyr to search out the city's weak-
nesses prior to an invasion, that could disrupt his
plans. He had to pursue this investigation with all
vigor, despite the fact that he did not believe for even
one moment that this Sorak was a simple herdsman.

He had caught a brief glimpse of the sword Sorak
wore beneath his cloak. It had a most unusual config-
uration, and though Timor could not be certain, for
the blade had been covered by its scabbard, it
appeared to be a metal one. A simple herdsman did
not carry such a weapon. It would be way beyond his
means. Moreover, a simple herdsman did not carry
himself the way Sorak did. The elfling had the bearing of a fighter. There was definitely more to him than
met the eye, and Timor wondered if he was not a
plant from Nibenay, sent to spy out any potential
weakness in the council.

He had assigned some templars to investigate the
claims Sorak had brought to the council, for he could
afford to take no chances. At the same time, however,
he had sent a team of templars to work in shifts and
have Sorak watched. As each watcher was relieved,
he reported back to Timor on Sorak's activities. The
most recent report had been especially enlightening.

Sorak had been escorted by Captain Zalcor and a

squad of city guard to the warrens, so that he might secure some cheap accommodations while ostensibly waiting for the investigation to confirm the validity of his claims. No sooner had Zalcor left, however, than Sorak had made his way straight to the Crystal Spider, and a short while later, Rikus himself had been seen entering the gaming house, as well. This could not be coincidence. It was a well known fact that the half-elf female who operated the gaming house had once been a gladiator, as had Rikus. Undoubtedly, they knew each other. And now Sorak was there, as well. It was a clear indication of collusion. Only, what was their plan?

Was it possible, Timor wondered, that Rikus and Sadira had somehow managed to get wind of his plans for the Night of the Scourging? Then, just as quickly as the thought occurred to him, he dismissed it. If that had been the case, he would surely have been arrested; even the absence of proof would not have stopped Rikus and Sadira from moving against him. Sadira was not above letting the end justify her means. No, it had to be something else. If he was plotting against them, then could they not at the same time be plotting against him?

Neither Rikus nor Sadira made any secret of their distrust and antipathy toward the templars. However, for the moment, the templars had strong support among the people of the city. If Sadira moved against them now, she would have difficulty justifying her actions, and she would be perceived as using Kalak's methods. On the other hand, if she could make a strong case against the templars. . .

"Of course," said Timor to himself. "She plans to accuse us of collusion with these so-called spies from Nibenay. The elfling is her cat's-paw. The whole thing was contrived to make the templars look like traitors to the city."

"My lord. . . ."

Timor turned around. One of his templars stood at the entrance to his chambers. "Yes, what is it?"

"We have apprehended two of the spies," the templar said. "We found one at the merchant house of Kulik, and the other was arrested in the elven market, coming out of the Drunken Giant wineshop. He was observed at several inns and taverns, making inquiries about the Veiled Alliance."

"Indeed?" said Timor. "Where are they now?"

"Downstairs, my lord, awaiting your pleasure."

"Excellent. Have them brought in."

He poured himself some wine and raised the goblet to his lips. A moment later, he heard shouting on the stairs, and then a scuffle. He frowned. There was more shouting, and the sounds of blows falling, then several of his templars entered, accompanied by soldiers from the city guard, dragging the two prisoners. Oddly enough, the prisoners were not so much resisting them as trying to get at one another.

"What is the meaning of this?" Timor said, his voice a whip crack. "How dare you create a disturbance in my home?"

The two men fell silent as they stared at him. Then one turned to glower at the other and spat out, "If you tell him anything, you misbegotten son of a silt wader, I shall tear out your tongue and feed it to you!"

"Silence!" Timor said sharply. "The only one to make any threats here shall be me." He turned to the soldiers. "Leave us."

"But, my lord, these men are dangerous. . . ." the sergeant of the guard protested.

"I said leave us. I shall interrogate these men myself. You are dismissed."

"Yes, my lord."

The soldiers left, leaving only Timor and his templars with the prisoners, whose hands were bound. Both men glared at him defiantly.

"What are your names?" asked Timor, raising the goblet to his lips once more.

"You tell him nothing, you miserable turncoat!" said the one who had spoken before. The second man lunged at him, and the templars had to grab them both to keep them apart.

"Very well, then," Timor said, fixing his gaze on the first man. "*You* shall tell me."

"I'll tell you nothing, templar!"

Timor stirred the wine in the goblet with his forefinger. He mumbled something under his breath. He looked up at the prisoner. "Your name."

The prisoner spat at him.

Timor grimaced with disgust and wiped away the spittle, then dashed the wine from his goblet into the man's face. Only it was no longer wine. As the droplets struck the prisoner's skin, they began to burn into his flesh, and the man screamed, doubling over in pain, unable to raise his hands to his smoking face as the acid ate it away. The second prisoner's eyes grew wide with fear as the first man fell to his knees, screaming in agony.

"Your name," said Timor softly, once again.

"Rokan!" screamed the prisoner. "My name is Rokan!"

Timor softly whispered the counterspell and made a languid pass with his hand. The prisoner abruptly felt the burning stop as the acid turned once again to wine. He remained on his knees, doubled over, whimpering and gasping for breath.

"There now, that was simple, was it not?" said
Timor. He turned toward the second prisoner and
raised his eyebrows.

"D-Digon!" the man sputtered quickly. "My name
is Digon!"

Timor smiled. "You see?" he said. "Things are so
much easier when people are cooperative." He turned
back to glance at Rokan, still kneeling, doubled over,
on the floor. "You two seem not to like each other very
much," he said. "Why is that, I wonder?"

"Because he was my chieftain, and he feels I
betrayed him," said Digon hastily.

Timor raised his eyebrows. "And did you?"

Digon looked down at the floor and nodded. "I had
no choice," he said. "My will was not my own. He
made me."

"Who made you?"

"Sorak, damn his eyes!" said Digon, spitting out
the name. "I curse the day I met him!"

"Sorak?" Timor said. "How very interesting. Tell
me more."

After seeing what Timor had just done to Rokan,
Digon let the story come tumbling out of him. He told
all about the plan the marauders had to ambush the
caravan, and how Sorak had run into them while they
were posted on lookout duty on the ridge overlooking the city. Timor listened intently as Digon described
how easily Sorak had dispatched the other lookouts,
leaving only Digon alive, and the templar looked
even more interested when Digon described how
Sorak had disarmed him and then probed his mind,
reading all his thoughts.

"There was nothing I could do, my lord," said
Digon as he finished the story. "He knew that if I tried

to go to Rokan and warn him, Rokan would kill me
for failing in my task. I had nowhere else to go except
to Tyr, for I could not rejoin my comrades, and I knew
that if my path crossed with his again, he would read
my thoughts and know if I had failed him. The task
that he demanded of me did not seem to be so difficult. Go to Tyr and make inquiries; contact the Veiled
Alliance and tell them he was coming. That was all,
and then I would be free."

"And you were so afraid of him you dared not disobey?" asked Timor.

Digon shook his head. "You do not know him, my
lord templar. The elfling is a powerful master of the
Way, and he fights like a fiend. It was worth my life to
disobey him."

"And you say he came down out of the mountains?" Timor asked.

"He must have," Digon replied. "From our vantage
point, we would have seen anyone approaching from
any other direction. We never expected anyone to
come down out of the mountains. There is nothing up
there, no villages, no settlements, nothing."

"And yet that is where he came from?" Timor
asked again.

"I can think of no other explanation, my lord templar," Digon said.

"Hmmm," said Timor. "Interesting. Most interesting. So the marauders had been sent to Tyr, to infiltrate spies into the merchant houses and attack the
caravan to Altaruk?"

"Yes, my lord."

"Where is the attack meant to take place?"

Digon told him the exact location where the
marauders waited.

"And who are the spies?"

Digon told him that, as well, and Timor was fascinated to discover that what he said matched Sorak's report to the council down to the last detail. That seemed to eliminate the possibility that Sorak himself was a spy from Nibenay, as did the fact that he came down from the Ringing Mountains. Nibenay was clear on the other side of the tablelands. So then what was his game?

"Please, my lord," Digon pleaded, "I have told you all I know. I beg you, do not kill me. I shall do anything; I am still of value. I can guide your soldiers to where the marauders wait to attack the caravan. I can identify those who are among the caravan party itself."

"You pathetic, groveling, piece of kank dung," Rokan said, his voice hoarse as he looked up at his fellow marauder with disgust.

Digon gasped. Rokan's face was a ruin. Not even his own mother would have recognized him. The acid had eaten deeply into his flesh, in some places clear through to the bone. His face was a horror. With his hands bound behind him, he had not been able to protect himself. By reflex, he had turned his face at the last moment, so that most of the damage had occurred only to one side. One eye had been dissolved, leaving a raw and empty socket. An exposed cheekbone gleamed whitely, and a corner of his mouth had been eaten away, giving him a frightening, permanent rictus, a death's head grimace. As the drops of acid had run down his cheek, they had etched trails in his flesh, so that it looked as if it had been raked by claws.

"You may kill me if you like, templar," Rokan said, his one-eyed gaze boring into Digon, "but if the dead can have one last request, set free my hands for but one moment."

Timor smiled. "I have no intention of killing you, my friend," he said. "I dislike to waste potentially valuable resources. You possess strong spirit. It is a mean spirit, but it is mean down to the bone. I can always use a man like you. But this pathetic wretch," he added, turning toward Digon, "has no perceptible value whatsoever."

"My lord templar, no!" shouted Digon. "I can help you! I can serve you!"

"Your sort would serve any master, for you have no backbone," Timor said. "I will not soil my hands with you. Your request is granted, Rokan."

He made a languid motion with his fingers, and Rokan felt his bonds fall away. With a snarl, he launched himself at Digon. His hands still bound, Digon was defenseless. He screamed and tried to kick out at his attacker, but Rokan moved too quickly. He had his hands around Digon's throat, and as he choked him, he forced him to his knees, then pushed him down flat upon his back and sat astride him. Digon's mouth was open wide as he gasped in vain for breath. Timor poured himself some more wine, then sat comfortably in a high-backed chair, watching as Rokan took revenge.

With one hand, Rokan continued to apply relentless pressure to Digon's throat, while with the other, he reached into the man's mouth and grasped his tongue. With a savage yank, he ripped Digon's tongue out, then crammed it back into his mouth, forcing it down his throat. The marauder screamed and gagged, both on his own blood and on his tongue.

"Your tongue always was too loose, Digon," Rokan said. Then his fingers dug in and wrapped themselves tightly around Digon's trachea. With an abrupt, powerful motion, he tore his throat out.

"I see you keep your word," said Timor, recalling the marauder's threat. "A commendable trait."

Rokan stood and faced him, breathing heavily. "If I thought I could, I would tear out your throat, as well, templar."

"I have no doubt that you would," said Timor, "if you thought you could. But why direct your anger at me? I am but the intermediary of your fate. It was Sorak who suborned your late, unlamented comrade and learned all your plans, and it was Sorak who exposed those plans to the Council of Advisors. He gave us your names, he gave us detailed descriptions of you, he told us where you could be found. He warned us of your plan to attack the caravan after it leaves Tyr. Our soldiers will be waiting for them, and they will all be slaughtered to the last man. Your fellow spies will all be brought before me, perhaps even before this night is through. You have journeyed from the Mekillot Mountains all the way to Tyr, only to meet your utter ruin, and it has all been brought about by just one man. Not even a man at that, but an elfling half-breed whom you have never even met."

"It was not the elfling who has ruined my face," rasped Rokan, his one eye filled with hate.

"No, that is quite true," said Timor, "but look at it another way. You and your confederates were all described to us in great detail, and that description was passed out to every soldier in the city guard. Your face was known. Now, no one would recognize you. When you consider it that way, I did you a favor."

"And you expect my thanks?"

"No, not really," Timor replied, "only your obedience, which I could easily compel. However, a man serves a master best when he serves himself, as well.

You have lost everything, Rokan. I offer you the chance to take revenge on the one who laid you low."

"Sorak," Rokan said violently.

"Yes, Sorak. I can tell you where to find him. And when the rest of your confederates are brought in, they shall have to choose between converting to my cause or dying. I think we both know which way they will choose."

"You desire this elfling's death?" said Rokan. "Consider it done. I need no help. I can take care of him myself."

"Oh, I think not," said Timor. "The elfling is a master of the Way, and apparently quite skilled with a blade, as well. It would be best to take no chances. Perform one service for me, and for yourself, and you will have proved your worth."

"And then?" said Rokan.

"And then you will find the rewards of serving me far greater than looting caravans or spying for Nibenay."

"What of my face?" asked Rokan. "Can you use your sorcery to heal it?"

"Perhaps," said Timor with a smile. His fingers played with the stem of the goblet. "In time."

"How much time?" Rokan asked. "Why should I believe you? You ask much, but promise little."

"I promise more than you could ever imagine, you fool," said Timor. "As for restoring your face, consider it an incentive."

"Defiler magic is still outlawed in Tyr," Rokan said. "I am sure the council would be fascinated to know that the senior templar is a secret practitioner of defiler sorcery."

Timor chuckled. "Yes, I am sure they would, but you will never tell them."

"What is to stop me? You could kill me anytime you wished. It would only spare me the suspense of waiting."

"Killing a man is a very simple matter," Timor replied. "Using him constructively is more creative, and ultimately more rewarding. As a leader yourself, you understand that as well as I. You may not be afraid of death, but you are a survivor. You are even arrogant enough to attempt bartering with your betters. I respect that. But I am the future of Tyr, Rokan, and without me, you have no future. Observe."

Timor reached out casually, and mumbling a quick spell, he brought his fingers and thumb together, as if squeezing something between them.

Rokan felt his throat constrict. He grabbed his neck and tried to cry out, but nothing except a feeble croak escaped his lips. He could not speak. All he could manage was a rasping, grunting sort of sound.

"Imagine your future, Rokan," Timor said. "Deprived of speech, your face a horrid ruin, you would be reduced to begging in the streets. Sitting there and croaking like a misshapen lizard, hoping some passer-by will not be too repelled by your appearance to pity you and drop a measly ceramic in your palm. There are worse punishments than death, Rokan. I could simply leave you like this, and let you live."

He pulled his fingers apart, and Rokan gasped for breath and broke into a fit of coughing.

"I think we understand each other, do we not?" asked Timor softly.

"Yes, my lord," said Rokan, finding his voice again.

"Excellent," said Timor with a faint smile. He spoke to his templars. "Take this man downstairs and see that he is well fed and rested. Prepare a room for him in the servants' quarters. He will require weapons. I am sure he is best qualified to tell you what he needs." He turned to Rokan. "They will see you to your quarters. Remain there until I send for you. And think about the elfling, Sorak. Your downfall was his doing. His will be yours."

As the templars took Rokan away, Timor poured himself some more wine. He was beginning to feel warm and satisfied inside. Things were progressing nicely, he thought. Very nicely, indeed.

TEN

Sorak watched the dealer shuffle the cards and pass them to the man next to him. The wine merchant cut the cards and passed them back to the dealer, a caravan trader from Altaruk. There were five men around the table, not counting Sorak. And one of them was cheating.

Sorak picked up his cards, fanned them out, and glanced at them.

The ante was ten silvers. As soon as everyone had put his coins into the iron cauldron, the wine merchant discarded three cards, and the dealer laid three new ones on the table before him. The wine merchant picked them up and slipped them into his hand. His jowly, florid face betrayed nothing.

The young, dark-haired noble took two. The burly beast trader took three. Sorak stood pat, and the balding ceramics merchant took two.

"Dealer takes two," the caravan trader said, dealing himself two cards.

The wine merchant opened with ten silvers.

"I will match your ten silvers and raise them ten," said the dark-haired noble.

"That's twenty to you," the dealer said to the beast trader. The brawny man grunted and looked at his cards once more. "I'm in," he said, counting out twenty silver coins and tossing them into the black cauldron at the center of the table.

"I will raise another twenty," said Sorak without looking at his cards. He dropped the coins into the pot.

"Too rich for me," said the ceramics merchant, folding his cards and putting them facedown on the table.

"I will match your twenty," said the caravan trader, his eyes meeting Sorak's with a level stare, "and raise it twenty more." The wine merchant folded. The beast trader and the dark-haired noble stayed in, as did Sorak.

"Call," said Sorak.

The caravan trader smiled as he laid his cards down faceup on the table. "Weep long, my friends," he said, leaning back smugly in his chair. He had a three and four sorcerers. The beast trader swore softly and threw down his cards.

"That beats me," said the noble with a sigh, as the caravan trader smiled and reached for the pot.

"Four dragons," said Sorak. He laid his cards down. The caravan trader jumped to his feet, sending his chair crashing to the floor.

"Impossible!" he shouted.

"Why?" asked Sorak, calmly gazing up at him.

The other players exchanged nervous glances.

"Indeed," the noble said. "Why?"

"He slipped it out of his sleeve!" the caravan trader said in an ugly and accusatory tone.

"No, in fact, I slipped it out of the top of your left boot," said Sorak.

The caravan trader's eyes grew wide and involuntarily, darted down toward his high, over-the-knee boot.

"The cards you discarded were a six of cups and a two of wands," said Sorak. "The cards you drew were a dragon of swords and a four of pentacles. That was how you knew it was impossible for me to have four dragons, because the dragon of swords and the four of pentacles were in the top of your left boot, where you concealed them when you made the switch."

"Liar!" shouted the dealer.

Two of the half-giant guards quietly came up behind him.

Sorak glanced at the other players. "If you look inside the top of his left boot, you will find the four of pentacles still hidden there. And inside the top of his right boot, you will find two sorcerers. He began with four, one of each suit."

"I think we had better check those boots," the young noble said with a hard look at the caravan trader.

The two half-giants came up behind the caravan trader to grab his arms, but the man moved too quickly for them. He drove his elbow hard into the solar plexus of one half-giant, forcing the wind out of him, and he brought his bootheel down sharply on the instep of the other. As the half-giant cried out in pain, the caravan trader drove a fist into his groin. He had moved so quickly, it had taken no more than an instant, and even as other guards moved in from the across the room, the trader's iron sword sang free of its scabbard.

Sorak's own hand darted for his sword hilt, but as his fingers closed around it, he suddenly felt himself falling away. A new presence surged to the fore within him, and Sorak felt the dizzying sensation of spinning away into the darkness. An icy chill suffused his body as the Shade stormed up from the recesses of his subconscious mind.

As the caravan trader brought his blade down with a snarl, aiming a devastating cut at Sorak's head, the Shade drew Galdra with lightning speed and parried the blow. The iron blade struck the elven steel with a ringing tone and shattered as if it had been made of glass. The trader gaped in astonishment, but recovered quickly and kicked the table over, sending cards and coins and goblets flying as the round table fell over on its side, making an effective shield between him and Sorak. The Shade raised Galdra and brought it down in a sweeping, overhead blow, slicing the entire table in half as if the hard and heavy agafari wood were no more substantial than a piece of cheese.

The caravan trader bolted, but found his way blocked at the door by a squad of armed half-giant and half-elf guards. He swore and turned back toward Sorak.

"Die, half-breed!" he shouted, drawing an obsidian dagger and hurling it at Sorak.

The Shade abruptly ducked back under and the dagger stopped, frozen in midair mere inches from Sorak's chest as the Guardian came to the fore. Sorak's eyes glittered as the dagger slowly turned end over end in midair, its point aiming back toward the caravan trader. The man's jaw dropped in astonishment, and then his amazement turned to panic as the dagger took off toward him like an angry hornet. He turned and tried to run, but the blade buried itself to the hilt between his shoulder blades, and he fell to the floor, sliding across the tile with his momentum. He crashed into a table, knocking it over, and lay there in a tangled, lifeless heap.

There was utter silence in the gaming hall, and then the patrons broke into an undertone of murmuring. Sorak walked over to where the cardsharp's body lay and nudged it with his foot. Then he bent down and pulled a card out of the top of the dead man's boot. It was the four of pentacles. He brought the card over to the other players and showed it to them.

"You may divide the pot amongst yourselves," he said, "according to how much each of you put in. As for the cardsharp's share, you may split that up in equal shares." He turned and scaled the card back toward the body. It landed on the cardsharp's chest. "Cheats are not tolerated in this house," he added. "You may take my share of the pot and divide it among you, by way of an apology for your inconvenience." He signaled one of the serving girls. "Please bring these gentlemen a drink on me," he said.

"Thank you," said the wine merchant with a nervous gulp.

The young nobleman stared down at the pieces of the table, then turned his gaze toward Sorak's sword. "That table was solid agafari wood!" he said, with disbelief. "And you cut it clean in two!"

"My blade is steel, and it has a keen edge," said Sorak.

"Keen enough to cause an iron sword to shatter?" said the beast trader. "Not even a steel blade could do that. But one that is enchanted could."

Sorak sheathed his sword and said nothing.

"Who are you?" asked the beast trader.

"My name is Sorak."

"Yes, so you said when we began to play," the beast trader replied. "But *what* are you?"

Sorak gazed at him. "An elfling."

The beast trader shook his head. "That was not what I meant."

Before Sorak could reply, one of the half-elf guards came up and tapped him on the shoulder. "The lady would like to see you," he said softly.

Sorak glanced up toward the second floor, and saw Krysta looking down at him through the beaded curtain of her office. He nodded and headed toward the stairs. Behind him, the patrons broke into excited conversation about what they had just witnessed.

The door was already open when he came down the hall. The half-elves in the antechamber gazed at him with respectful silence. He went through the curtained archway into Krysta's office. She stood behind her desk, waiting for him.

"I am sorry for the damage," he began.

"Never mind that," Krysta said, coming around the desk. "Let me see your sword."

He frowned. "My sword?"

"Please."

He drew it from its scabbard.

"Elven steel," she said softly. "Please . . . turn it so I may see the flat of the blade."

He did as she asked and heard her sharp intake of breath as she read the inscription on the blade. "*Galdra!*" she said in a voice barely above a whisper. She looked up at him, eyes wide and awestruck. "I never dreamed . . . " she began. "Why didn't you tell me?"

"My lady . . . " said one of the half-elf guards, parting the curtain behind them. "Is it true?"

"It's true," she said, gazing at Sorak with an expression of astonishment.

The guard stared at Sorak, then he came into the room, followed by the others.

"What is this?" Sorak said. "Is *what* true?"

"You carry Galdra, sword of the ancient elven kings," said Krysta. "The blade that nothing can withstand. Could the old myth possibly be true?"

"What myth?"

"The one that every elf thinks a mere wives' tale. 'One day, there will appear a champion, a new king to bring the sundered tribes together, and by Galdra you shall know him.' Even half-breed elves raised in the city know the legend, though none would believe it. No one has seen the sword for a thousand years."

"But I am no king," said Sorak. "This blade was a gift to me from the high mistress of the villichi, into whose care it was given."

"But she gave it to you," said Krysta.

"But . . . surely, that does not make me a king," protested Sorak.

"It makes you the champion of which the myth spoke," Krysta replied. "Galdra's power would never serve one who was not worthy to bear it." She shook her head. "I'm not sure I myself believe, but if I had but known, I might not have been so insolent."

Sorak turned toward the half-elf guards, who were staring at him in awe. "This is absurd. Please, get out, all of you. Get out, I said!"

They turned in a jumbled mass and backed out the door.

"When word of this spreads," said Krysta, "every male and female in the city with elven blood running through their veins will begin to wonder about you, Sorak. Some will want to make you what you wouldn't be. Others to steal your fabled blade. And if the nomad tribes out in the desert hear of it—"

"Now wait," said Sorak. "Merely because some sort of myth has grown up around a sword does not mean I am the fulfillment of it. I did not come here to assume some mantle of authority. And if I am to be anybody's champion, then I shall fight for the Sage."

"What of the myth?" asked Krysta, somewhat amused.

"For the last time, I am no king!" protested Sorak. "I am not even a full-blooded elf! The line of elven kings died out with Alaron. I do not even know who my parents were."

"And yet you know Alaron's name," said Krysta.

"Only because I heard the story from a pyreen elder," Sorak said with exasperation, "just as you have heard this bit of folklore. Perhaps this may have been his sword, but the mere fact of its possession doesn't make me Alaron's heir. What if some human were to steal it from me? Would that make a human king of all the elves? If it was yours, would the title fall to you?"

"Let me hold it for a moment," Krysta said, extending her hand.

He sighed. "As you wish," he said, handing her the sword.

Her fingers closed around its hilt. She bit her lower lip as she held it, gazing down at the blade as if it were a holy thing, and then she took a deep breath, spun around, and brought it down with all her might in an overhand blow upon her desk. The blade bit deep into the wood and lodged there.

"Gith's blood!" said Sorak. "What are you doing?"

She grunted as she struggled to pull it free, and on the third try, she finally managed it. "I once fought in the arena," she said. "I am not some weak female who cannot handle a blade. My guards will attest that not one of them could have struck a stronger blow. Now you try."

"What is the point in scarring your desk any further?" Sorak asked.

"Humor me."

He shook his head, took back the sword, and swung hard at the desk. The heavy desk buckled in the center and collapsed as the blade cut it completely in two.

"According to the legend, the blade's enchantment will not serve anyone else," said Krysta, "and if it were to fall into the hands of a defiler, it would shatter. The enchantment will serve only the champion, because his faith is true. Perhaps you are that champion. You *are* the rightful king."

"But I have said that I am not a king!" said Sorak. "I do not believe it! Where, then, is my faith?"

"In the task that you have set yourself, and the course that you must follow," Krysta replied. "The myth speaks of that, as well."

"It does?"

"It says, 'Those who believe in the champion shall hail him, but he shall deny the crown, for the elves have fallen into decadence. They must first rise above their downfall and deserve their king before he will accept them, for like Galdra, sword of the elven kings, the scattered tribes must likewise become strong in spirit and be forged anew in faith, before they can be true in temper.' Whether you like it or not, you fulfill all the conditions of the myth."

"I am no king," Sorak said irately. "I am Sorak, and whatever any myth may purport, I have no intention of ever being a king or wearing any crown."

Krysta smiled. "As you wish," she said. "But you may find it thrust upon you just the same. If you do not want me to speak of this, then I shall not, but you cannot deny your fate."

"Whatever my fate may be," said Sorak, "for the moment, it is bound up in my quest for the Sage. You said that you would make inquiries about the Veiled Alliance."

"And so I have," she replied. "I am told that members of the Veiled Alliance can be found almost anywhere, but a good place to make contact is the Drunken Giant wineshop. It is not far from here. But you must be discreet. Do not make any inquiries aloud. The signal that one wishes contact is to pass your hand over the lower part of your face, as if to indicate a veil. If any Alliance member is present, you will be watched and followed, and someone will make contact with you."

"The Drunken Giant wineshop," Sorak said. "Where can I find it?"

"I will have my guards take you," Krysta said.

"No, I would prefer to go alone," said Sorak. "They will probably be suspicious of me as it is. If I went with an escort, it would only make things worse. I want to draw these people out, not scare them off."

"I will draw you a map," said Krysta, turning toward her desk. She stared at the two halves of the desk for a moment. Everything that was on top of it had scattered on the floor. "On second thought," she said, "perhaps I should just give you directions."

After Sorak had left, her guard captain returned to her and said uncertainly, "What should we do? Should we follow him?"

She shook her head. "I do not think he would like that."

"But if any harm should come to him. . ."

"Then the myth is false," she said, "just as we always thought it was." She stared down at what was left of her desk. "Besides, I would hate to be the one who tried to harm him, wouldn't you?"

* * * * *

A group of beggars sat against a wall across the street from the Crystal Spider. Despite the overhanging awning, all six of them were bundled up in their filthy, threadbare, hooded cloaks, huddling together against the evening chill. As Sorak came out of the gaming house, one of them nudged his companions.

"There he is," he said.

Rokan raised his head and pulled his hood back slightly on one side so he get a better look with his one good eye. "Are you sure that's him?"

The templar who had nudged him nodded, but kept his gaze averted. He didn't want to look at the hideously scarred marauder any more than was absolutely necessary. "I've been watching him, haven't I?" the templar said irritably. He disliked having to deal with scum. The sooner this was over, the better he would like it. "Go, get him! He is alone."

"I will make my move when I am ready, templar," Rokan replied curtly. "This half-breed has cost me much. I do not want him to die too quickly."

"But he is getting away!"

"Calm yourself," said Rokan. "We shall follow him, but at a discreet distance. I will pick the time, and the place."

After giving Sorak a good head start, Rokan nodded to the others, and they rose as one, following in the direction Sorak had gone. The templar started to hurry after him, but Rokan grabbed him by his cloak and yanked him back. "Where do you think you're going?" he asked.

"Why, with you, to see you kill the elfling, of course," the templar said.

"Of course, nothing," Rokan said, shoving him back hard enough to make him land on his rump in the middle of the street. "Stay here and keep out of the damn way."

"But I am to watch . . ."

Rokan turned without another word and stalked
off with his men. The templar picked himself up out
of the dirt and glared at Rokan's back with loathing.
There had been a time when no one would have
dared to treat him that way. However, those days
were gone. Kalak was dead, and the templars had lost
their magic. In Kalak's time, the templar had struck
fear into the hearts of anyone he even looked at
harshly. Now he knew enough to be afraid of a man
like Rokan, and the feeling did not sit well in the pit
of his stomach. He remained behind, watching as the
marauders disappeared down the street. He nervously moistened his lips. Timor would not like it,
but Timor was not here, and Rokan was.

One of the marauders sidled up to Rokan as they
followed Sorak at a distance. "What happens after we
kill the half-breed?"

"Then the job is finished, and you will be free to
go," Rokan replied, keeping Sorak in sight as they followed him through the twisting streets.

"How do we know we can trust this Timor?"

"You don't," said Rokan. "But never fear, Vorlak.
He is not interested in you. We are insignificant in his
scheme of things. He has a much bigger game to play.
We are but tools he will use briefly to serve his immediate needs, and then he will cease to be concerned
with us."

"This was a bad venture all around," grumbled
Vorlak. "We never should have come here to begin
with."

"We were well paid."

"Not nearly well enough to compensate us for
what has happened," Vorlak replied sourly. "Nor
shall we receive the balance of our payment from our
Nibenese patron now that we have been exposed as

spies. The caravan for Altaruk has already left the city, and they have a full day's head start. Even if we managed to secure a string of swift crodlu, which we cannot, we would never reach the others in time to warn them. They shall attack the caravan as planned, and ride straight into a trap."

"You think I don't know that?" Rokan replied in a surly tone. "What do you expect me to do?"

"There is nothing to be done," said Gavik, one of the other marauders. "It is finished. Even if some of our comrades should manage to escape, they will still have to cross the tablelands, and if the desert does not kill them, what is there for them to return to? What is there for any of us to return to?"

"We still have our camp in the Mekillot Mountains," Rokan said, "and we still have our women, and the men who did not come on the journey."

"A mere handful," Gavik said. "Not even enough to ambush a small caravan."

"I began with less than that," said Rokan, "and I can start again. Nothing is finished."

"Then you do not plan to take this templar's offer and remain here in his service?" Vorlak asked.

"Rokan serves no one but Rokan," the bandit leader said, his voice practically a growl.

"But . . . what of your face?" asked Gavik. "You said the templar promised to heal your wounds if you served him faithfully."

"An empty promise," Rokan said bitterly, "which I am sure he never intended to keep. He thinks it has given him a hold on me. He shall find he is mistaken."

"Then . . . why bother with this elfling?" another marauder asked. "Why not simply accept our losses and leave the city now?"

"Devak is right," said Tigan, the fifth man of the group. "Let us quit this city now, before we run afoul of the city guard or treachery from the templars."

"When this is finished, the rest of you can do whatever you damn well please," said Rokan. "If you want out, then go suffocate in the Sea of Silt for all I care. But the elfling is going to pay for what he has done. And when I am finished with him, I am going to go back and kill that templar."

"Go up against a defiler?" Devak said. "Not I."

"Nor I," said Gavik. "You know better than any of us what Timor can do, and yet you still think you can kill him?"

"He will think I am his man, held in thrall by his promise to heal my face and make me rich," said Rokan. "I will act the part of his lackey, and when the moment comes, I will snap his neck or drive a blade into his ribs."

"Leave me out of it," said Vorlak. "I have had enough of this whole thing. I am done with it."

"You will be done with it after the elfling is dead, and not before!" said Rokan, grabbing him by the throat. "After that, you can all rot for all I care!"

"All right," said Vorlak in a constricted voice. "The elfling dies. But I want no part of trying to kill the templar."

"None of us do," said Gavik.

"Suit yourselves," said Rokan, releasing Vorlak and continuing on Sorak's trail. He was almost out of sight now, and they had to quicken their pace to close the distance. The streets had become very dark and almost completely deserted. Lamplight burned in only a few of the buildings. Sorak turned down another street, and they hurried to catch up with him. As they came to the corner, they saw that he had entered a narrow, winding street that ended in a *cul de sac*. There were several alleyways leading off to either side, between the tightly clustered buildings. It was a perfect place for an ambush.

"Let's get it over with," said Vorlak, moving forward and reaching for his blade.

"Wait," said Rokan, grabbing his arm. Sorak had gone into a wineshop, the only building on the street that still had lights burning within. Several people came out as he went in. The marauders watched quietly as they passed.

"We shall wait until he comes out," Rokan said. "Vorlak, you and Tigan get ready in that alley over there." He pointed to the dark and refuse-strewn alleyway across the narrow street. "Devak, you and Gavik take your posts in the alley on the other side. I will wait in the street, beside the entrance to the wineshop, and pretend to be a drunk. When he comes out, I'll let him pass and then come up behind him while the rest of you come out and cut him off."

"What if he should not come out alone?" said Tigan. "What if anyone is with him?"

"Then it will be their hard luck," said Rokan.

* * * * *

Sorak paused briefly outside the entrance of the wineshop. It was an aging, two-story building of plastered, sun-baked brick, and like many of the buildings in the area, much of the plaster had worn or flaked away, exposing the bricks and mortar beneath. The entrance was not protected by an overhang. A short flight of wooden steps led to an arched, recessed opening with a heavy, studded wooden door. Above the door hung a wooden sign on which was the image

of a drunken giant, rather inexpertly painted. There
were two windows in the wall on either side of the
door, now tightly shuttered against the night chill and
the swarms of nocturnal bugs.

A couple of patrons came out of the wineshop and
passed by Sorak. They were walking a bit unsteadily.
As they came out, Sorak heard shouts and laughter
coming from inside the shop. He went up the steps
and through the doorway.

He paused a moment within the alcove and looked
around. The shop was laid out in a long, open rectan-
gle, with battered wooden tables and benches to the
left and a long bar to the right. Behind the bar were
crude, dusty wooden wine racks holding a vast array
of bottles. A few oil lamps provided illumination in
the bar area. Large, square candles, thick enough to
stand by themselves, stood in the center of each table,
dripping wax onto the tabletops. The interior walls,
as those on the outside, were made of plastered brick,
with the plaster flaking off in many places. The wood-
planked floor was old and stained.

The atmosphere was a far cry from the elegance of
Krysta's dining room, and the patrons seemed to fit
the atmosphere. It was a rough, surly-looking crowd,
and Sorak noticed a couple of brawny half-giants at
each end of the bar, keeping an eye on the customers.
Each of them had a club within easy reach, and several obsidian-bladed knives tucked into his belt. The
one nearer the door gave Sorak an appraising glance
as he came in. His gaze lingered for a moment on the
sword, its hilt just visible beneath Sorak's open cloak.

A number of people looked up at him as he came
in. Sorak paused and glanced around, then passed his
hand over his mouth, as if rubbing his chin absently.
If anyone recognized the signal, they gave no sign of

it. He walked up to the bar.

"What'll it be, stranger?" asked the bartender, casually wiping down the bar in front of him with a dirty rag.

"Could I have some water, please?"

"Water?" said the bartender, raising his bushy eyebrows. "This is a wineshop, friend. If you want water, go drink from a well. I've got a business to run here."

"Very well," said Sorak. "I will have some wine, then."

The bartender rolled his eyes. He indicated the racks of bottles behind him. "I've got all kinds of wine," he said. "What kind would you like?"

"Any kind," said Sorak.

"You have no preference?"

"It makes no difference," Sorak said.

The bartender sighed with exasperation. "Well, would you like a cheap wine, a moderately priced wine, or an expensive wine?"

"Whatever this will buy me," Sorak said, laying down a couple of silver pieces.

"That will buy you just about anything you like in here," the bartender said, sweeping up the coins with a smooth, well-practiced motion. He set a goblet down in front of Sorak and then picked up a small footstool, moved a bit farther down the bar, and climbed up to reach one of the bottles in the top rack. He blew a layer of dust off the bottle, opened it, and set it down in front of Sorak.

"Was that enough for a whole bottle?" Sorak asked.

The bartender chuckled. "Friend, that was enough for most people to drink in here all night and then some. I don't know where you're from, and I don't really care, but you're obviously new here in the city. Take some friendly advice: get yourself a better idea of what things cost. I could've robbed you blind just now."

"It is good to meet an honest man," said Sorak.

"Well, it hasn't made me any richer," said the bartender.

"Will you have a drink with me?"

"Don't mind if I do." The bartender got himself a goblet and poured for himself and Sorak. "What shall we drink to?"

Sorak passed his hand over the lower part of his face. "How about new alliances?"

As he spoke, Sorak ducked under and the Guardian came to the fore.

The bartender shrugged. "Suits me." He clinked his goblet against Sorak's and drank. "My name is Trag."

"Sorak," said the Guardian. Then, speaking internally to Sorak and the others, she said, "*He knows the sign, but he is wary.*"

Trag saw that Sorak set his goblet back down without drinking from it. He frowned. "You propose a toast, then you don't drink?"

"I don't like wine."

Trag rolled his eyes. "Well then, why in thunder did you buy one of my most expensive bottles?"

"Because you did not have water, and as you said, you have a business to run."

Trag laughed. "You're a strange sort, my friend. You come to a wineshop, but you do not want wine. You buy my most expensive vintage, but you do not even condescend to try it. Still, customers who pay as well as you do are entitled to their eccentricities."

The Guardian probed his mind as he spoke. He knew about the Veiled Alliance, and he had caught Sorak's not-so-thinly veiled remark, but he was not part of the underground group and had no connection with it other than knowing that his wineshop was a frequent contact point for them. Secretly, he was in sympathy with the aims of the Alliance, but they had purposely kept him ignorant of their affairs so that he could not betray them to the templars if he were arrested and brought in for questioning.

"This man cannot help us," Eyron said. *"We are wasting our time with him."*

"Time is never wasted," Sorak replied. *"It simply passes. Trag recognized the sign. Someone else may have recognized it as well."*

"You seem to get an interesting crowd here," said the Guardian.

Trag shrugged. "I open late and close down late. That attracts the night people."

"The night people?"

"Those who sleep during the day and remain awake all night," said Trag. He smiled. "I can tell that you're not city bred. In the outlands, people rise with the sun and go to bed when it sets. In a city, things are different. A city never sleeps. I like the night, myself. It's cooler, and darkness suits my temperament. And night people tend to be more interesting. I get all kinds in here."

"What kinds do you mean?" the Guardian asked.

"Oh, just about any kind you can imagine," Trag replied, "except what they call the better class of people. Tramps, thieves, traders down on their luck, common laborers, bards. . . . A small wineshop such as this can hardly compete with places like the Crystal Spider. You will find no dancing girls or high stakes games in a place like this. Most of my customers can barely afford a goblet of wine to keep them warm. Beggars often come in to get out of the chill night air. I don't mind, so long as they spend a

ceramic or two. Some will buy themselves a goblet of
cheap wine and nurse it for as long as possible, others
will spend every ceramic they've managed to beg
during the day and drink themselves insensible.
Times are hard in Tyr these days, and when times are
hard, people like to drink." He shrugged. "Come to
think of it, people always like to drink. It makes the
world seem less oppressive for a while. Except for
you, apparently. You did not come here to drink, so
what's your reason?"

"No reason in particular," the Guardian replied. "I
am new in the city, and I heard this might be a good
place to make some interesting contacts."

"Really? Who did you hear it from?"

"*He is distrustful*," said the Guardian. "*He thinks we
might be an agent of the templars.*"

"*But if he knows nothing, what reason should he have to
be concerned?*" asked Eyron.

"*I'm getting bored*," Kivara said.

"*Be quiet, Kivara*," Sorak said, irritably. He did not
need to deal with Kivara's childlike impatience at
such a moment.

"Oh, I heard it mentioned somewhere," the
Guardian replied aloud.

"And where was that?" asked Trag casually, taking
another drink.

"*He is suspicious because we are not drinking, and
because someone has been in here recently, asking about the
Veiled Alliance*," the Guardian said, abruptly picking
up the thought from Trag's mind. "*The man was obvious and clumsy . . . wait. I see his image as he thinks of
him. . . . It was the marauder.*"

"*Digon?*"

"In the market, I think," the Guardian replied to
Trag's question. "Yes, it must have been one of the

traders in the market."

"*Trag did not seem to recognize my name,*" said Sorak.

"No," the Guardian replied. "*He has not heard it before.*"

"*Then Digon must not have mentioned it when he came here to make inquiries,*" said Sorak. "*But at least he did as I bid him.*"

"*If he was obvious and clumsy, then he did not do you any favors,*" Eyron replied. "*This man Trag is clearly on his guard.*"

"What sort of . . . contacts were you interested in making?" Trag asked, watching him intently.

"*He is thinking that if we make our intent any more clear, he will ask us to leave,*" the Guardian said. "*He will say that the Alliance is almost a criminal organization, and that he knows nothing of such things, nor does he wish to know, for he obeys the law.*"

"*We have made this man uneasy,*" Sorak said. "*Perhaps it would be best for us to leave.*"

"*Good! I want to leave,*" Kivara said. "*This place is dull. I want to go back to the Crystal Spider and play some more games.*"

"I had nothing specific in mind," said Sorak, coming to the fore again. "I merely sought a drink of water and a bit of friendly conversation. However, as you seem to have no water, and there is little point to paying for wine I do not drink, perhaps I had best be on my way. It is getting late, in any case, and I am not, as you have correctly deduced, accustomed to staying up all night." He put down another silver coin. "Thank you for your company."

Trag pushed the coin back across the bar, toward Sorak. "Keep it," he said. "You already paid more than enough for the wine you did not drink, and there is no charge for conversation."

Sorak picked up the coin, not wishing to insult the man by offering it again. "Thank you."

"Come again."

As Sorak turned away from the bar, he once more passed his hand over the lower part of his face, then headed toward the door. He had no idea if anyone recognized the sign or not.

"You think anyone saw?" asked Eyron as Sorak stepped into the street and headed back the way he had come.

"If they did, I saw no reaction," Sorak replied, allowing the Ranger to handle the task of getting them back through the dark and winding streets to the Crystal Spider. Lyric whistled softly as they walked. Kivara sulked.

"That wasn't any fun," she complained.

"It was not meant to be fun, Kivara," the Guardian replied. *"We have a task to perform. If you cannot contribute, then at least keep silent."*

"Why do I always have to keep silent? I never get to come out anymore. It isn't fair."

"Kivara, please," said Sorak. "You will get your chance to come out and have some fun, I promise. But not now."

"We are being followed," said the Watcher, breaking her accustomed silence.

"Who?" asked Sorak. *"I cannot see."*

"There was a man sitting in the street, leaning back against the building wall when we came out of the wineshop," said the Guardian. *"He appeared to be drunk."*

"And now he's following us?" said Sorak. "Interesting. We may have made contact after all. We shall continue on as if we do not know we are being followed. Let him make the first move."

* * * * *

In the darkness of the alleyway, Vorlak and Tigan waited patiently. Vorlak stood by the corner of the building, peering out into the street.

"Do you see anything yet?" asked Tigan anxiously.

"The elfling's coming. And Rokan's right behind him. Get ready."

They both drew their weapons.

"Take him fast," said Tigan. "Remember what the templar said. The elfling's dangerous."

"He's already dead," said Vorlak, stepping away from the wall.

There was a whoosh as something whistled through the air, followed by a soft thud as something fell to the ground behind Vorlak and rolled to touch his foot.

Vorlak glanced down. "Quiet, you fool! You want to . . . " His voice trailed off as he saw what had rolled up against his foot. It was Tigan's head.

He gasped and spun around just in time to catch a brief glimpse of a dark, shadowy figure standing behind him, and the last thing he felt was the impact of the sword plunging through his chest.

* * * * *

Rokan tensed and swore softly under his breath. The elfling had reached the first alleyway. Where were Vorlak and Tigan? They should be rushing out to the attack. If those two had fallen asleep in there, he would slit their throats. His hand went to his own weapon, and then he saw Devak and Gavik come rushing out from the opposite alleyway, their weapons already in their hands. . . .

What happened next occurred so quickly he almost couldn't follow it. The elfling moved with blinding

speed. His sword seemed to suddenly appear in his
hands. Devak swung his blade, the elfling parried,
holding his sword in both hands, and Devak's blade
shattered. It simply burst apart, as if it had exploded.
In one smooth motion, the elfling brought his blade
down from the high parry at an angle, and Devak was
sliced cleanly through from the shoulder to the hip.
He screamed as his body fell in two sections to the
street. Without pausing, the elfling brought his blade
up once again, parrying Gavik's blow, and the same
thing happened. Gavik's blade broke on the elfling's
sword, erupting with a shower of sparks, and then
Gavik was literally cleaved in two, from head to
groin.

Rokan's hand darted toward his sword hilt, and it
was only that motion that saved his life. In reaching
for his sword, he had turned slightly so that the crossbow bolt that came whistling out of nowhere struck
him in the shoulder instead of in the heart. He gasped,
stumbled, swore, and then turned and ran back the
way he had come, clutching at the arrow that was
buried in his shoulder.

* * * * *

The Watcher had cried out an internal warning
when the two marauders rushed from the alley, then
Sorak experienced that cold and dizzying, spinning-
away sensation as the Shade came storming up out of
his subconscious like a leviathan out of the depths.
No more than a moment had passed, but it was a
moment Sorak had not witnessed. Now, as the Shade
retreated back to the subconscious depths from which
he came, Sorak stood in the street, staring down at the
grisly remains of his attackers, their blood making

large, dark puddles on the hard-packed ground. For a moment, he felt disoriented, then he heard running footsteps behind him and turned quickly to face the potential threat. However, he caught only a brief glimpse of someone running down the street and ducking into the alleyway behind the Drunken Giant.

"Well, if that was our contact from the Veiled Alliance, then I fear we've scared him off," said Sorak.

"Has it occurred to you that our so-called contacts from the Veiled Alliance might very well be these men, lying here before us in the street?" said Eyron.

"You think so?" Sorak replied. "But why would they attack us?"

"Because we were making inquiries in the wineshop," Eyron said. *"The Guardian sensed Trag was suspicious. If he thought you were an agent from the templars—"*

"No," said the Guardian. *"Trag is not a part of the Alliance, and even if he were, he would not have had time enough to send a message to these men to ambush us. They were already waiting when we came out of the wineshop."*

"That is true," said Sorak. "Besides, the Alliance uses magic. It would make more sense for them to launch a magical attack. These men were armed with swords and knives. The Shade is an efficient killer, but he does not pause to think. If he had left one of these men alive, we would know who sent them and why."

There was the sound of a shutter opening and then closing quickly with a slam. Sorak glanced up and saw several unshuttered windows where people looked down at him. When they saw him look up, they quickly disappeared back inside their rooms.

"We had best not linger," said the Guardian. *"It would prove awkward if the city guard should come upon us."*

"It was self-defense," said Sorak. "But you are

right. There is no point to antagonizing Captain Zalcor. Or the Council of Advisors."

He started walking quickly and purposefully
through the dark, deserted streets, back toward the
Crystal Spider. No one called after him or tried to stop
him. Indeed, had anyone seen how quickly he'd dispatched those men, that would have been discourage-
ment enough, but in the elven market, people had a
tendency to mind their own business, for their own
good.

*"If those men were not from the Alliance, then who were
they, and why did they attack us?"* Eyron asked.

"I do not know. Perhaps they were merely cutthroats, after our money," Sorak suggested.

"They did not have the look of common cutthroats," the
Guardian replied, *"and they were armed with iron
blades."*

*"If they were not Alliance members or cutthroats, then
whom does that leave?"* asked Eyron.

"Soldiers?" Lyric said.

Sorak stopped. "Soldiers?"

"Soldiers are well armed, after all," said Lyric, and
then promptly lost interest in the discussion and
started whistling a jaunty tune.

Soldiers, Sorak thought. Indeed, those men could
have been soldiers in disguise. And that, of course,
implied that they had been sent by the council, or perhaps the templars. But why would they want him
dead? To avoid paying him a reward for his information? Surely, that was much too petty a reason. There
had to be some other explanation. If, in fact, they truly
were soldiers. Sorak had no proof of that, though it
suddenly seemed the most likely possibility. And that
would explain their being disguised as beggars. It
would not do for the new government to have sol-

diers of the city guard seen assassinating someone in the streets. Krysta had cautioned him about the templars. But what did the templars have to fear from him?

"*The templars once served the defiler king,*" said Eyron. "*Perhaps they have not truly forsaken their old ways.*"

"But it is said the templars lost their magic when Kalak was slain," said Sorak. "And defiler magic is outlawed in the city."

"*Outlawed does not mean eliminated,*" Eyron reminded him. "*Under Kalak, the templars had a great deal more power. They were once the law in Tyr. Now the council has superseded them. They may not be satisfied with their new, diminished role.*"

It made sense, Sorak thought. But it still did not explain why the templars would see him as a threat. Unless, of course, they knew that he was seeking the avangion. However, he had not mentioned that to anyone but Rikus and Krysta, and he knew neither of them would share that knowledge with the templars.

Somehow, without intending to, he had stumbled into some sort of an intrigue. The balance of power in Tyr was teetering precariously, and without really understanding how or why, he found himself at the fulcrum of that balance point. What, exactly, was the nature of his involvement? The question kept gnawing at him as he made his way back to the gaming house, and he was so preoccupied with his thoughts that he did not notice the tattered beggar who was following him discreetly, at a distance.

* * * * *

The templar made certain he kept as much distance as possible between himself and the elfling, just enough to keep him in sight. After what he had just seen, he had no intention of getting any closer. He had followed Rokan and the others, for it was his responsibility to report back to Timor, and much as he feared Rokan, he feared Timor even more.

He dreaded having to go back to Timor and tell him what had happened, but he knew that he would have no choice. He would put the blame on Rokan. The marauder and his underlings had bungled it. Watching from the shadows at the far end of the street, the templar had seen two of the marauders rush out at the elfling, and he had seen the devastating, terrifying swiftness with which the elfling had dealt with them. He had seen Rokan, ready to join the fray, stumble in the street, though he had not seen the crossbow bolt that struck the marauder leader. He had simply assumed that Rokan had stumbled as a result of trying to stop his forward momentum when he saw what the elfling had done to his men. The coward had turned and fled, and the other two marauders had never even come out of their hiding place in the alleyway. Doubtless, thought the templar, they had fled, as well. That was what came of using scum like that on such a job, he thought. They were criminals, and criminals could not be trusted. But the elfling. . .

The templar had withdrawn deep into the shadows when the elfling passed, and he had heard the elfling talking to himself—a disjointed conversation, as if he were speaking with invisible spirits. The templar had heard nothing but the elfling's voice, but the elfling seemed to be speaking to someone and giving answers. The templar had shuddered when he heard that. The elfling was insane, or else he was inhabited by spirits. Either way, he was incredibly dangerous.

The templar had never seen anyone move so quickly, and he had never seen anything like the way the marauders' blades had shattered on the elfling's sword. Those had been iron blades! Iron simply did not shatter like that. And that sword! Even in the darkness, the templar had seen the glittering blade, and it was *steel*! Shaped like no sword he had ever seen before. A steel blade like that would be worth a fortune, and it was no ordinary steel, at that. Iron did not break on ordinary steel. The templar knew magic when he saw it.

He followed the elfling and watched him go back into the gaming house, then he made his way back to the templars' quarter. It was very late, and Timor would undoubtedly be asleep at this hour. He did not relish the thought of having to wake the senior templar, but this new information would not wait, and Timor would want to know of it at once. The templar did not know who this elfling was or what he intended, but he was clearly someone very extraordinary. And he had met in secret with Councilman Rikus at the gaming house.

This meant trouble, certain trouble for the templars and for Timor's plan. Perhaps Timor had underestimated Rikus and Sadira. In particular, perhaps he had underestimated Sadira. How much did they really know about the sorceress? She had risen from obscurity to become the most powerful woman in Tyr, and though she had forsworn her former defiler ways, she possessed powerful magic. What had she done to accumulate such power? And what forces had she been in contact with while she had been away from Tyr?

It was rumored that she had traveled with the Sun Runners, one of the most fearsome of the elf tribes.

And now, out of nowhere, an elfling appears in the city, posing as a simple herdsman who has inadvertently discovered a plot to infiltrate Nibenese spies into Tyr. And this self-proclaimed "herdsman" has a clandestine meeting with Sadira's pet mul, Rikus, and then suddenly he is working at the Crystal Spider, whose owner is half-elf. Suddenly, in the middle of the night, he goes to a wineshop known to be a contact point for the Veiled Alliance, and when attacked, he demonstrates a skill for fighting that none of the soldiers of the city guard could hope to match, and with an enchanted blade, at that.

No, thought the templar, there are too many coincidences here. Rikus and Sadira are clearly plotting something, and this elfling is the key to it. Killing him had seemed such a simple thing. Well, now he has demonstrated that it won't be so simple. Brute force won't get the job done.

It will take magic.

ELEVEN

The gatekeeper of the Crystal Spider greeted Sorak with a slight, respectful bow when he came in. The entire staff of the gaming house knew him now and treated him with friendliness and courtesy. Nevertheless, the attitude of the gatekeeper seemed different, more than courteous. He had never actually bowed to him before. Sorak ducked under briefly and allowed the Guardian to probe his mind.

"*He knows*," the Guardian said.

Sorak grimaced inwardly. The guards must have talked. That meant everybody on the staff probably knew by now. This nonsense about his being Alaron's heir because he carried Galdra had to stop before it could spread any farther. They didn't want a king, and he didn't want to *be* a king—

"*Someone is lurking in the shadows by that pagafa tree,*" the Watcher said.

Sorak stopped. He was about halfway down the brick-paved path leading through the courtyard to the entrance of the gaming house. The path curved through a garden planted with desert shrubs and wildflowers. Several tall succulents with long spines stood like twisted giants in the courtyard, and small, night-blooming kanna trees swayed gently in the

251

evening breeze, their fragrant white blossoms, closed
during the day, now open to perfume the garden. Just
in front of him was a small, artificial pool, with a foot-
bridge running across it, and to the right of the foot-
bridge stood a thick blue tree, its branches spreading
out to shade the path. As Sorak watched, a cloaked
and hooded figure stepped out from behind the trunk
of the tree and stood on the path before him.

"Greetings, Sorak," said the stranger. The voice was
male. Resonant and deep. It was a mature voice,
relaxed, confident. "You have had a busy night."

"Who are you?" Sorak asked, remaining where he
was. He ducked under so that the Guardian could
probe the stranger.

"I fear that will not avail you," the stranger said. "I
am warded against psionic probes."

"*He is telling the truth,*" the Guardian replied. "*I cannot detect his thoughts.*"

Sorak glanced back toward the gate.

"The gatekeeper can neither see nor hear us," said
the stranger, as if reading his thoughts, though he
obviously only interpreted his backward glance.

"What have you done to him?" asked Sorak.

"Nothing," said the stranger. "I have merely created
a temporary veil around us, so that we may speak un-
disturbed."

"A veil?" said Sorak. "As in the Veiled Alliance?"

"May I approach?"

Sorak nodded, but kept his hand near his sword,
just in case.

"You have nothing to fear from me," the stranger
said. "Unless, of course, you come as an enemy of the
Alliance."

"I come as a friend."

The stranger came closer. "We have been watching

you," he said. Sorak could see that the lower part of his face, beneath his hood, was veiled. "There is little that happens in the city that we do not know about. You have been anxious to make contact with the Alliance. Why?"

"I need to speak with your leaders."

"Indeed," the stranger said, "there are many who would like to do so. What makes you different from all the others?"

"I was raised in the villichi convent. I am sworn to follow the Way of the Druid and the Path of the Preserver."

"The villichi are a female sect. There are no male villichi."

"I did not say I was villichi, merely that I lived among them and was trained by them."

"Why would they accept a male among them? That is not their way."

"Because I possess psionic abilities, and because I was cast out by my tribe and left to die in the desert. A pyreen elder found me and took me to the convent. I was accepted there at her request."

"A pyreen elder, you say? What was this elder's name?"

"Lyra Al'Kali."

The stranger nodded. "The name is known to me. She is one of the oldest of the peace-bringers. And the wishes of a pyreen elder would carry considerable weight with the villichi. Perhaps you are telling me the truth. But you still have not told me why you wish to see our leaders."

"I seek information that will aid me in my quest to find the Sage," said Sorak.

"You have set yourself quite a task," the stranger said. "Many have tried to find the Sage. All have failed. What makes you think you will succeed?"

"Because I must."

"Why?"

"Elder Al'Kali told me that only the Sage could help me learn the truth about my origins. I have no memory of my early childhood, nor of my parents. I do not know where I came from, or what became of them. I do not even know who I truly am."

"And you believe the Sage can help you learn these things? That is all you wish from him?"

"I also wish to serve him," Sorak said. "I believe that in doing so, I may find the purpose that has been lacking in my life."

"I see."

"Can you help me?"

"No. I do not possess the information that you seek. Nor would I give it so easily if I did. However, there are those among us who may be able to help you, but you will first have to prove yourself."

"How can I do that?"

"We shall let you know. We had thought you might be an agent of the templars until they tried to have you killed tonight."

"Then it *was* the templars," Sorak said.

"The men they sent against you were the very spies from Nibenay whom you exposed to the council."

Sorak frowned. "The marauders?" He might have recognized them from the images he had picked up from Digon's mind except that it had been dark, and there had not been much left to recognize after the Shade got through with them.

"One of them ran away," the stranger said. "And you were followed coming back here."

"I was followed?"

"You did not see the beggar trailing you at some

distance?"

"No," Sorak admitted. "I was preoccupied."

"The beggar was a templar," said the stranger. "They have been watching you ever since you appeared before the council. When the templars are on your trail, it is a wise thing to watch your back."

"I am grateful for the warning," Sorak said.

The stranger nodded. "We will speak again," he said.

"How shall I get in touch with you?" asked Sorak.

"When the time is right, we shall contact you," the stranger said.

"Why do the templars wish me dead?" asked Sorak.

"I cannot say," the stranger replied, "unless, perhaps, you have told them of your quest to find the Sage."

"I have told only two people," Sorak replied, "Krysta and Councilman Rikus."

"Rikus has no love for the templars," said the stranger. "He would have no reason to tell them anything. Krysta looks to her own interests first and foremost, but she has wealth enough not to be tempted by any reward the templars might offer for information about you. She also has a strong allegiance to Rikus and would not go against his wishes. Unless you have reason to believe otherwise."

"Krysta would not betray me to the templars," Sorak said.

"Then I cannot account for why they would want you dead," the stranger said. "They clearly perceive you as a threat, but I cannot say why. However, I shall endeavor to discover their motives. The enemy of our enemy is our friend. Sometimes."

"And is this one of those times?"

"Perhaps," the stranger said. "In Kalak's time, alignments were much more clear. These days, however, things are not simple. We shall speak again."

The stranger passed him and went back toward the gate. Sorak watched him go, then turned back toward the entrance to the gaming house. It occurred to him that he should probably thank the man, and he pivoted about to do so, but the path leading back to the gate was suddenly deserted. The stranger had moved quickly. He ran back toward the gate, hoping to catch him.

"The man who just passed by here," Sorak said to the gatekeeper. "Which way did he go?"

The gatekeeper frowned. "What man?"

"The man in the hooded cloak. He passed by you not a moment ago."

The gatekeeper shook his head. "You are mistaken," he said. "No one has passed by here since you came through the gate."

"But he had to have gone past you!" Sorak said. "There is no other way out!"

The puzzled gatekeeper shook his head. "I have not left my post, and no one has passed this way since you came through the gate," he insisted.

"I see," said Sorak slowly. "Well, never mind. I must have been mistaken."

He turned back toward the entrance. Magic, he thought, with a certain amount of trepidation. He knew very little of magic. He had a feeling that his education was about to begin.

* * * * *

Timor glared at the templar who stood, trembling, before him. "You mean to tell me that *five* men, all expert murderers, were unable to dispose of *one* miserable, half-breed peasant?"

"He is no mere peasant, my lord," the templar replied, biting his lower lip in his anxiety. He fervently hoped that Timor would not blame the failure of the brigands on him. "I, myself, saw him cut down two of the marauders with such speed and ferocity that it was breathtaking. Only Rokan escaped him alive. He ran, like a coward."

"That makes three," said Timor. "What of the other two?"

"I found their bodies in the alley where they had hidden, waiting to ambush the elfling. One had been beheaded, and the other killed with a single sword thrust through the heart."

Timor frowned. "But you told me that you saw the elfling come of out the wineshop and walk up the street, as if he were unaware of any ambush."

"That is true, my lord."

"Then who killed the two men in the alley?"

The templar looked puzzled. "I . . . I do not know, my lord. I had assumed the elfling had. . . ."

"How could the elfling have done it if he was in your sight from the time he left the wineshop to the moment he was attacked in the street? When could he have disposed of the two in the alley?"

The templar shook his head. "I do not know, my lord. Perhaps he suspected somehow that the ambush would take place and left the wineshop by the back door, then came up behind the two marauders in the alley and surprised them."

"Then why would he return to the wineshop and come out the front door again? Why invite the ambush?" Timor frowned. "No, it does not make any sense. If you are telling me the truth—"

"I am, my lord, I swear it!"

"Then someone else killed those two men in the alley," Timor said. "It is the only possible explanation. It seems the elfling has a guardian. Perhaps more than one."

"I cannot see why he would require one," the templar said. "The way he handled that sword of his, and the way the other blades broke upon it . . . "

"What?" said Timor.

"I said, the way he handled that sword of his—"

"No, no . . . you said the other blades *broke* upon his sword?"

"Yes, my lord. They simply shattered when they struck the elfling's blade."

"What do you mean, they shattered? They were iron blades! I saw to it personally that Rokan and his men were equipped with them."

"Nevertheless, my lord, they shattered. Perhaps there was some flaw in their construction—"

"Nonsense," Timor said. "In one blade, perhaps, but surely not in both. Besides, even if there were a flaw, the blade would crack and break, not shatter. You are *certain* that they shattered?"

"They burst apart as if they had been made of glass," the templar said.

Timor turned away and stared out the window, deep in thought. "Then the elfling's blade must be enchanted," he said. "There was a report from one of my informers concerning how the elfling killed a man in the Crystal Spider. That report, too, spoke of his antagonist's blade shattering against his own, but it could have been obsidian, and obsidian will shatter on a well-made metal blade. There was also something about his cleaving an entire table in two, and turning the man's own knife against him . . . obvious exaggerations. Or at least, so I thought at the time."

"I know what I saw, my lord," the templar said. "The elfling is a highly skilled and dangerous fighter. I will wager that he is the match of any gladiator in the city."

Timor rubbed his chin absently. "It seems to me I heard something once, many years ago, about a sword against which other blades would shatter . . . a very special sword." He grimaced. "I cannot recall it now. But it will come to me." He turned back to face his minion. "At the very least, this is clear proof that the elfling is not the simple herdsman that he claims to be. And proof that, whatever he is up to, he is not working alone. I cannot proceed with my plans until I am certain they have not been compromised. And time is growing short. I do not trust Rikus and that damned sorceress. They are up to something, I am sure of it, and this elfling is involved somehow."

"What do you wish me to do, my lord?" the templar asked.

"Resume watch on the elfling for the time being," Timor replied, and the templar sighed with relief that he was apparently not going to be blamed for the failure of the ambush. "Keep me advised of every move he makes. I will let you know if I have any further instructions."

The templar bowed and gratefully withdrew, leaving Timor alone in his chambers.

That wineshop is a known contact point for members of the Veiled Alliance, Timor thought, *considering this new information. And the elfling carries an enchanted blade. It all seemed much too convenient for coincidence. He was involved with them, with the Alliance, without a doubt. And he had met secretly with Rikus. What did it all mean?*

Clearly, it was a plot of some sort. Sadira had to be
behind it. Rikus was her confidant, just as Kor was
his. Was it possible that Sadira was a secret member
of the Veiled Alliance? But, no, he thought. She had
once been a defiler, and even if she had forsworn
defiler magic and repented of it, the fact that she had
once defiled would be enough to prevent the Alliance
from accepting her. Still, that did not necessarily
mean they could not work hand in glove, to the
advantage of both parties. What would be served?
What could both Sadira and the Veiled Alliance want?

Obviously, the destruction of the templars. Just as
Timor himself wanted more than anything to wipe
out the Veiled Alliance as the sole threat to his power,
so would the Alliance look upon the templars. To the
Alliance, the templars would always be enemies.
They would always be Kalak's enforcers. He could
work to change the image of the templars in the
minds of Tyr's citizenry, but the Alliance would
always remain firm in its relentless opposition. And
the only other threat he had to face, the only other
power in the council, was Sadira. Without her and
that mongrel gladiator, he would be in complete control. The rest of the advisors were nothing more than
saplings that bent with the prevailing wind.

Yes, he thought, Sadira had to see that, too. She was
no fool. He would not make the mistake of underesti-
mating her. She had brought down Kalak, after all.
There was a great deal more to that pretty wench than
met the eye, though what met the eye was pleasing.
Under the right circumstances, with her made properly pliable . . . but no. He pushed the thought from
his mind. Better to have her safely dead, but in such a
manner as no blame could befall the templars. And
she, of course, was most likely thinking the selfsame

thing about him at this very moment.

She cannot move against me openly, thought Timor, so she has found herself this elfling as a cat's-paw. He was to approach the Alliance where she could not. What was he? Where had she met him? What had she promised him in return for his mercenary services? Was it possible that he could be bought off? No, Timor thought, the time to have tried that would have been before the attempt on his life was made. Now it was too late for such measures of expediency. Now the only thing to do would be to finish the job Rokan had bungled.

The corners of his mouth turned down as he thought of that traitorous brigand. He was not through with Rokan yet, not by any means. By now, the marauder could be halfway across the desert, only he wouldn't do that. He might flee from a battle he knew he could not win, but he would not give up the war. Not that one. Besides, there was still the matter of his face. Timor smiled. Rokan would remain, so long as there was the promise that he might be healed. And if that promise were not kept, then Rokan would do everything in his power to kill him. Oh yes, Timor knew his man. Rokan was a man he could understand. And he could still be useful, but as to what extent, well . . . that depended to a large degree on Rokan.

For the present, Timor had to concern himself with the one wild card in the game—the elfling, Sorak. He did not know to what extent the elfling might upset his plans, but he had no intention of taking any chances. He had sent five well-armed and dangerous men to kill the elfling, and they had failed. If you want a job done properly, he thought, do it yourself.

He pulled out a key he wore around his neck, then

went over to a small, wooden chest he kept on the sideboard. He unlocked the chest and opened it. Within it, on a bed of black velvet, lay his spellbook. He tucked the spellbook within the folds of his tunic and put on his cloak. It was late, but the night was not yet over, and he had much to do before the dawn.

* * * * *

Rokan winced as the healer gently probed the wound around the crossbow bolt. "Stop messing about and pull the blasted thing out!" he said, gritting his teeth.

"Bad enough you woke me in the middle of the night and threatened to slit my throat if I did not see to your wound," the healer said wryly. "I have already gathered that I am not going to be paid for this. I do not need the added burden of your body to dispose of. That bolt may be the only thing holding a blood vessel together. If I were to simply yank it out without a careful examination, you could start leaking like a sieve."

"You talk too much," Rokan muttered sullenly. "Be on about your business."

"I will if you stop squirming. Now sit still."

Rokan scowled, but complied.

"What happened to your face?" the healer asked as he continued to examine the wound.

"It was burned away. Can you restore it?"

"I have not that sort of skill. The old templars had that level of power, but not me."

"Never mind my face and see to my shoulder. Or is that beyond you, too?"

"Hold still," the healer said.

He took hold of the crossbow bolt and pulled.

Rokan cried out with pain and grabbed the arms of his chair with all his might. The healer pulled the arrow free and held it up.

"There," he said. "Did that hurt much?"

"Yes, damn you!"

"Good. You are a lucky man. It could have been much worse. Some healing salve and a bandage to cover the wound and you should recover completely. That is, of course, unless someone shoots you again. And I can't imagine why anyone would want to do that to such a pleasant fellow as you."

Rokan grimaced. "I can do without your witticisms," he said. "Maybe this will dull your humor." He tossed a silver coin to the healer.

The man caught it, glanced at it with surprise, and grunted. "Well . . . consider me the soul of humorlessness. This is rather more than I expected."

"It is meant to buy your silence, as well."

"This is the elven market, my irksome friend," the healer said dryly. "I see similar injuries, and worse, every day. Discretion comes with the treatment, else I would not stay in business long."

Rokan winced as the healer applied the salve to the wound. "Pah! It smells worse than kank dung!"

"It's nothing compared to what your wound would smell like in a few days if I did not apply the salve," the healer replied. "I will give you some to take with you. Bathe the wound and apply some every day, as I am doing now, and change the bandage before it becomes dirty. If you have any difficulties, come and see me. Or, better yet, go threaten someone else in the middle of the night. There, that should do it."

Rokan glanced down at the bandage and tentatively moved his arm and shoulder.

"Are you left-handed?" asked the healer.

"No, right."

"Good. If you must kill someone, use your right arm. Try not to move the left too much."

"I am grateful to you, healer," Rokan said.

The healer shrugged. "I am grateful to be paid, and so generously, to boot. It makes me not mind losing my sleep so much."

"There are more coins where that one came from," Rokan said.

"Are there, indeed? And what dastardly thing would I have to do to earn them?"

"What do you know of poisons?" Rokan asked.

"A man in my profession, in this neighborhood? A good deal. But I will not *supply* you with any poison to kill someone. I *am* a healer, after all."

"Fair enough, I ask only for the knowledge. I can obtain the poison elsewhere."

"In the elven market, you could obtain it on almost any street corner," said the healer dryly. "As for the knowledge you require, that should be worth at least another silver coin."

"Done."

"Hmm. I should have asked for two. What purpose do you want this poison to serve?"

"I want something I can smear upon a crossbow bolt, like this one," Rokan said, picking up the bloody arrow the healer had pulled out of his shoulder. "And it should be strong, strong enough to drop a kank in its tracks."

"I see," the healer said. "I am no expert on poisons, but I knew a bard who taught me a little. I would recommend the venom from a crystal spider. It is thick enough to smear upon an arrow, though I would not do it with my fingers, and it paralyzes at once. Death follows in moments."

"Venom from a crystal spider," Rokan said with a smile that gave his ravaged face a hideous expression. "How very fitting." He tossed another silver coin to the healer. "You can go back to sleep now."

* * * * *

Timor rode the kank through the Grand Gate and disappeared out into the darkness beyond the city walls. The guards on duty at the gate passed him through without remarking on his leaving the city at such an unusual hour. It was not their place to question a templar, much less the senior templar himself, and if they wondered what errand he was on in the middle of the night, they kept it to themselves.

With his cloak wrapped around him against the night chill, Timor turned the kank and followed the outer city wall, going past the king's gardens and the templars' quarter, past the stadium and Kalak's ziggurat, toward the brickyards and the old slave pens, now standing empty. He turned east, away from the city wall, and followed a dirt road for several miles beyond the work farms until the road began to rise, leading up into the foothills.

The road did not continue up into the mountains. It stopped at their base, at a wide plateau that spread out beneath the foothills. During the day, hardly anyone ever came here. At night, the place was always deserted. The only sounds were the whistling of the wind blowing over the desert and the scrabbling of the giant kank beetle's claws on the hard-packed soil. Timor tapped the beast's antennae with a switch and got down from its back. He dropped the switch and then tied the creature's leads to a rock outcropping. The kank simply stood there, docile, its huge pincers opening and closing as it scanned the ground around it for some food.

Timor gazed out at the deserted cemetery. This was where Tyr buried its dead, in simple, mounded graves marked by nothing other than red clay tablets with the names of the deceased incised upon them. The heaped dirt mounds stretched out across the wide plateau and up the hillside. A cool dust cloud, making ghostly undulations in the night breeze, obscured many of them from view.

Timor found a small, rocky knoll and climbed up on it. He pulled back the hood of his cloak and took out his spellbook. If he could not find living men to do the job of killing the elfling, then he would raise the dead to do it. He looked around cautiously. He had no reason to expect anyone to be out here at such an hour, but it would hardly do for him to be seen not only practicing defiler magic, but defiling graves, as well. Only the guards at the Grand Gate had seen him leave the city, and he would place them under a spell of forgetfulness when he returned, thereby ensuring that his part in this would remain unknown. The dead would not talk.

He opened the spellbook to the correct page and quickly reviewed its patterns. Then, lifting his eyes to the sky, he began to intone the words of the spell in a sonorous, chanting tone. The wind picked up, and there was the distant boom of thunder in reaction to the disturbance in the ether. The dust cloud upon the ground began to swirl, as if agitated by a current underneath it.

The kank raised its chitinous head and swiveled its antennae curiously in reaction to the strange vibrations that suddenly permeated the air. The wind picked up. It plucked at Timor's cloak, causing it to flap around him, and as it grew stronger, it blew the cloak out behind him like a cape. Thunder rolled. Sheet lightning flashed across the sky. There was a smell of ozone in the air . . . and something else, the rising, heavy stench of sulphur. The dust cloud upon the ground, in contravention of all logic, common sense, and natural law, started to grow thicker, despite the strong wind that should have dissipated it.

Timor raised his right hand high over his head as though drawing power from the heavens, then he slowly brought his hand down as an aura of crackling blue energy played around his fingers. He aimed his outstretched arm, with hand held so that the palm was facedown, fingers splayed, toward the ground around him. His voice rose, the wind increased, and the aura of energy that crackled around his outstretched fingers grew alternately brighter and dimmer. The power began to pulsate with regularity, each succeeding pulse growing brighter than the one before, each drawing more life out of the vegetation all around him.

The waving, brown desert grasses that had grown up on and around the mounds and all across the plateau turned black and shriveled into compost. The wildflowers that grew on the hillsides and gave a beautiful array of bright colors to this barren world withered and died as the life was leeched from them.

Timor trembled as the energy he robbed from the vegetation around him flowed into his outstretched hand and spread throughout his entire body. He felt exhilarated, vibrant with power. The lifeforce of the plants infused him, sluiced through him, filled him with a warmth and vitality that was addicting. He wanted more. He wanted it never to stop.

The desert succulents, the long-spined cacti that stood four times as tall as a man and took at least two centuries to reach full maturity, softened and became flaccid, flopping over onto the ground with loud thuds and decomposing in a matter of seconds. The jade bushes drooped and shed their fleshy, paddle-shaped leaves as they turned first brown, then black, then crumpled to the ground like bits of ash. The blue pagafa trees growing on the slopes, their thick, dense trunks and branches almost as hard as rock, dropped their tiny, blue-green leaves and began to split as the moisture was drained out of them. With loud, popping cracks, they splintered and fell, as if struck by invisible bolts of lightning. In a wide swath all around the templar, everything withered and died and decomposed, leaving behind a desolation even more barren than the sandy washes of the tablelands.

Timor gave no thought whatever to the wanton destruction that he caused. He was focused solely on the sheer, lustful pleasure of feeling all that warm, life-giving energy surging through his being. This was the lure of true sorcery, he thought, the heady rush of sensual power that the preservers, with their pathetic, weak philosophy, would never understand. *This* was what it meant to truly feel alive!

It was a pleasure that could only dimly be perceived in the consumption of an excellent meal prepared by the finest cooks, or in the exquisite release of sexual fulfillment. This was the full measure of the satisfaction that could be found in the complete satiation of the senses. It was the ultimate indulgence, the intoxication that only a true mage could ever know. It was what drove the sorcerer-kings to follow the painful route of metamorphosis that would turn them into dragons, whose capacity for power was greater because their hunger and their need for it was also greater. He wanted it never to end.

But it had to end. He was not yet king, and there was only so much energy he could contain. When he felt that he could absorb no more, he stopped and simply stood there for a long moment, wanting to stretch it out, vibrating with the force that filled him, his muscles spasming so hard he thought his bones would break. Every nerve fiber in his body sang with an exquisite pain. His lips were drawn back from his gums, his features twisted in ecstasy as he stood with his head thrown back, gasping for breath and trembling. Not yet, not yet—he thought—make it last! Hold onto it for just a little while more. . . .

And then when he could not bear it any longer, he had to release it all or risk being consumed by it. With an effort, he brought his gaze back down to his spell-book. His hand was shaking so hard that he could barely hold it still. He reviewing the last words of the spell, he closed his eyes, finished the incantation, and released the power.

The power surged through his outstretched arm and burst from his fingers in sheets of blue flame. It struck the ground and made fissures in the earth that spread out like a fine network of veins and capillaries all through the cemetery. Timor's breath whooshed out of him and everything started spinning around him as he teetered on the edge of consciousness. It was like the most profound sexual release, only magnified a hundredfold. It left him feeling utterly drained as he collapsed to his knees and gulped in great lungfuls of air. His fingers dug at the barren ground, as if he were trying to grab onto the earth to keep from floating away. His chest rose and fell as he tried to breathe, and for a while, it was all he could do to simply manage that.

Slowly, his strength returned to him, but it was still a paltry feeling compared to the sheer force that had surged through him moments earlier. As he gradually recovered, he regained his normal state, a feeble state compared to what he had just experienced. He felt let down, crushingly disappointed. He felt cheated. This was not life. What he had felt when all that energy surged through him, *that* was living! But it had been so brief a taste. . . .

He forced himself to his feet. Control, he thought. For a wizard, self-control was everything. He did not dare try it again so soon. He would not survive it. Nor would he survive if he remained here much longer. He stood, breathing heavily. The spell was nearly finished; now it had to be directed. He visualized the elfling in his mind as he spoke the words that would command the spell to work his will. He had waited almost too long. Even as he finished saying the words, the ground around the grave mounds began to crack and buckle.

He picked up his spellbook and hurried back to where he had left the kank tied up. The beast had frayed the rope; it had pulled frantically to break free during the height of the spell. Fortunately, kanks were stupid insects, for it could easily have cut the rope with its pincers had it the intelligence to do so. He untied the kank and mounted, then urged the beast back down the hill on the road leading to the city. The antlike creature needed little prodding. As it started down the slope, the first of the grave mounds burst open, and a bony hand covered with strips of rank, decomposing flesh appeared, clawing its way out.

TWELVE

It was nearly dawn. The gaming house had shut down for the day, and the cleaning staff had not yet begun their work. They would begin shortly after sunrise, working throughout the morning and into the afternoon, preparing the Crystal Spider for yet another night of gaming, dining, and entertainment. The place was deserted when Sorak came in and went up the back stairs to his quarters.

Tigra had grown anxious and restive in his absence and had torn apart the bed. The tigone had also gnawed through two chair legs, upended a table, clawed up the rug, and torn down the curtains over the window. Fortunately, Sorak had left the heavy window shutters closed and bolted, and Tigra had not been able to open the door—otherwise the damage surely would have extended beyond his room.

"What have you done?" he asked when he came in.

Tigra stopped rubbing up against him and looked up contritely. "*Lonely,*" the beast communicated to him, psionically. "*Sorak gone. Left Tigra alone.*"

"I thought we had an understanding," he said. "You were supposed to behave yourself. Look what you've done."

"*Tigra sorry.*"

Sorak sighed. "Well, I suppose I shall have to pay for all this."

"*Tigra hungry.*"

"Very well. Let's go down to the kitchen and see if we can find you some raw meat."

"*Lyric hungry, too,*" said Lyric, mimicking the cat. "*Find Lyric some raw meat?*"

"Stop that," Sorak said.

"*Lyric has a point, though,*" Eyron said. "*The rest of us have all been very cooperative with you through all this, but city life does not exactly suit us, nor does your diet of kank food.*"

"*Eyron is right,*" Kivara added. "*It has been a long time since we have enjoyed a fresh kill.*"

"You know that I do not meat," said Sorak.

"*That is your choice,*" said Eyron, "*or rather, your rationalization. You may try to deny your elf and halfling needs because of how the villichi raised you, but the rest of us have never accepted their ways. The Ranger holds his peace, but he has not hunted since we came to this city, and he does not feel comfortable here. Screech also hungers for the taste of flesh, as do we all.*"

"What of the Guardian?" asked Sorak. "Does she feel the same?"

"*I am less bothered by your choice not to eat flesh than are the others,*" said the Guardian, "*but it is not wise to disregard their wishes and their needs. They have always kept their agreements with you and refrained from coming out without your knowledge or consent.*"

"And in return I give them access to all that I know, feel, and experience," said Sorak, "and I allow them time to come out whenever possible."

"*But lately, you have allowed them to come out less and less,*" the Guardian replied.

"*That's right,*" Kivara said. "*I have not been out in a*

*long time. I am tired of being kept under. You have not been
fair."*

"Perhaps you are right," said Sorak. "We must all
live together and strive for balance. Perhaps I have
been too selfish. Very well, then. Since Kivara has
complained the most, let her come out and share a
meal with the others. As for me, you know that eating
meat offends me, so I shall duck under and go to
sleep. It has been a long day and an even longer night,
and I am weary."

He opened the door and Tigra trotted out into the
hall, but it was Kivara who stepped from the room,
not Sorak. As Sorak ducked under and went to sleep,
Kivara came out and moved quickly down the hall
after Tigra, toward the stairs leading to the first floor
and the kitchen.

Outwardly, nothing about the elfling had changed,
but a keen observer who was familiar with Sorak
would have noticed a slightly different, lighter gait,
almost catlike, with a playful bounce in his step and a
somewhat more self-conscious carriage. The expression on his face, too, had undergone a change.
Whereas, under most circumstances, Sorak's expression was a rather neutral one—if anything, one of
brooding and contemplation—now Kivara gave his
features a more animated cast. A slight, crafty smile
played about the lips, and the eyes seemed to dance
with mischief.

In the kitchen, she found some game birds hanging
in the smoke room and tossed them out on the floor
for Tigra. The tigone greedily began to gobble them.
Without wasting any time on such niceties as table
settings, Kivara grabbed a large hunk of raw z'tal
meat and tore into it. It was not the same as a fresh
kill, and the thrill of the hunt was absent. The heady

rush of warm blood spurting down her throat was missing, too, but the pleasure of eating raw, still-bloody flesh, only recently butchered, was undiminished. Both Kivara and the tigone made sounds of satisfaction deep in their throats as they gobbled their food.

"Decided to have a late night snack?" asked Krysta.

Kivara looked up to see the half-elf standing in the kitchen doorway, wearing a long, sheer, gossamer-thin nightgown.

"I thought you did not eat flesh," she said with a mocking smile. "Something about a . . . spiritual vow, was it?"

"I was hungry," said Kivara, unable to think of a better explanation for the discrepancy between her halfling appetites and Sorak's asceticism.

"So I see," said Krysta in a low voice. She was coming closer. She moistened her lips. "I told you once vows can be broken . . . especially when one is hungry."

She reached up and touched Kivara's cheek gently, running her fingertips down along her jawline to her lips.

"Kivara, make her stop," the Guardian said, and the Watcher echoed her distress with a surge of alarm.

"There is blood on your mouth," said Krysta.

Kivara raised her hand to wipe it off, but Krysta caught it in hers and said, "No, don't. Let me. . . ." And she brought her face closer. . . .

"Kivara!"

. . . So close that Kivara could feel her warm breath. . . .

"Kivara, what are you doing? Stop it!"

. . . And gently, Krysta's tongue flicked out and licked the blood from her lips.

"Kivara! No!"

The Watcher fled, abandoning her post in her panic and ducking deep under, where the Guardian could no longer sense her presence. Alarmed, the Guardian shouted and pressed at Kivara from within, but Kivara was out now, and she had been under for a long time. The unwillingness to relinquish control and the fascination of the new sensations she was experiencing were combining to create resistance. At the same time, that resistance—a child's rebellion against an overbearing parent—and what Krysta was doing with her mouth were tremendously exciting. It was a new sensual experience, and Kivara was unable to let go of it.

Krysta was pressing her body up against her now, and the warmth of the touch flowed through Kivara. She could feel Krysta's smooth, sinewy flesh beneath the sheerness of the nightgown, and it was soft and pleasant to the touch. Krysta's flesh responded as Kivara touched her, and she felt it tremble. Krysta's tongue was probing between her lips now, and Kivara, interested to see where this would lead, opened her mouth to it.

She struggled to block out the Guardian's protests as Krysta's fingers twined themselves in her hair and evinced a wonderful, tingling sensation. Their tongues met, and Kivara followed Krysta's lead, learning quickly with a hunger for experience that only the truly innocent could know. Krysta's hands were on her chest now, fingernails scratching lightly, caressing, moving lower. . . .

Sorak was jerked out of his slumber by a jolt from the Guardian. His first, disoriented perception was that they were all in danger, for he felt the Guardian's tremendous agitation and alarm, and then suddenly he realized what was happening. Angrily, he yanked

Kivara back under and rose to the fore. . . .

"No! No, not yet! It isn't fair!" Kivara protested, but Sorak ignored her as he suddenly found his arms full of passionate, half-elf female, hungrily devouring his lips and lashing her tongue against his. He felt her left hand reaching down his leg, while the fingers of her right hand fumbled at his breeches. . . .

"No," he said, quietly but firmly, and pushed her away.

"What?" said Krysta, staring at him with sudden confusion. "What is it? What's wrong?"

"This is wrong," said Sorak. "I cannot do this."

"How can it be wrong when it feels so right?" asked Krysta. "Besides, you were doing just fine a moment ago. . . ."

She came up close to him and put her arms around his neck. Sorak took hold of her arms and gently but firmly removed them. "Krysta, please . . . you do not understand."

She stepped back away from him, her puzzled expression turning to one of anger. "What?" she demanded. "What do I not understand? I understand that a moment ago, you were willing . . . more than willing, eager, and now this sudden change of heart comes upon you inexplicably. Is it me? Am I not good enough for you, now that you know who and what you are? Is that it? Is a former slave not a fit consort for a king?"

Sorak shook his head and sighed wearily. "That has nothing to do with it," he said. "I have already told you what I think of this idea of yours about my being some sort of mythological elven king. It is utter nonsense. I reject it."

"Then what?" she demanded. "What *is* it? Tell me I did not excite you! Tell me that you did not want me!"

Sorak sighed. "You did not excite me," he said. "I did not want you."

"Liar!"

"As I said, you do not understand. You did not excite *me*. It was not *I* who wanted you; it was not *I* who became excited over new and unfamiliar physical sensations. It was Kivara."

"*Who?*" said Krysta. "What are you talking about?"

"Kivara," Sorak said. He took a deep breath. "Kivara is . . . another entity who inhabits my mind and shares my body with me. She is not *me*. She is a different person."

Krysta gaped at him. "*She?*"

"Yes, she. Kivara is a female. A halfling female."

Krysta stepped back another pace, utter confusion on her face. "What are you telling me?" she asked. "Are you trying to say that you think you are a . . . female?"

"No," said Sorak. "*I* am male. But Kivara is a female, as are the Watcher and the Guardian. My other aspects are all male."

Krysta shook her head. "You are trying to confuse me."

"No. I am simply telling you the truth."

"Then . . . you are insane?" Krysta asked with disbelief. "Is this what you are trying to tell me?"

"Perhaps I am insane, in a way," Sorak replied. "Most people, knowing what I am, would undoubtedly think of it that way. But my mind is not unbalanced, Krysta. It is merely divided into a multiplicity of different personalities. At least a dozen that I am aware of. That is one of the main reasons why the villichi took me in. They have encountered this sort of thing before, though it is exceedingly rare. They call what I am a 'tribe of one.' "

Krysta stood, shaking her head, staring at him with astonishment. "But . . . how can that be?"

"The villichi believe it comes about in childhood," Sorak explained, "through suffering and abuse that is so intense that it becomes unbearable, and the mind seeks refuge by splitting apart, creating new and separate entities out of itself, personalities that are as real and fully manifested as I am. That is why I took a vow to remain celibate, Krysta, because I am not merely one male. I am at least a dozen different people, some male, some female, all sharing the same mind and body. And not all of them see things alike, as Kivara has just unfortunately demonstrated. I am sorry. I was not present when it happened. I was . . . sleeping. Had I known, I would have stopped it before it even began. Please . . . forgive me."

Krysta stared at him with a stricken expression. "You are really telling me the truth?" she asked.

"I would not lie to you," said Sorak. "There was someone once . . . a young villichi female, for whom I cared more than I can say. We grew up together as brother and sister, though we were not related by blood. In time, the feelings between us became stronger, grew into love . . . a sort of love, I suppose. *I*, Sorak, loved her, at any rate, and I still do. But we could never consummate that love. The Guardian is female, and could not make love with a woman, nor could the Watcher, who is also female. In this, my male and female aspects exist in a conflict that cannot be resolved."

"But . . . you said this Kivara is a female. . . ." Krysta began, looking confused.

"Yes, but Kivara is a child who does not truly understand. To her, everything new that pertains to the senses is exciting, and she cannot help but to explore it. However, she grows bored very quickly. If not stimulated by some novelty, her attention tends to wander."

"But . . . it was *you* I kissed!" Krysta insisted. "It was not some . . . girl child in my arms!"

"No, not if you speak of the body," Sorak said. "The body is male, of course. But the intelligence guiding it, at that particular moment, was that of an immature female. I was not there, Krysta. I was not present. It was not *me*. I do not even know how it all began. I shall not share the memory unless Kivara or the Guardian bestows it on me."

"You mean . . . but how . . . the Guardian?"

"She is the one who seeks to maintain a balance in the inner tribe," said Sorak. "It was the Guardian who controlled the dice the first night that I came here. I, myself, possess no psionic skills."

"It makes my head hurt just to think about it," Krysta said, staring at him wide-eyed. "How can you *live* this way?"

Sorak shrugged. "I have never known any other way to live," he said. "I have no memory of what I was like, or even who I was, before this happened to me."

"How terrible for you!" said Krysta, with sincere concern. "If I had only known . . . "

"What difference would it have made?" asked Sorak. "Even now, you do not fully understand. You may grasp the idea of it, but you could never truly know what it is like. No one could. That is why I must remain alone. Yet, in another sense, I can never really be alone. I am a tribe of one."

"And that is why you seek the Sage," said Krysta. "You hope that he may cure you."

"I seek the Sage for the reasons that I gave you and

Rikus," Sorak said. "I do not know that I can be cured, or even if 'cure' is the proper term to use under the circumstances. I am not sick. I am merely . . . different. Nor am I sure I would wish to be any other way."

"But . . . if the Sage could help you, would you not accept his aid?"

"I do not know," said Sorak. "If I were to become simply Sorak, what would become of all the others? What would happen to them? Where would they go? They are a part of me, Krysta. I could not let them die."

"I see," she said, looking down. "I think, perhaps, I understand." When she looked up again, her eyes were moist. "Is there nothing I can do?"

Sorak smiled. "You have already given me two things that I prize above any material gain or comfort. Your friendship and your understanding."

"I only wish that there was—" A horrible scream cut through the stillness of the night. "What was that?"

Sorak was already moving. "It came from outside."

"The gatekeeper!"

They ran through the dining room and into the empty gaming hall. Sorak drew his sword. Even as he did so, the heavy front door burst off its hinges and three ghastly apparitions came stumbling through. They were encrusted with dirt, and rags hung from them in tatters, as did rotting flesh. Empty eye sockets, writhing with worms, turned in Sorak's direction. The breeze blowing through the doorway carried the rank stench of decomposing flesh into the room. Krysta blanched.

"Undead!" she gasped.

"They look very dead to me," said Sorak.

The rotting corpses stumbled toward them.

"Guards!" shouted Krysta, running for the stairs.

All three corpses ignored her and came straight for Sorak.

"Tigra!" Sorak said.

The tigone roared and took a running leap, bringing the first corpse down. It jerked convulsively as Tigra tore it apart, and the scattered parts continued to twitch and writhe upon the floor.

Sorak swung his sword as the second corpse came stumbling toward him, its rotting fingers, with bones poking through, reaching for him. Galdra whistled through the air and cleaved the zombie completely in two, and where the magic blade had passed, acrid smoke issued from the twitching flesh and bones.

The third zombie lurched toward him, its burial clothes in rotting tatters, its feet nothing but bones, its face little more than a grinning skull. Sorak swung his sword again, knocking the head clean off the shoulders. Smoke issued from the zombie's neck, or what was left of its neck, but still the body came lurching forward, arms stretched out, skeletal fingers grasping. Sorak swung his sword again, chopping off one arm. It fell to the floor, smoking and twitching, but still the corpse came on. Then it fell as Tigra leapt upon its back, claws and teeth rending it apart.

Sorak heard the sound of running footsteps; guards on the stairs. He was about to tell them that it was all over when he saw two more zombies stumble through the doorway, followed by a third, and yet a fourth.

And as he watched, the scattered remnants of the first corpse Tigra had torn apart writhed toward one another across the floor and began to join themselves together once again.

"Gith's blood!" said the guard captain, as the walking dead lurched and swayed toward Sorak across the gaming hall. And two more were coming in.

Sorak lunged to meet them, and the guards drew their weapons and joined the fray. The zombies were unarmed, and they did not move quickly, but as each one fell, hacked to pieces by Sorak or one of the guards, another came in to take its place. And, moments later, the ones that fell came up again, their rotting body parts joined back together. The guards and Sorak laid about them with their blades, and Tigra leaped from one walking corpse to the other, savaging them and rending them to pieces.

Sorak noticed that the ones he had dismembered and struck down twitched for a short while, then grew still, nothing but rotting flesh and bones on the floor. The others, torn apart without Galdra, always reshaped and attacked again. A severed arm lay twitching, then began to drag itself across the floor to rejoin itself to its torso. A skull that had been split apart became magically fused back together. One of the guards ran a zombie straight through the chest with his sword, but the blade passed through the corpse's ribs with no apparent effect, and the zombie kept on coming, impaling itself on the sword until its bony fingers closed around the guard's throat and started squeezing. The half-elf screamed, but the others could spare no time to save him, and he went down beneath the corpse's weight.

Krysta came running back downstairs, having quickly grabbed her blade. Several more zombies came lurching through the doorway and Sorak charged them, chopping his way through, swinging Galdra like a scythe. As they fell, he encountered three more in the garden just outside the door. They went down before his blade and became nothing more than rotting bones and body parts upon the ground, but another was coming down the path toward him.

Krysta's voice cried out behind him, "Sorak, look out!"

He swung around and chopped out with Galdra just as another zombie came stumbling back out of the gaming hall toward him. The corpse was cut in two by the elvish steel, and the smoking, severed halves of its body collapsed to the ground.

Sorak saw Krysta cut her way through several of them and come running up to his side. Three more of the zombies followed her out the door. Together, she and Sorak cut them down, but only the ones that Galdra struck remained dismembered on the ground. The others, it seemed, could not be stopped.

"Running them through does not do any good," said Krysta, gasping for breath. "You can cut them to pieces, but the pieces keep coming back together. Five of my guards are already dead, and the others are hard pressed. But it's you they're after. See, here come two more."

As she spoke, two more zombies came stumbling out the door, heading toward them. With a roar, Tigra flew out behind them and landed on both in a flurry of claws and teeth. But Sorak knew it was, at best, a temporary reprieve. Only Galdra, it seemed, could truly be effective against them. Behind them, inside the gaming house, the sounds of fighting were diminishing. There was a scream, followed by another, and yet another as Krysta's guards were overwhelmed.

"Kank's blood!" said Krysta, looking beyond Sorak and pointing, her eyes wide with horror. "*Look!*"

Sorak turned to gaze in the direction she was indicating. He looked out through the open gate, the strangled body of the unfortunate gatekeeper lying on the ground beside it, and saw that the entire street beyond was full of walking dead. There were dozens of them, shambling down the street like specters, some recently dead and still recognizable as human, some no more than skeletons. And even as he looked, the sounds of struggle in the gaming house behind him stopped completely. The last of Krysta's guards had fallen. The corpses started coming back out toward them.

"We are going to die," said Krysta.

Not if I awake the Shade, thought Sorak, and wondered if even the Shade, for all his fearsomeness, could deal with such a sheer weight of numbers. "No," he said, aloud, "not you. It's me they're after."

"They killed all my guards," she said.

"Only because they were in their way," Sorak replied. "Get away from me! Run, and you'll be safe!"

"I won't leave you," Krysta said, hefting her sword as the zombies closed in on them from both directions. Tigra brought two of them down, but more were coming.

"I have no time to argue with you," Sorak said. He quickly transferred Galdra to his left hand and, with his right, struck a sharp blow on Krysta's chin. As she collapsed, he caught her, then dragged her off the path and dumped her behind a rock outcropping in the garden.

"If you hadn't done that, I was about to hit her myself," said a familiar voice.

Sorak spun around and his jaw dropped as he saw a young villichi priestess standing behind him, dressed for battle, her white hair tied back, sword in one hand, dagger in the other.

"*Ryana*! How . . . what are you doing here?"

She slashed out with her sword and knocked the

head off a walking corpse, then kicked the still-ambulatory body back into the pool. "Someone had to watch out for you," she said.

"Behind you!"

But with the sharply honed instincts of a villichi fighter, she was already spinning around, sword flashing, and another zombie fell as she sliced through its rotting waist with one vicious stroke.

"I'd already dropped that one before," she said. "They don't stay down, do they?"

"They do if Galdra strikes them," Sorak said, wondering why the Shade wasn't manifesting. There were more of them coming, far too many, even for the Shade.

"Galdra?"

Then Sorak became aware of a curious, warm, floating sensation stealing over him, suffusing him. A lilting voice that sounded like an echo from some far-off canyon came to him, speaking in his mind, saying, "*Sorak . . . let go.*"

"Kether," he whispered.

"Sorak . . . we have a lot of company," said Ryana, her voice betraying anxiety despite her outward bravado.

"*Let go, Sorak. Let go.*"

"Ryana!" he called out. "Use this!"

She quickly sheathed her dagger and caught his blade as he tossed it to her, and then he felt himself fading away gently into a lulling, soothing warmth. He knew now why the Shade had not responded to the threat. There was a still-greater power within him, something that seemed to be a part of him, and yet was not a part of him, an entity that seemed to come of its own volition, not from within him, but from . . . somewhere else. As his vision faded into a stark yet

comforting white haze, he could dimly hear Ryana
calling out to him, and then her voice was fading, too.

"*Sorak!*" Ryana shouted.

She saw him standing there, absolutely motionless,
his eyes closed, not a single weapon in his hand. And
then there was no time to do anything else but defend
herself and him, as four corpses advanced toward
them down the path, and six others came out of the
gaming house behind them. The one she had kicked
into the pool stood up, dripping and still headless,
and began to splash its way toward her. Tigra roared
and leaped onto the one in the pool, but the others
kept coming. There were far too many of them,
thought Ryana, holding her sword in one hand and
Sorak's in the other. She could not fight *and* use her
psionic powers at the same time. It was hopeless.

"Coming here was *not* a smart idea," she muttered
to herself, and slashed out with Sorak's sword at the
nearest corpse. The zombie's flesh emitted smoke as
the blade passed through it effortlessly and cut the
torso completely in half. The dead thing fell and
walked no more. Ryana whistled to herself softly.
"Nice sword," she said.

The zombies were coming closer. She backed away,
looking for some room to fight in, and then she saw
them turn and head for Sorak, disregarding her completely.

He simply stood there, unarmed, doing nothing.

"No," she whispered.

They closed in around him, obscuring him from
view.

"*No!*" she screamed.

She was about to launch herself at them when she
saw something that froze her to the spot. The corpses
simply fell apart. What little flesh remained on their

bones disintegrated, and then the bones themselves clattered to the ground like a rain of dry twigs. In the wink of an eye, they turned to ash and blew away on the breeze.

Sorak simply stood there, where once a throng of undead clustered. His arms hung loosely at his sides, and an expression of utter calm and serenity was on his face.

Ryana realized suddenly that it wasn't Sorak, at all. It was one of the others, but not the Guardian or the Ranger, not Screech or Lyric. . . . She had never seen this one before.

The entity in Sorak's form walked slowly out onto the path. The zombies kept coming toward him, ignoring Ryana now that she was not between them and their quarry. And as they came up to him and reached out to seize him, they all collapsed and fell apart, drying up and blowing away just like the others. They kept pouring through the gate, shambling in from the street, grim and terrifying in their decay and lifelessness, and Sorak—or whoever it was—simply allowed them to come to him. As each and every one touched him, the same thing happened.

Ryana stood there, watching it all with a sense of awe and wonder. What sort of power *was* this? What entity possessed him now?

There were still dozens of the zombies shambling and dragging themselves down the street, heading toward the gate. Sorak moved out to meet them. But as he reached the gate, the street outside was abruptly illuminated by brilliant blue light. Small globes of azure fire came hurtling out from several alleys at once, striking the zombies and wreathing them in glowing, incandescent auras. One after the other, the corpses were consumed, and the hail of energy continued for several minutes, until the street was once again completely clear.

Ryana came running up to stand beside Sorak at the gate. As she looked at him, she could see that it *was*, in fact, Sorak once again. His face looked somehow different, transfigured, but it was the same face she remembered, that same, stoic, neutral expression of a male determined to keep everything inside.

"It is done," he said.

"What happened?" she asked.

"Reinforcements," he said. "Look."

A dozen or more figures stepped out of the shadows into the street. They all wore long, white, hooded robes and veils across the lower part of their faces. The sky was beginning to get lighter. It was almost dawn.

"The Veiled Alliance," Sorak said.

"Your sword," said Ryana, handing it back to him. "Quite a weapon. Know where I can get one like it?"

"It worked for you?"

"Like no other blade I've ever held," she said, watching as the hooded figures approached them.

"Then your spirit is strong and your faith is true," said Sorak, with a smile. "Either that, or you're king of all the elves."

"What?"

"Never mind. I will explain later."

The robed and hooded figures came up to them and Sorak nodded to them. "Thank you," he said.

One of the men stepped forward. "We would have come sooner if we could have," he said, "but we did not receive the summons until the attack was already in progress."

"Summons?" said Ryana.

"They have had me watched," said Sorak, "to see if

I would prove myself to them."

"And so you have," the speaker for the others said. He reached into his robe and pulled out a slim scroll, bound up in a ribbon. "This is the information that you seek from us," he said, handing the scroll to Sorak. "It will not, regrettably, give you the answer that you wish, but it is all we know, and perhaps it will help set your feet upon the path. Burn the scroll once you have read it, and scatter the ashes."

"What is he talking about?" Ryana asked.

"Later," Sorak said.

"Yes, later he can explain. Right now, it would be best for you to leave the city. You have become a marked man, Sorak. What happened here tonight was merely the beginning. Wherever you go, look to the Alliance for your allies. You will find them nowhere else, I fear. We think we know who unleashed the undead plague on you, and if our suspicions are correct, then—"

Something whizzed past the mage, coming at a sharp, downward angle, and Sorak felt the breeze as the crossbow bolt flew by him, missing him by scant inches. There was a yelp behind him, and Sorak turned to see Tigra topple over onto the ground.

"Tigra!"

The Alliance members turned, looking to see where the attack had come from, but Sorak, heedless of his own safety, rushed to the tigone's side and knelt beside the beast.

"There! On the roof!" one of the wizards cried, pointing to a building across the street.

Rokan had already fitted another bolt to his crossbow. As he pulled back on the bow, Ryana drew and threw her dagger in one swift motion, guiding it psionically to its target. The dagger struck him in the chest, and he fell from the roof to the street below.

"Well done," said the Veiled Alliance leader, with an approving nod. They moved toward the body.

Rokan was still alive, but only barely. "Damn shoulder," he muttered, through clenched teeth. "Made me miss. . . ."

"Who sent you?" asked the Alliance leader, bending over him. "Was it the templar? Was it Timor?"

"Timor . . . " Rokan's voice was little more than a croak. "Lousy sorcerer. . . . Ruined me. . . . Ruined everything. . . . Kill the bastard. . . ." His last words escaped in a long, rattling exhalation, and he died.

"Who is Timor?" asked Ryana.

"Leave him to us," the Alliance leader said. "He is our problem. We will solve it. See to it that Sorak leaves the city safely. And the quicker, the better." He reached up to clasp her shoulder. "It was an honor, priestess. Guard him well."

They split up and scattered quickly into the early morning shadows. Ryana hurried back to Sorak, who was crouched over the wounded animal.

"Sorak . . . " The tigone's thoughts were weak.

"It will be all right, friend," Sorak replied, stroking the huge beast's flank. *"The wound is not a fatal one."*

"Cannot move. . . . Tigra hurt. . . . Great pain. . . ."

Sorak felt the beast's body stiffening beneath his touch. His gaze shot down toward the arrow. There was something smeared upon the shaft. He took hold of it and pulled it out, careful not to touch the part of the shaft that was smeared. He sniffed it. Poison. Spider venom. It paralyzed first, and then a painful death swiftly followed.

"Nooo!" he moaned.

"Sorak . . . Sorak . . . "

He could feel the tigone's agony. As its mind

touched his, he shared the searing pain, and it washed over him like fire.

"*No, Tigra, no . . .* " he groaned, not protesting the animal's pain that he was sharing, through their psionic link, but the fate of his lifelong companion.

"*Sorak . . .* " The pain he felt was ebbing quickly now as the tigone's own life ebbed, and the link grew weaker. "*Friend . . . protect. . . .*"

And then the beast was gone.

Sorak felt it die. He experienced its death, and for a moment, he was numb with shock and loss, as if a part of him died too. And then he threw back his head and howled, a sound that was utterly inhuman, a sound that came from both his broken heart and Screech, the beast entity within him. The cry echoed through the once-again deserted streets, and Ryana stood there beside him, tears in her eyes as the dark sun slowly rose over the city.

EPILOGUE

Timor stopped just inside the entrance to the small council chamber and looked around. All the councilors were already present, sitting at the table. Everyone was silent, staring at him. All except for Kor, who pointedly gazed down at the surface of the table before him.

"You have heard what the people are saying," Sadira began without preamble, even before he had sat down. "The entire city is outraged over the defiling of the graves in the cemetery," she continued. "The count is still inexact, but we know that over three-score dead were raised. Raised by defiler magic," she added redundantly, merely to emphasize the point. Rikus sat beside her, glaring at him.

Timor was about to reply, but Sadira continued without pause. "The entire hillside and plateau where the city cemetery is located was rendered completely barren by the foul spell," she said, her gaze never wavering from him. "Moreover, the walking dead were sent into the city itself—*into the city itself!* There are scores of witnesses. People barricaded themselves in their homes in panic. Children were traumatized, to say nothing of those whose loved ones were buried in that cemetery, and were raised to walk again as foul flesh imbued with deadly and repellent purpose. An entire complement of guards was murdered at the Crystal Spider gaming house before members of the Veiled Alliance neutralized the threat."

"Yes, a tragic thing," Timor began smoothly, shaking his head as if in commiseration. "It is fortunate that—" but he never finished, for Sadira's next words brought him up short.

"The people are saying it was you who are responsible," she said, drilling him with her gaze.

"*I?*" said Timor. "Surely, it was the city guard who were responsible, for being derelict in their duties. The templars—as you well know, since you were the one to draft the edict—no longer bear an active role in law enforcement in the city. We support the city guard, of course, but—"

"They are saying it was you, Timor, who raised the dead," said Sadira flatly.

Timor felt a chill, but he recovered quickly. "That is absurd," he said. "Everyone knows we templars lost our powers when Kalak was slain. Surely you, of all people, do not believe such nonsense?"

"What I believe or do not believe is not at issue here," Sadira said.

"What, precisely, *is* at issue?" he demanded, but she ignored him and went on.

"Also found dead upon the scene was one Rokan, said to be the leader of the Nibenay marauders, and one of the spies arrested by the city guard and given over to your custody. How is it, Timor, that a criminal in your custody, a known murderer and spy, was not only free to walk the streets of Tyr, but was able to do so armed with dagger, sword, and crossbow? Why was he not brought forthwith before the council?"

Crossbow? I gave him no crossbow, Timor thought.

He must have obtained that for himself. Doubtless because he feared to meet the elfling face-to-face. Still, no matter. It was clear now how things stood. They were seeking to pin it all on him. Obviously, they had their suspicions, but if Rokan was dead, they could not possibly have any proof.

"Rokan . . . " Timor said, as if trying to place the man. "I am not certain I recall which one he was. In any case, I was not informed that he had managed to escape. Clearly, the fault lies with those who were in charge of him, and I shall be sure to ascertain who was responsible."

"It is clear who was responsible," said Rikus, his voice a growl.

"What are you suggesting?" Timor countered in an affronted tone. "Your remark implies some sort of accusation."

"I don't need to imply anything," said Rikus. "It is all clear to me. All five of the Nibenese spies were apprehended by the city guard. All five were given over to the custody of the templars. Specifically, they were brought directly to *your* estate. All five conveniently escaped to make an attempt on the life of Sorak, the elfling. Their remains have all been positively identified."

"That they escaped is regrettable," said Timor smoothly, "and they clearly sought to take their revenge on the man responsible for their capture. It is fortunate the elfling knows how to take care of himself. He would seem to be quite a fighter for a mere herdsman. But I fail to see what all this has to do with me, unless you are seeking to hold me personally responsible for the regrettable escape of those spies. Granted, I did interrogate them, but then—"

"We are holding you personally responsible for

turning those spies loose with orders to kill Sorak,"
Rikus said. "And for a great deal more, as well."

"You must be insane. Why should I do such a
thing? Moreover, I do not know who began the perni-
cious rumor about my being responsible for the
undead plague, but it is clearly ludicrous, nothing but
malicious and totally unfounded gossip. I am no sorcerer."

"So then you deny practicing defiler magic?" Rikus
asked.

"Of course I deny it! It is against the law!"

"And you deny using coercion, magical or otherwise, to set the marauders on the elfling?"

"I repeat, why should I wish to do such a thing?
What could I possibly have to gain?"

"The elfling's death, if you saw him as a threat to
some plot you were hatching," Rikus said.

"Ridiculous!" said Timor. "I coerced no one, magically or otherwise! I refuse to sit still for these ludicrous and insulting accusations! It is no secret that
you have both long harbored resentment for the templars. This is merely a ploy to make the templars fall
into disfavor with the people and to oust me from the
council!"

"The man Rokan was badly disfigured when he
was found," Sadira said.

"So? What of it?"

"Bring in the first witness," said Sadira.

"Witness? Witness to what?" asked Timor angrily.

A soldier of the city guard entered.

"You were one of those who took the Nibenese
marauder, Rokan, into custody?" Sadira asked him.

"Yes, my lady, I was."

"Was he in any way disfigured at the time?"

"No, my lady, he was not."

"Was he in any way disfigured during your capture of him?"

"No, my lady."

"Was he in any way disfigured when you left him in the private quarters of the senior templar?"

"No, my lady."

"Thank you. You may go."

The soldier turned and left.

"So what?" said Timor scathingly. "What does that prove? Merely that he was not disfigured when he was brought to me. Obviously, it must have happened to him during his escape, or else soon afterward."

"Send in the next witness," said Sadira.

A man entered whom Timor had never seen before.

"You are a healer in the elven market?" asked Sadira.

"I am, my lady."

"And you treated the marauder named Rokan?"

"He never told me his name, my lady, but I recognized him from being shown his body. He came to me in the middle of the night and threatened to slit my throat if I did not treat him for an arrow wound. A bolt shot from a crossbow, to be precise."

"For the record, this was the same night that the attack took place on the elfling, Sorak," said Sadira, glancing around at the other council members, "to which other witnesses have already testified." She turned back to the healer. "Was Rokan disfigured when he came to you for treatment?"

"Yes, my lady, most terribly so," the healer said. "His face was as I saw it when I was shown his body."

"Did he happen to mention how he came by this disfigurement?"

"He asked if I was able to restore his normal

appearance," the healer said. "I told him that was
beyond my skill. He replied that it was a sorcerer who
had disfigured him, but he did not name the sorcerer."

"So you treated him for his arrow wound and then
he left?" Sadira asked.

"We had one other small transaction," said the
healer. "He wanted to know about poisons. Something very strong, that would kill quickly. I told him
that I was a healer and did not deal in poisons, but as
I did not wish my throat slit, I named one that would
serve. He could easily have been able to obtain it in
the elven market, so I did not tell him anything he
would not have found out somewhere else, in any
case. I saw no point in withholding mere information."

"What was the poison that you named to him?"
Sadira asked, ignoring the healer's equivocation.

"Venom from a crystal spider, my lady. He wanted
something with which an arrow could be enven-
omed."

"An arrow such as this crossbow bolt?" Sadira
asked, carefully holding up the object.

"Yes, my lady."

"This arrow was recovered from the carcass of the
tigone belonging to the elfling," said Sadira. "It was
fired at the elfling by Rokan, but missed him and
killed his beast, instead. Healer, would you examine
this pasty substance left upon the bolt?"

The man came up to her, bent over, and cautiously
sniffed the arrow. "It is venom from a crystal spider,
my lady."

"Thank you. You may go."

The healer nodded to her and left the chamber.

"What is the point of all of this?" demanded Timor.

"So Rokan tried to kill the elfling. What have I to do with it? You have proven nothing with these so-called 'witnesses.' You merely produce them to add the appearance of some weight to your baseless insinuations."

"Rokan was disfigured by sorcery," said Sadira. "He was not disfigured when he was brought to you."

"Well, so he was disfigured by sorcery! That *proves* I could not possibly have done it! I am not a sorcerer! My power came from Kalak during his reign. I knew nothing of magic myself. I know nothing of defiler spells!"

"Send in Captain Zalcor," said Sadira.

A moment later, the captain of the city guard came into the chamber.

"Captain Zalcor, you have conducted your search?"

"I have, my lady."

"Search?" Timor said uneasily. "What search?"

"And what have you found?"

"This, my lady," Zalcor said, withdrawing a small chest from beneath his cloak.

Timor's eyes grew wide when he saw it.

"And where was it found?"

"In the private chambers of the senior templar, my lady."

"And what did it contain?"

"After the hinges on the lid were broken and the chest was opened, it was found to contain a spellbook, my lady. This spellbook." He tossed it on the table so that it landed in front of Timor.

"Lies!" said Timor. "This is a conspiracy! That chest was planted in my home!"

"You mean it is not yours?" Sadira asked, raising her eyebrows.

"I never saw it before in my life!"

She nodded to Zalcor, and the soldier suddenly seized Timor from behind, pinning his arms. As Timor cried out in protest, Rikus got up from his chair and started searching him.

"Zalcor found no key," said Rikus. "With what that chest contained, if it were mine, I would not let the key out of my sight. Aha! What have we here?"

He tore open Timor's tunic and revealed the key the templar wore around his neck. With a jerk, Rikus tore it off and inserted it into the lock on the chest. It fit perfectly. He turned it, and the lock snapped open.

"I suppose that key was planted on you, as well?" Sadira said dryly. She closed her eyes a moment, inhaled deeply, muttered something under her breath and made a pass with her hand. The spellbook opened by itself, and the pages fluttered for a moment. Then they stopped, and the spellbook remained open on the table.

"Captain Zalcor, if you will be so kind as to look upon the page at which the book has remained open?"

Zalcor glanced down over Timor's shoulder. "It is a spell to raise the dead, my lady."

"I never knew he planned this," Kor said, still staring down at the tabletop. He swallowed hard and shook his head. "I swear, I never knew that he would go this far!"

"Kor!" cried Timor. "*Shut up*, you imbecile!"

"Whatever he says could make no possible difference now," Rikus said. "You already stand convicted."

From outside the building, there came the sounds of a commotion. Many voices shouting angrily. The tramp of many feet. The sound of ominous chanting, growing closer and closer. Timor froze. They were chanting his name.

"*Ti-mor! Ti-mor! Ti-mor! Ti-mor!*"

"News travels fast, it seems," Sadira said. "Can you hear them, Timor? The very mob you sought to turn against us. The voice of the people, Timor. And they are crying out for you."

Timor paled. "You won't turn me over to them? You can't! You mustn't! They would tear me limb from limb!"

"And what a pity that would be," said Rikus, his voice dripping with sarcasm.

The crowd was rapidly growing closer. The chanting was louder now, and more insistent. Rocks were hurled through the open windows. Those sitting in the line of fire quickly moved away as more missiles struck the table and the walls behind them. The council members scrambled out of the way. One of them risked a quick glance out the window.

"There is going to be riot," he said. "There are hundreds of them out there! The guard will not be able to keep them out!"

"I should be with my men," said Zalcor.

A fresh fusillade of rocks came through the windows, and everybody ducked. Everyone except Timor, who seized the opportunity to break away from the distracted Zalcor. He shoved the soldier hard, then bolted. Rikus started after him, but the barrage of stones through the windows slowed him down. Several large rocks struck Rikus in the head, and he stumbled, throwing up his arms to protect his face.

Timor ran out into the hall. He had no idea where he would escape to; he only knew he couldn't let that crowd get their hands on him. Behind him, Kor cried out his name.

"Timor! Timor, quickly! This way!"

Timor turned and swore. Then, hearing footsteps running out of the small council chamber, he realized he had no other alternative but to follow Kor. They ran around a corner and Kor grabbed him by the arm, pulling him down a corridor.

"This way!" he said. "Quickly, quickly!"

"Where are you taking me?" demanded Timor. "To that screaming mob out there?"

"I'm only trying to help you," Kor protested.

"You've helped me enough! All you care about is saving your own miserable skin!"

"There was nothing I could do. You were finished before you walked into the chamber." Kor pulled him into a small sitting room. "Here, quickly!"

"This leads nowhere, fool! We're trapped!"

"No, watch," said Kor. He pressed a hidden stud by the mantlepiece, and the back wall of the fireplace swung aside to reveal a secret passageway. "Through there, hurry!"

"Where does this lead?"

"It's an old escape route leading beyond the city walls," said Kor as they ducked through, shutting the entrance to the passageway behind them.

"I never knew of this," said Timor, hurrying through the narrow passageway, bent to keep from striking his head on the low ceiling.

"It was kept a secret from Kalak and the templars," Kor said. "When Kalak ruled, the council had much to fear. This passageway was built to allow them an escape route from the sorcerer-king's wrath in the event he ever turned on them."

"How did you know of this?" asked Timor, cursing as he swept away the cobwebs in his path.

"My grandfather was the architect who designed

the small council chamber," said Kor. "He was a prudent man."

"If you know of this passage, then the others will know of it, also!"

"No, Rikus and Sadira know nothing about it, and I am the only one left now on the council whose family had served in Kalak's time."

"I cannot see a thing in this infernal darkness!"

"Just follow the passageway," said Kor. "It leads to a hidden door concealed in a rock outcropping, outside the wall of the king's gardens."

"Why help me now, Kor, when you threw me to the carrion eaters back there?"

"Because I, myself, would have been next," said Kor. "They knew I was your man, and they would have made me share your punishment."

"So, craven coward to the very end, eh?" Timor said.

"You ran as well," said Kor. "Besides, I do not find a desire for survival to be cowardly. And it was not I who brought you down, Timor. You did that to yourself. I supported you, but I never dreamed you'd go so far as to release a plague of undead upon the city!"

"I did not release them on the city, you fool! I sent them after that misbegotten elfling!"

"You should have left well enough alone," said Kor. "That elfling was your downfall."

"And I fully intend to be his," Timor replied through gritted teeth. "I shall not rest until I find him and make him pay for his interference! His death will be a slow and excruciating one!"

"Wait, slow down," said Kor from just ahead of him. "I think we are almost there. Yes, here is the doorway!"

Timor waited.

"It sticks," said Kor. "It has not been used for years. Here, help me push. . . ."

Positioning himself beside Kor, Timor put his shoulder to the door. "If it wasn't so close in here, I'd blow this blasted door right off its hinges!"

"And give away our position to anyone who might be watching from the city walls?" asked Kor. "Now who's being the fool? Push!"

Both men grunted with effort, and the door slowly gave way. A crack of daylight appeared, and then grew wider as the door swung open on protesting hinges. Timor felt a fresh breeze on his face and inhaled deeply. The stale, musty air inside the passageway had made him feel faint. He stepped out through the door and straightened up. "Ahhh! My back was beginning to ache from being hunched over like—"

With a creaking, scraping sound, the door swung closed behind him. Kor had not come out. He was still inside the passageway, behind the door.

"Kor! Kor! Come out! What are you doing?"

Timor looked for a way to open the door, but he could find nothing that would open it from the outside.

"Kor! Open this door! Can you hear me? Kor!"

"Your friend is gone," said a voice behind him. "He has performed his task, and has returned the way he came."

Timor spun around. Behind him, just beyond the outcropping, stood a group of white-robed, hooded figures, gathered around him in a semicircle. All of them wore veils. Timor's eyes bulged. The Alliance! Kor, that miserable traitor. . . .

"If you think to fight us with your defiler spells, then try," said the preserver wizard who had spoken.

"We would welcome the test."

Timor licked his lips and glanced around fearfully. He no longer had his spellbook, and his memory suddenly refused to give up any spell that would serve this horrible occasion. Besides, they outnumbered him. He might get two or three of them, if he was lucky, but the others would quickly finish him. His mind raced to find a way out of this predicament, but he could find no solution. There was no escape.

Several of the hooded figures moved aside, and the elfling came forward, accompanied by a beautiful young villichi priestess.

"You!" said Timor.

Sorak simply stood there and gazed at the templar with a puzzled expression. "Why?" he said. And as he spoke, the Guardian probed the templar's mind, and Sorak had his answer.

Timor gave an inarticulate scream of rage and launched himself at Sorak. Ryana quickly stepped forward and clubbed him down with her staff.

"*So that was all it was?*" said Sorak. "*A mistaken assumption?*"

"*He attributed his own foul and devious motives to everyone around him,*" said the Guardian. "*He plotted against the others, so he believed they plotted against him. He was drunk with the idea of power, so he believed that others were no different.*"

"*He has only received his just desserts,*" said Sorak, looking down at the templar, on his hands and knees upon the ground.

Timor gazed up at him, blood running from the cut on his head where Ryana had struck him. "Go ahead, you misbegotten, bastard, half-breed spawn! Go ahead and finish it! Kill me, damn you, and have done with it!"

Sorak gazed down at him and shook his head. "No, templar, not I," he said. "You have brought me more pain than you could ever know, but their cause takes precedence." He glanced around at the men in the white robes and veils.

"No!" said Timor. "Not them! I know only too well what they can do!" He grasped at Sorak's leg. "Kill me! Strike me down! It was *I* who raised the dead against you! It was *I* who sent Rokan and his men to cut your throat!"

Sorak jerked his leg out of the templar's grasp and turned away.

"Nooo!" screamed the templar. "Kill me! Use your sword! Kill me, damn you! For pity's sake, kill me!"

Sorak kept on walking, away from the city, with Ryana at his side. Neither of them looked back as the hooded men closed in around the templar and he began to scream in earnest.

* * * * *

On a hill overlooking the city, Sorak and Ryana sat before a fire. Ahead of them, the desert tablelands seemed to stretch out into infinity.

"Why did you follow me?" asked Sorak softly as he held the scroll the Veiled Alliance had given him.

"Need you ask?" Ryana said.

"The mistress gave you leave?"

Ryana looked down and shook her head. "When I came out of the tower and learned that you had gone, I knew I had to follow."

"You mean you left the convent without permission from the high mistress?"

"Yes," she said. "I broke my vows. I cannot be a priestess any longer. Nor do I want to be. I just want to be with you."

"You tracked me? All the way to Tyr?"

She smiled. "I am villichi. Following your trail through the mountains was not very difficult, but it took a while to find you once I reached the city. However, your reputation had spread quickly. Many spoke about the fearsome elfling fighter and master of the Way who worked at the Crystal Spider gaming house. I knew that it could only be you. But when I saw you with that half-elf girl, I thought. . . ." Her voice trailed off.

"You of all people should have known better," Sorak said.

She nodded. "Yes, I know. I know only too well. Still, you left without even telling her good-bye. I am sure she pines for you."

Sorak glanced down at his sword. "If she pines at all, it is for an ideal, not for me."

"You cannot always walk alone, Sorak, despite your name. No one can. You need me."

"It would be better if you were to go back."

"I cannot."

"Cannot, or will not?"

"Both," she replied. "You can tell me that you do not want me to go with you, Sorak, but it will make no difference. I will follow you whether you want me to or not. No one knows you as I do. No one understands you as I do. No one cares for you as I do. And no one can watch your back as well as I," she added, thinking about the two men she had killed back in the alley as they waited to attack him. She would not tell him about that. She did not want him to feel obligated. She only wished her aim with the crossbow had been better, and that she had killed Rokan, as well. Then Tigra would not have died. She would not tell him about that, either.

He smiled wanly. "Why waste yourself on a male who cannot love you properly?"

"Why waste myself in a villichi convent, where I would never even see a male, much less love one?" she countered.

"But you have forsaken your vows, and you are no longer a priestess. You have no more vows to keep, while I have a vow I cannot break, no matter how much I might wish I could."

"I will be satisfied with whatever you can give," she said. "If I cannot be your lover, then I shall be your sister, as I once was."

"And always shall be," Sorak said. "Very well then, little sister. Since I cannot dissuade you, we shall both go out to seek the Sage together. Somewhere out there."

He looked out across the vast Athasian desert, slowly fading from golden orange to bloody red as the dark sun sank on the horizon.

The Penhaligon Trilogy

If you enjoyed *The Dragon's Tomb*, you'll want to read —

The Fall of Magic   Book Three
A sinister mage unleashes the power of an ancient artifact on Penhaligon, an artifact that drains the world of all magic except his own. In a final, desperate gambit, Johauna and her comrades set out on an impossible quest to stop the arcane assault and save the world of Mystara! *Available in October 1993.*

ISBN 1-56076-663-8
Sug. Retail $4.95/CAN $5.95/£3.99 U.K.

The Tainted Sword
Book One
The once-mighty knight Fain Flinn has forsaken both his pride and his legendary sword, Wyrmblight. Now Penhaligon faces a threat only he can conquer. All seems hopeless until . . . Flinn regains his magical blade. Yet even Wyrmblight may not be powerful enough to quash the dragon! *On sale now.*

ISBN 1-56076-395-7
Sug. Retail $4.95/CAN $5.95/£3.99 U.K.

Novels

DUNGEONS & DRAGONS and the TSR logo are trademarks owned by TSR, Inc.
©1993 TSR, Inc. All Rights Reserved.